Anissa's Redemption

by

Zack Love

This is a work of fiction. Any references to historical events, real people, or real places are used fictitiously. Other names, characters, places, and events are products of the author's imagination, and any resemblance to actual events, places, or persons, living or dead, is entirely coincidental.

www.ZackLove.com

ISBN: 978-1514227190

Cover by Ashley Byland

Contents

Acknowledgements v

Chapter 1: Anissa 1

Chapter 2: Julien 8

Chapter 3: Anissa 21

Chapter 4: Julien 26

Chapter 5: Anissa 30

Chapter 6: Anissa 37

Chapter 7: Anissa 42

Chapter 8: Julien 54

Chapter 9: Anissa 61

Chapter 10: Anissa 70

Chapter 11: Anissa 74

Chapter 12: Julien 78

Chapter 13: Anissa 81

Chapter 14: Julien 84

Chapter 15: Anissa 90

Chapter 16: Julien 93

Chapter 17: Anissa 96

Chapter 18: Anissa 98

Chapter 19: Julien 104

Chapter 20: Anissa 107

Chapter 21: Julien 111

Chapter 22: Anissa 116

Chapter 23: Julien 119

Chapter 24: Anissa 123

Chapter 25: Julien 128

Chapter 26: Anissa 131

Chapter 27: Julien 137

Chapter 28: Anissa 142

Chapter 29: Julien 146

Chapter 30: Anissa 149

Chapter 31: Julien 154

Chapter 32: Anissa 158

Chapter 33: Anissa 169

Chapter 34: Anissa 171

Chapter 35: Anissa 175

Chapter 36: Anissa 182

Chapter 37: Anissa 187

Chapter 38: For You, My Dearest 190

About the Author 191

Acknowledgements

I am immensely grateful to have the enthusiastic help and advocacy of several wonderful individuals. I am especially thankful for:

Author Nadine Silber, for her warm and loyal friendship, enthusiastic support (including countless giveaways and efforts to promote this novel and my other books), assistance with my newsletter, excellent production of promotional materials/graphics (including the trailer for the first book in this series), helpful advice, sponsoring ads, and so much other support.

Anita Viccica Toss for being such an early, loyal, and hugely helpful fan who has consistently provided tremendous promotional support on Facebook, Goodreads, and other book forums; for helping me to stay organized and upbeat, despite whatever frustrations or obstacles presented themselves along the way; and for readily offering a helping hand with so much research and countless other projects.

Daina Lazzarotto and her awesome company, EPIC Literary Promotions, for organizing a release party and launch blitz for this book that were (true to her company's name) epic, and generously sponsoring prizes to help generate buzz, assisting with so many research projects, acting as my de facto publicist in many ways, and otherwise promoting my books at every opportunity.

Author KM Golland, for her early friendship; general, mood-lifting hilarity and encouragement; editorial feedback; giveaways and other efforts to promote my work; and helpful advice.

Phala Theng, for donating her graphical talents to create so many beautiful teasers for this series, and for her other promotional efforts.

These fans who promoted my work with such kind and supportive enthusiasm: Donna Lorah, Jessie Duchannes, Heather Howard Lewis, Louisa Gray, Jo Turner Field, Nancy Zavala, Elena R. Cruz, Erin McFarland, Janet Wilkie, Julie Garlington, Alessandra Melchionda, Letty Sidon, Amy Cobb Pope, Sarah Mae Mink, Verna McQueen, Lily Maverick Wallis, Maggie Welsh, Crystal R. Solis, Jessica Lynn Leornard, Jennifer Pou, Diana Cardonita, and Jennifer Cothran.

I am also very grateful for the feedback of the following beta readers who helped me to improve the manuscript: author KM Golland, Danielle Goodwin, author Nadine Silber, Christy Wilson, Anita Viccica Toss, author Anne Conley, Amy Cobb Pope, Jenna Hanson, Letty Sidon, Nancy Palmer, Louisa Gray, Elena Cruz, and Crystal Solis.

To the Christians, Yazidis, and other persecuted minorities of the Middle East, and those working to bring them security and dignity.

Detailed Synopsis of Book 1

(for Readers Starting with Book 2)

In Book 1, *The Syrian Virgin*, Anissa Toma, is a 16-year-old girl living in the city of Homs, as the Syrian Civil War rages. Anissa's father, Youssef, is a hospital doctor and businessman, as well as a leader of the local Christian community. As Islamist fighters increasingly terrorize the Christian minority in Homs, Youssef realizes that he must do whatever he can to protect his four children. After Christmas 2011, he sends Anissa's older sister and younger brother to stay with their uncle in the northern Syrian city of Raqqa, which is far safer. Anissa's older brother will stay in Homs to help their parents manage the family pharmacy and medical device business, and Anissa, who is academically gifted, will relocate to New York and stay with her uncle who lives there, after Youssef uses his professional contacts to secure a Canadian visa for her.

During their last hours together, Youssef asks his daughter for a solemn promise: fulfill your personal potential and help our persecuted community. Anissa vows to do this, and, after packing all of her things, takes the family dog out to the front yard one last time. But her world shatters when five armed Islamists suddenly show up at her house to punish her father's decision to fire a doctor who had been purloining supplies from Youssef's hospital for their benefit. After seriously injuring her father in a shootout that leaves Anissa's dog dead, the gunmen present Youssef with a stark choice: renounce the Christian faith and become a Muslim, or die.

As a proud man and one of the leaders of the Homs Christian community, he refuses their demand that he convert to Islam. Horrific carnage ensues. Anissa narrowly escapes the murderous rampage by fleeing through the backdoor, across their backyard, and over a fence to the house of Mohammed, who is her neighbor, a trusted family friend, and a Sunni Muslim.

A few days later, with Mohammed's help, Anissa is able to get past Sunni rebel checkpoints to her flight departing from Damascus. Her uncle in NY picks her up from the Montreal airport, and then drives her across the US-Canada border, back to his home in NY, where she must restart her young life while seeking asylum. Traumatized and devastated, Anissa tries to find the will to go on, even though all that remains of her family is her host uncle and cousins in NY, and her older sister, younger brother and other uncle in Raqqa.

During her last year and a half of high school, Anissa focuses on adjusting to life in a new country, while overcoming the traumas she recently endured with the help of her therapist, Monique. As part of her strategy for coping with the horrific loss of her parents and older brother, Anissa lies to everyone (except her therapist) about how her parents died, claiming they were all killed in a car crash, which gives them a "more normal" death. She suffers from horrible nightmares about her trauma in Syria but can manage them in part with her nightly ritual of whispering to her imaginary parents and convincing them not to get into the car that will end up crashing. Anissa also intensively pursues martial arts and running to improve her confidence and mood.

While searching for a place where she can study self-defense with other Mideast Christians, Anissa meets Michael Kassab on Facebook. She quickly develops a crush on Michael, who is a twenty-six-year-old doctoral student at Columbia University, and a political activist fighting for the rights, security, and dignity of Mideast Christians facing Islamist persecution.

Michael is helpful to Anissa but never shows any romantic interest in her, so Monique eventually advises her to stop trying to maintain her Facebook relationship with Michael. Anissa follows her therapist's advice and focuses on self-healing and completing her last year of high school. She keeps a diary in an effort to battle the demons that haunt her, and it is through this personal record that she tells her story. Anissa struggles with depression and nightmares related to her trauma and Monique tries to help her manage PTSD. Anissa resists the temptation to take her own life so that she can honor the promise that she made to her father in their very last conversation. Not only does her vow sustain her will to live, but it also fuels her drive to succeed academically. Her hard work and unusual intellect secure her a full-merit scholarship at Columbia University, which she enters at the age of eighteen.

During her first semester, Anissa stays focused on her studies but is regularly reminded of how different her concerns are from those of her classmates. They escape their academic pressures by indulging in campus parties, carefree fun, drinking, and dating. But Anissa clings to her conservative attitudes towards sex and, when she's not studying, remains anxious about the situation in Syria – especially in Raqqa, where her surviving family lives under increasingly perilous conditions. She resolves to become politically involved, during her second semester, with the Mideast Christian Association (MCA), the non-profit that Michael founded and leads.

On the first day of her spring semester classes, Anissa goes to a campus rally organized by the MCA, where she meets her longtime Facebook crush in person for the first time. Hoping to impress Michael while helping the cause by soliciting donations and petition signatures, Anissa approaches a stylishly dressed man in his late thirties, just as he is about to make a phone call, but he brusquely rebuffs her request. Michael resentfully points out that he is the wealthiest man associated with the university but never donates anything or shows any other form of support.

After the MCA rally, Anissa heads to the first lecture of her Psychology & Markets course, only to learn that her new professor is the same man who just rejected her solicitation: Professor Julien Morales. She awkwardly avoids his gaze throughout his introduction to the class, and tries to remain unnoticed for the next few lectures. At one point, Julien announces that the three students with the highest midterm exam results will be invited to a special office tour of his twenty billion-dollar hedge fund, JMAT. He notes that most of the students selected in the past have gone on to secure high-paying jobs with his prestigious fund. Anissa suddenly starts to dream big, and is excited by the rare opportunity to help herself (and eventually her community), and resolves to be among the top three students in the class.

A few days later, she sees her professor speaking on a Spanish-language financial news program on TV while helping Michael with some MCA-related tasks. Anissa learns that Michael also speaks Spanish, in addition to her native Arabic and several other Mideast languages. She realizes that she is drawn to both men for different reasons, but – after discovering that Michael actually has a girlfriend – she tries to distance herself from him, as her therapist advises.

Meanwhile, Julien continues to receive unwanted messages from one of his ex-lovers, threatening to publicly shame him if he doesn't pay her a substantial "breakup fee." Julien refuses to do so on principle, but realizes that his playboy lifestyle may have gotten too reckless and decides that he needs to start seeing a shrink about that issue and his recurring nightmares.

Anissa's friend Maya, who was in Julien's class the year before, confirms that his course is very difficult and admits that she received a poor grade in his class, but adds that she gained something far more valuable than a good grade: Julien's friendship and regular invitations to his VIP parties, which are attended by the political and financial elite, and some of the city's most eligible bachelors. Anissa is intrigued when Maya suggests that she join her as a guest but Anissa declines the invitation, noting that she doesn't want to show up at Julien's home unannounced unless she's already proven herself on his midterm exam.

Julien selects a young and sexy therapist, Lily, who eventually gets him to open up to her more than he has done with any prior therapist. He admits to Lily that he chose an attractive therapist in part because he needs to learn self-control, and what better way to do so than with someone to whom he is drawn and who can study his behavior as it goes astray? He also reveals that his estranged father is the principal cause of his nightmares but reveals little else about what took place during his troubled childhood.

Michael eventually breaks up with his girlfriend and starts to see Anissa more frequently. They grow closer while discussing his dream of founding a Mideast Christian state – an inspiring goal that makes her hopeful about someday protecting her beleaguered community. Michael asks Anissa to go ice skating with him on Valentine's Day, and the two start dating.

A few days later, Anissa and Michael are again at an MCA rally, collecting donations and signatures despite the cold weather. As luck would have it, Julien again walks by them. This time, however, Julien stops and explains to Anissa his reasons for rarely getting involved with politics, but then takes out a $100 bill and hands it to Anissa, joking that they should buy an outdoor heater to keep themselves warm with it. Michael is amazed that Julien finally showed some generosity and realizes that it's entirely thanks to Anissa's spell over the man.

Anissa continues to worry about the safety of her siblings and uncle in Raqqa, where ISIS has taken over and imposed Sharia law, persecuting Christians and other religious minorities. But she withdraws from world events and everyone around her in order to focus intently on midterms – especially the exam for Julien's class, which she prepares the most for, at the expense of her other classes. Her efforts pay off when she learns that she has received the highest grade in the class and secured for herself an office tour of Julien's hedge fund.

Julien's therapist finally gets him to share something he's never told anyone else: a detailed account of his horrific nightmares. They involve his bed blanket transforming into hooks or blades that cut him open to the point that he begins drowning in his own blood, until he throws the covers to the floor gasping for air. He eventually also reveals that he is a strict vegetarian after being traumatized at a young age when watching his father work as a butcher. Julien's love of animals is also apparent from the lengths to which he goes to care for and heal Icarus, the sparrow that he accidentally stepped on when getting out of his car once and subsequently adopted as a pet.

Anissa goes on the tour of JMAT and is dazzled by the stunning offices full of alluring possibilities that, until that moment, had seemed so removed from her reality as a refugee: wealth, abundance, prestige, success. But when she shows up late to the MCA meeting that night and shares her excitement about the JMAT office tour, Michael clearly resents everything that Julien represents and fears that Anissa could end up forgetting her ideals and values if she is seduced into pursuing some materialistic American Dream. She and Michael have their first quarrel, which is further aggravated by Anissa's jealous suspicions that Michael has not completely cut ties with his last girlfriend.

Meanwhile, Julien grows increasingly intrigued by Anissa, and — realizing that it would be risky and inappropriate to pursue her in any way — he throws a small VIP party at his triplex penthouse (occupying the 63rd through the 65th floors) in the hope of finding himself a new crush, to help him take his mind off of Anissa. To that end, he asks Maya to bring a young, smart beauty with her to his party. Much to his surprise, she shows up with Anissa, who — after her stellar exam performance — is no longer wary of showing up uninvited.

But Anissa, who has since made up with Michael (after he apologized and brought her a charming gift), goes out of her way to do as her boyfriend suggested: limit her interactions with Julien at his party, in order to set herself apart from the countless young women throwing themselves at the billionaire playboy. Michael convinces Anissa that if she plays her cards right with Julien, she will be uniquely positioned to help Middle East Christians by gaining the support of an extremely wealthy and well-connected benefactor.

Michael's plan works and Anissa's aloofness intensifies Julien's budding fascination with her. To avoid revealing any of this interest to his current student, Julien plays it cool in class and pretends not to notice Anissa, who similarly seems indifferent towards her professor during the lectures that follow their party encounter.

But Julien is determined to get some quality time with Anissa, so he invites Maya to another party, and suggests that she bring Anissa again. This time at his party, Julien chats privately for a few minutes with Anissa and invites her out to dinner later that week.

The next day, at a political rally in Union Square for the protection of Mideast Christians, a counter-protest erupts and Michael comes to Anissa's physical defense when she is accosted and threatened by three much bigger men. A trained martial arts fighter, Michael knocks out the biggest man in the group and the others cower away as he escorts Anissa away from the area. She ends up going back to his apartment, where they passionately kiss and Anissa reveals her breasts to a man for the first time in her sexually inexperienced life. But after Michael notices a scar on Anissa's hip, they stop their heavy petting. She tells him that the mark is from what happened to her in Syria but prefers not to elaborate, having shared the details of her ordeal with no one besides her therapist. Anissa wants to explore their intimacy more, but Michael notes that he would rather take things slowly, given that she's still a virgin and he's about to leave for Syria on a dangerous mission for the MCA.

When Anissa tells Maya what happened with Michael, her more experienced friend tells her that Michael's relationship with his last girlfriend might not be as finished as Anissa would like to think. They also discuss the whole question of giving one's virginity to the right person. Anissa notes how freely and frivolously women in the USA seem to do so, particularly when drunken fraternity parties are involved. But Maya points out that some U.S. women have auctioned off their virginity for six-figure payments.

The next time Anissa speaks with Michael (over Skype, when he calls to let her know that he's safely arrived in Syria), she confronts him about whether he still has any relationship with his ex-girlfriend. Michael responds by suggesting that he and Anissa keep their relationship light and open because he is too focused on the cause they both care so much about for him to be involved in anything very serious. He encourages her to cultivate her relationship with Julien, adding that the cause is much more important than any particular jealousies, and gaining Julien's support is too important an opportunity for them to miss. But Michael emphasizes that he wants Anissa in his future and trusts her to stay true to that hope; it's clear that Michael is torn about having Anissa charm Julien into being more supportive. Michael resents Julien's materialistic values and views him as a romantic rival, even though the MCA desperately needs a wealthy supporter.

A few days later, Julien takes Anissa on their dinner date. They have a long and very open chat during their time together, covering everything from Anissa's experiences in college, to the plight of her community, to the current geopolitics of the Middle East. He is more impressed than ever by her intellect and knowledge of topics about which he knows little. They also discuss how different her traditional and more conservative background is from the sexual mores of American culture, at which point she jokingly mentions that she would have premarital sex with someone who wasn't going to become her husband only for a donation of ten million dollars to the MCA, the cause she holds dearest. Julien humorously congratulates Anissa on not undervaluing herself and – noting that Michael may still be in the picture – muses that the whole idea, albeit theoretical, seems to him like a philanthropic version of the Demi Moore film *Indecent Proposal*.

Anissa's older sister (who is still staying with their uncle in Raqqa, Syria) shares some ominous news: they fear that a Christian who owes their uncle money may accuse them of blasphemy to the ISIS authorities, as a way to avoid his debt. She reports hearing that the man had befriended the Islamist authorities to avoid other debts in this manner, even though the other Christian creditors he accused of blasphemy all ended up dead. Anissa begs her sister not to lose hope, noting that Michael is well connected with key players in Syria and may be able to help them flee very soon.

A few days later, the mysterious consequences that Julien's harassing ex-lover has been threatening are finally unveiled. She sold the shirtless selfies that Julien had sent her when they were dating (a few months earlier) to the New York tabloids, and Anissa's professor is now the object of ridicule throughout all of the New York area, as his selfies are splashed across the front pages of the local papers. A man who was always associated with good judgment, prudence, class, and prestige now looks laughably undignified and even desperate. Later that day, when Anissa overhears some students mocking him just as Julien's lecture ends, she tries to defend him, reminding them that everyone makes mistakes and that they shouldn't judge so harshly a professor that everyone had loved and admired so much up until that point.

Full of shame, Julien slips away after class, clearly trying to avoid everyone as he makes his way back to his driver. But Anissa wants to comfort him and follows him until no one else is around to see her approach him. She tries to reassure him that the scandal hasn't altered her view of him in any way. He wants to escape public view as soon as possible, and suggests that they speak in his car.

Anissa decides to join him for his ride to the Brooklyn Bridge, which she's always wanted to visit. On the way there, they discuss the dinner they had together, and Julien eventually admits that he is struggling to keep their relationship strictly teacher/student, particularly because of her charm and exceptional intellect, and the unusual openness that her presence inspires in him. He confesses to her that he shares more with her than with many people he's known for far longer.

On the other hand, his recent scandal is a painful reminder of how risky his adventures with women can be, although he notes that he strangely trusts her more than he can fully explain – in part because of her authenticity and refugee experience, which is so unlike the social-climbing, money-grubbers of whom he's grown weary and wary. He also doesn't want to break her heart but fears that such an outcome is inevitable, given his lousy track record with women and relationships generally. He concludes that the only way to have a sexual relationship where no one gets hurt is to keep their relationship strictly "transactional," as she had jokingly mentioned when she said that it would take a ten-million-dollar donation for her to give her virginity to someone other than her future husband. Julien points out that, under such an arrangement, each person gains nothing more or less than what each expects: he would enjoy the taboo-filled thrill of sex with his current and much younger, virginal student, and she would secure a large donation for the MCA. Julien also notes that if it were really set up as a transaction, he would donate five million dollars before they have sex, and five million after.

But Julien adds that he has never had to pay for sex and refuses, on principle, to start now. He concludes the discussion by asking Anissa never to mention any formal arrangement again. Julien says that if he does decide to donate to the MCA, then it's not to pressure her into having sex with him, but because he genuinely wants to support her cause, which he has come to respect and care about. And similarly, if Anissa ever decides to lose her virginity to him, then it should be because she deems him worthy enough to receive that honor, and not because of some obligation.

When they get to the Brooklyn Bridge, they get out of the car and walk towards the middle, as his driver waits for Julien's call to pick them up nearby. On the bridge, Julien reveals the suicidal thoughts that he's had on those occasions when he's hit bottom, and describes the struggles he had with himself to stay on the bridge. He admits that the public humiliation following the photo scandal has brought him back to his nihilistic despair.

Julien walks Anissa back to the car and instructs his driver to take her back to her dorm at the Columbia University campus. He decides to return to the bridge, so that he can just think and be alone and contemplate his own life, the way he has on every other such despair-filled occasion.

A few days later, Julien never shows up to class. His social media accounts are all quiet and there is no way to reach him or any sign that he is alive. After nearly a week of this eerie silence, Anissa begins to worry that Julien has taken his own life.

She grows even more distraught when Michael, who's still in Syria, misses their scheduled Skype call – after not communicating for several days either. She starts to fear that she has lost both men in her life. Hours after she was scheduled to speak with Michael on Skype, she receives an email indicating that both he and Julien are actually alive. The email is from Michael, and it congratulates her on a job well done: the MCA bank account just received a wire transfer of five million dollars. That is where book one ends.

NOTE: Due to space limitations, the above summary is highly condensed and not always in chronological order. For the full experience, with all of the drama and details, please read *The Syrian Virgin*.

Chapter 1: Anissa

(Diary)

∾ Friday, April 11, 2014 ∽

To My Dearest,

Last Tuesday brought a powerful reminder of why I should never lose hope in life, no matter how bleak things seem to get sometimes. The danger of prolonged despair is its tendency to cloud the gift of a new beginning that every tomorrow offers.

With all of the mounting anxiety and bad news of last week, I had almost forgotten this truth. And then, last Tuesday, my worries and depression were suddenly flipped on their heads, leaving me full of promise and joy. I learned that Professor Morales and Michael are both alive, and that my efforts to help my family and other persecuted Christians in Syria have borne fruit in ways that exceeded my wildest optimism.

After seeing all of the good news in Michael's email, I eventually calmed down enough to get to Professor Morales' class, although he embarrassed me a bit for showing up about an hour late.

"Anissa – so nice of you to join us!" he said, as he noticed me trying to enter the room as inconspicuously as possible. "Did you personally decide to end daylight savings time about six months early?" he asked jokingly, to the class' amusement. I was glad to see that he was back to his usual self and that the class was apparently responding well to him. The moment flustered me a bit, but I was strangely relieved by the net result: the class saw that Professor Morales doesn't play favorites and that I'm still on the hook – as much as every other student is – for the standards that he had established for everyone.

I caught only the last thirty minutes of his lecture – the first one that he gave since mysteriously disappearing for a week. Judging from that half hour when I was present, he seemed to have regained his confidence, and maybe even some new wisdom or perspective. His apparent renewal naturally increased my eagerness to speak with him again – if only to find out what brought about his epiphany or changed outlook. Of course, I also wanted to thank him for his five-million-dollar donation to the Mideast Christian Association (MCA). But when I went up to him after class to try to talk to him, he was rushing out. As he quickly walked to his car, he spoke on his cell phone for most of the time, so it was hard to communicate much with him while hurrying alongside his stride.

He eventually noticed me there, waiting for the right moment to address him. "I'm sorry, Anissa. I'm in a terrible rush right now. Guys like me have no business disappearing for an entire week without planning for it a solid year in advance."

"Right, sorry… I'm just glad you're OK," I replied, continuing at a brisk pace that matched his. "And I wanted to thank you for that unbelievably generous donation you sent to – "

"No thanks are needed," he replied with a smile, as we reached his car. "Let's do this properly, after I've put out the biggest fires," he added, as he opened the door and entered the luxury sedan.

"So when can I see you again, outside of class?"

"Hopefully by the end of Friday, things will be more manageable. I just need to get through this week somehow," he said, closing the door.

* * *

Then, on Wednesday, I finally spoke with Michael on Skype and learned more about my professor's big MCA donation, the change in plans requiring him to stay in Syria longer, and other details.

"Was there any note or anything with the five-million-dollar wire transfer?" I asked out of curiosity.

"No, it arrived anonymously from a foundation, which I'm sure is his," Michael informed me, his face beaming with pride and gratitude.

"Yes. He didn't deny sending the money when I tried to thank him for it yesterday," I noted with a smile.

"High five, Wonder Woman!" he said, putting his palm up against the screen. I mirrored his action so that our hands virtually touched on my laptop. "Or should I call you 'Incredible Inās?' Or maybe just my future Finance Minister for Antioch?" he added with a wink.

"I'm so happy and excited that this all worked out."

"Yes, it did. And guess what? I'm leaving soon to help your family."

My face lit up with an even bigger smile. "What do you mean?"

"I finally had a chance to talk with your uncle, Luke, in Raqqa last week but – until yesterday – I wasn't sure how I could help, mostly because he hadn't yet decided where he wanted to relocate his family, and I didn't have any cash to finance whatever assistance he needed."

"And now?" I asked, eager for the latest update.

"Well, that wire from your professor changed everything. After I sent you that email update yesterday, I called Luke to let him know that I could arrange for a secure transport with moderate Sunni rebels who are my contacts, and that I could help him with any expenses related to his move."

"It means so much to me that you're doing this," I confessed, my eyes welling up with tears and my heart beating faster. I wanted to give him a huge hug and had to restrain myself from wrapping my arms around my laptop.

"Well, your uncle sounded very relieved and anxious to leave Raqqa. He kept saying how his family could be targeted any day, and my call gave him the extra confidence he needed to uproot all of his immediate relatives from their hometown. When we spoke yesterday, he requested another day to think about where exactly he wanted to relocate everyone. And today he gave me his answer, just a few hours ago."

I wiped away tears. "So where does he want to go?"

"To Kessab."

I looked up as I tried to recall what I knew about that place. "Isn't that a Christian-Armenian village?"

"Yes. It's about a five-hour drive west of Raqqa, and is just south of the border with Turkey. Actually, it's roughly where historical Antioch was located, but it's been an Armenian village for centuries."

"Why there?" I asked, tilting my head slightly. It seemed odd for my family to be moving to an Armenian village, although the fact that the village is Christian certainly made the decision more understandable.

"So many places, like Homs, are now out of the question with fierce battles raging between Islamists and the Syrian Army. Many non-Armenian Syrians – especially from the war-torn cities of Raqqa and Aleppo – have been seeking refuge in Kessab, and in other coastal cities like Latakia and Tartus. I personally suggested Latakia to him, because there are more Alawites and regime protections there, so it seemed like a safer bet. But nothing is guaranteed, and Luke said that he has a very good friend in Kessab and some business contacts, so he thinks that village would be his best option at this point."

"And you're going to be personally involved in this relocation?" I asked, amazed at Michael's courage and self-sacrifice, yet fearful for his safety.

"Yes, I trust these Sunni rebels, but it'll be even safer for your family if I am there with them, because they know and respect me. And

I promised them $50,000 once your family is safely resettled, so they have every incentive to facilitate a successful move. I'm getting up at the crack of dawn to travel with them to Raqqa, where I'm supposed to meet your uncle at his house by 10 a.m."

"My Christian Hero," I said, touching the part of my laptop where his face appeared. "Just be safe. And thank you so much for this."

After we said goodbye, I thought for a moment about how Michael would be the first of my friends from the United States to meet my family in Syria. I also couldn't help wondering if he had ever met his ex-girlfriend's family, since he had dated Karen for twice as long as he had known me.

I shook my head in disapproval of my own petty competitiveness and proceeded to call my sister. It was so wonderful finally to contact her with a positive development that we could both appreciate.

"This is indeed good news," Maria said, with a forced, tired smile. "Life here is unbearable. Christians are worse than second-class citizens in Raqqa. Many have been beheaded and a few have even been crucified – horrors that darken your memories forever. We are all subject to Sharia law here and it's the most oppressive and medieval system you can imagine. There is no music allowed," she began fighting back tears. "I can't even remember the last time I played the violin." I thought of the pain and frustration that Maria must feel, knowing that her talent was going to waste, and her musical skills atrophying by the day. "Women must wear a full niqab veil and cannot go out in public without a male escort. They amputate the limbs of accused thieves here. Even some Sunni Muslims quietly complain that ISIS is just bastardizing Islamic law as a way to impose its authoritarian rule over the people of this city. So it's really just about power and control."

"I'm so glad you're finally leaving that Hell," I said. "But what do you think about going to Kessab?"

"Inās, nowhere is really safe. Syria is becoming one giant graveyard. Uncle Luke thought about Turkey too, but none of us speaks Turkish, and there are so many Sunni Islamists from all over the world flocking to Turkey on their way to fight here, that I don't even know if we'd feel safe there as Christians – especially since he doesn't know anyone there."

"And what about Lebanon?" I asked, even though our discussion was entirely theoretical anyway, since Uncle Luke had already decided on another location in Syria.

"Uncle Luke has better contacts in Kessab. But I think he plans to explore other options in Latakia and maybe also Lebanon, once we settle down a bit. The situation is changing all the time, so we have to be ready for anything, and we'll need to see what makes the most sense at any given moment. The main thing is to get out of this nightmare where we live now."

"Yes – just the fact that Kessab is a Christian village should make your lives easier and safer."

"You have no idea how much we're all excited about that, after getting a very long taste of life under Sharia law."

"I'm so happy you're leaving there tomorrow," I affirmed. "And guess who will show up to escort you with armed security guards so that your relocation is more secure?"

Maria seemed touched and surprised that someone was actually going to be coming to protect them in transit. "Escort us? I didn't get all of the logistics and details from Uncle Luke," she noted, as she tried to guess who it might be. "Who? That guy Michael, your boyfriend?"

"Yes. Well, he's not really my boyfriend, but we're very close. It's complicated. Anyway, he personally knows the moderate Sunni rebels who will escort you from Raqqa to Kessab. And he also speaks Armenian, in case that's needed, although I'm sure everyone in Kessab speaks Arabic."

"You have no idea what your help means to us."

"It's the least I could do. I always feel terrible that I don't do more, and that I'm not there helping you in person. But sending a close friend feels like the next best thing."

"You see, Inās? You're already doing things for us from there that we couldn't do for ourselves here."

"This is just the beginning. Please don't ever give up hope, Maria. And tell the rest of the family and every Christian you meet that they have a very powerful friend now."

"What do you mean?"

"The details aren't important. The main thing is that you and other Christians in Syria realize that you are not alone – that there are people outside who are working to help in any way they can. This movement is just starting, but it holds great promise. You just have to try to stay strong and keep your faith in God and in yourself."

"Thanks, little sister," Maria said playfully. "I have to call you that to remind myself you're actually younger than I am! You sound so grown up now – Mom and Dad would be so proud of you and what you're doing. I wish I could give you a big hug."

"Me too. I really miss you and Antoun."

"And we really miss you."

* * *

After my Psychology and Markets class yesterday, it took all of my willpower not to go up to Professor Morales and speak to him. I knew he was still stressed out and short on time after his unplanned absence from work, but after seeing all that he had done for my family and the cause of persecuted Christians in the Middle East, I needed to show him my gratitude in an unforgettably special way. I wanted to give him something that he would truly cherish and that no one else could give him – not just because doing so would probably deepen our connection, but because it seemed like the right thing to do. The kind of goodness he had shown should be rewarded. He made the generous donation anonymously and hardly let me thank him for it – as if to preserve my dignity and downplay his munificence. As much as I had already grown powerfully attracted to him in recent weeks, his goodness and largesse have made him absolutely irresistible – particularly when I have to keep my distance and let him catch up on his busy life.

But I'm still a bit torn about giving him my virginity – much the way I was when I wrote to you a few weeks ago, trying to decide if I should propose a transaction to him. Like the last time I wrestled with this question, I still find myself vacillating between him and Michael, because Michael really has been my Christian Hero, with all the help he's given to my family at great personal risk.

Two hours ago, I spoke with Maria again briefly, after they had just settled into a temporary guesthouse in Kessab. She said that there was one very tense moment, at the final checkpoint to exit Raqqa, when the armed guards demanded a final, surprise payment – in addition to the payment that Michael had already made when arranging my family's departure. ISIS wanted to facilitate their acquisition of "Christian war booty" as they often referred to the confiscated property of Christians who had left the city. Their related demands created a moment of dramatic uncertainty, because no one was sure how Uncle Luke would react to the surprise exit requirement: his signature on a legal document, transferring ownership of his house and business to ISIS.

Their convoy pulled over to the side, to let the other traffic through while Uncle Luke decided on his response. There were two large minivans standing idle with all of his relatives (and whatever possessions they could bring), in addition to two SUVs full of armed rebels that Michael had brought along for security.

Uncle Luke was appalled at the idea and, for a moment, the tension in the air could have exploded in some unpredictable way – if the ISIS guards had reacted violently or one of Michael's armed rebel escorts had misread the situation and started firing his weapon.

But in the end, Maria told me how Michael managed the situation and asked the ISIS men to give him a few minutes to talk to Uncle Luke privately. Apparently Michael convinced Uncle Luke that this was a lost cause, and that his property was essentially worthless under ISIS rule anyway. Michael patiently and gently set forth the tragic facts that Uncle Luke, in his emotional attachment to all that he had built, was too blind to see: that he was eager to leave the area, that he had no one strong enough to protect his property from ISIS confiscation in his absence, and that nobody would ever pay him a fair price for his property, knowing that he is a Christian who is desperate to leave the city. In the end, Uncle Luke listened to Michael's reasoning. Maria said that she and the rest of our family all watched from the van as Uncle Luke broke down in tears, reluctantly signing over his home and business to the Islamist thugs who had taken over the city where he had lived for over half a century. It was a heartbreaking moment, but necessary for my family's liberation from the barbaric rule that had destroyed their hometown.

Anyway, there is so much more I could write to you about so many related topics, but I have to stop now so that I can get ready for my date with Professor Morales. His extra hectic work week is finally over, and I was delightedly surprised to answer an unknown number on my cell a few hours ago, only to discover that it was my professor! He called to see if I wanted to join him for dinner at another high-end vegetarian restaurant – this one near his penthouse. During and after our brief conversation, the butterflies in my stomach went into overdrive. With so many conflicting desires and considerations, I still don't know how intimate I should be with him, or even – if I were to stay with him at his place – how I would manage my nightly (and rather private) ritual of falling asleep by begging my parents not to enter their car. But I guess that will all just figure itself out as the night unfolds.

Chapter 2: Julien
(Journal)

Saturday, 4/12/14 at 23:15.

Because of everything that's happened, I haven't written anything in almost two weeks, but I'm going to cover just the last week or so. I had my meeting with Dean Butterworth about the selfie scandal and was given a disciplinary warning, which means that I'm basically on thin ice with the university. The JMAT fund suffered some losses during my seven-day absence, and – outside the fund – most people seem to have moved on from the incident, even if I still hear a derisive or rude remark on occasion. If I maintain a low profile, hopefully the whole thing will soon be forgotten.

I still need to record everything surrounding the week that I was away. But that's such an involved journal entry and I'm so behind on everything else in my life (workwise and otherwise) that I'll need to leave that story for another time. It's obvious from the fact that I'm now writing anything at all in my journal that I stayed on the living side of the Brooklyn Bridge. But I did feel the vertigo of death's invitation, beckoning me towards the dark waters below. Only a newfound perspective and desire steadied my wavering soul. I came to realize, just in time, that suicide was far too easy – and obscenely cowardly – after someone I knew, not even half my age, had been through so much worse and still marched gloriously on. Indeed, I don't know if my visit to the Brooklyn Bridge would have ended the same had I gone there alone, as I had originally planned.

My time with Anissa, including our last conversation on the way to (and on) the bridge, gave me so much perspective – as did the week that I spent following her advice – dispensed to me half in jest – that I try homelessness. I don't know if, when she made and later repeated that joke, she seriously thought I would ever even consider "trying homelessness," much less do it. But I did, and I became a new man as a result.

In addition to my new outlook on life, in some absurdly simple way, Anissa gave me several new reasons to live. Above all, I had to see her again and find out what, if anything, would happen between her and me. Oddly, there was another reason that might be called "The Icarus Reason" – the sense that she needed me, even more than my injured bird did. She was somehow this damaged creature I had fortuitously encountered along my path and now cared about as a result. Granted, I didn't cause her harm, as I did with Icarus, but I somehow began to feel responsible for her welfare.

So it's fair to say that Anissa probably saved my life. Of course, I had to hide all of this on my first day back in class, and even went out of my way to mock her tardiness, to mislead other students about my true feelings for her. When I saw her in class again last Thursday, she just smiled at me politely and left without trying to talk to me, and it nearly killed me. I was glad that she respected my space – I really did need every available moment to catch up on everything. But seeing Anissa and knowing that we wouldn't be interacting – at my own request – also reminded me how badly I want to be with her.

By the time market hours closed last night, the fund seemed to have recovered from some of its losses during my week away, and I exhaled a huge sigh of relief after getting to the end of an insanely stressful week. Anissa was the first non-work phone call I had made since I returned from my absence. There was something exhilaratingly risky – like the adrenaline a criminal must feel when taking the first steps of a crime – about using my privileged access to the university's student database in order to look up her phone number for a forbidden purpose. It felt as if I had already breached a taboo just by exploiting my position to acquire Anissa's personal information, knowing that I would be using it to pursue her romantically, rather than for the only permissible reason: to discuss something relevant to her performance in my class. Such an improper approach wasn't really necessary, because I could have just given her my business card when we spoke after class last Tuesday. But that would have left me very distracted with thoughts about when she might get in touch with me at a time when I really did need to focus. As if that weren't reason enough, I was also enthralled by the taboo aspect of contacting her in this prohibited way.

To my delight, she also sounded pleasantly surprised to get my call, so any impropriety quickly dissolved into irrelevance. I kept our call brief, and she readily agreed to meet me for dinner at The Jade Buddha – the best, upscale vegetarian restaurant near my apartment.

She showed up in that same white sleeveless dress that looked so stunning on her when she unexpectedly showed up to my party. As we shared our second sumptuous meal, with our usual banter and several glasses of wine (which she now drinks with a little less hesitation), the intimacy and comfort level between us seemed to increase steadily. About mid-way through the various specialty dishes served at this high-end, Asian-fusion restaurant, when she tried again to thank me for my donation to the MCA, I cut her off and told her that it was she who needed to be thanked – for basically saving my life. I didn't admit to her that I was so eager to see her again or find out what would happen between us. But I thanked her for my newfound perspective, and told her about the general sense of responsibility that I felt for those I could help. I didn't mention her specifically – only Icarus.

"That's funny, I never noticed your bird on either of the two times I was at your place," she noted, as she subtly pushed her breasts outward.

The gesture was innocent, but my response wasn't and I felt my heartbeat quicken. "Well, just before that first party you attended, I had put him away in a locked room on the sixty-fifth floor, to make sure that he was safely away from all the commotion. And, shortly before the second party, I ended up moving him into my bedroom. That was my therapist's recommendation actually. And a good one."

Her face lit up in a smile of surprise at my disclosure. She seemed honored that I would share such a private fact with her. "You have a therapist too?"

"After you saw me on the bridge, how could that possibly surprise you?" I asked dryly.

She shook her head in amusement. "I guess I just didn't realize that we were members of the same club this whole time."

My face suddenly turned sober and devoid of any emotion. "Oh that reminds me. Did you prepare your final entry before the deadline next week?"

Anissa's eyes widened and the color drained from her face, as her Type A Personality emerged with puzzled concern about a potentially missed time. "What deadline?" she asked.

"For next week's Who's-the-Most-Broken Competition?" I replied with an ironic grin.

She laughed in amused relief and playfully rejoined. "I thought our therapists were supposed to submit our entries for us."

"Do you really think they know better than we do just how fucked up we are?"

We shared a hearty laugh, and then she added, "Speaking of which, how on Earth are you sleeping with a bird?"

We laughed again at how preposterously kinky her question sounded.

"OK, that's clearly *not* what I meant – you *know* what I meant!" she added, almost embarrassed.

"No, tell me. What *did* you mean by that?"

She finally controlled her chuckles and clarified. "I mean, doesn't the chirping and other noise keep you up?"

"Well, I'm usually up anyway, so it doesn't matter all that much. And somehow Icarus gives me a certain solace. It's hard to explain, but he's a special little guy, and it's just nice to have him around. I guess you'd have to meet him before you could possibly understand what I mean."

She moved her long dark hair behind her ear, exposing her neck – another innocent gesture that aroused me even more. "And when can I meet him?"

"Assuming his calendar of appointments hasn't changed since I last checked it this morning, he's free tonight," I replied with a playful smile, as I placed my hand on hers. "So you could meet him after dessert, if you like."

Anissa lightly licked her lips, clearly unaware of what she was doing to me. "I *would* like that."

The waiter came by with our after-dinner treat, bananas and lychees in sweet coconut milk. Anissa's eyes widened with impatient curiosity. I took a spoon and scooped up a bite for her, raising the spoon to her mouth.

"Mmmm." Her eyes shut for a moment as she savored the deliciousness.

I smiled at her enthusiastic enjoyment of the dish. "I must say that I get an almost perverse pleasure out of exposing you to new things, which actually reminds me of some bad news I've been meaning to tell you."

Her face grew puzzled and more serious, bracing for the unknown. "What news?"

I gave her a subtly suggestive smile and continued. "I know how much reading you already have to do this semester, but I'm afraid I need to assign you one more book."

Anissa smiled in relief, after hearing my bad news. "What book is it?"

"*Lolita* by Vladimir Nabokov."

She raised her eyebrow slightly. "It's funny you should say that…
I've heard about it a few times, and have actually been meaning to read
it."

"Good. I'll be very curious to hear your thoughts about it."

About thirty minutes later, we entered the elevator of my apartment
building. When the doors closed, I felt her smaller hand curl in mine. I
pushed the button and entered the authorization code. As the lift began
its ascent to the sixty-fifth floor, I turned back towards Anissa, taking
her other hand so that both of our palms were clasped together. "It's
great to take this ride with you – very different from the ride we took to
the Brooklyn Bridge," I said, feeling a bit overcome by the memory of it.

"But that one was special too, Professor Moral – "

"At this point, I think you're going to have to call me 'Julien' –
except when we're around other students."

"I like the sound of 'Julien,'" she said, as we gradually moved closer
to each other. I felt my pulse quicken with the burst of adrenaline that
accompanies the violation of a rule; I was about to expose myself to
disciplinary sanction by the university for having romantic relations with
a student. But somehow I couldn't stop the chain of events that had
been set into motion. My head dipped down and the space between us
kept shrinking, until our lips touched, as the elevator continued speeding
its way skyward. Our mouths met for a kiss that began ever so subtly,
while my hands slowly released hers so that they could find their way to
her deliciously curved hips, as I pulled her in a bit closer while feeling
her hands clasp around my lower back. Soon our lips pressed up against
each other more passionately, and the tip of my tongue began with
small, tentative swipes to tease her, seeing if she would invite me inside
further. She did. Her small tongue quickly grew adventurous, exploring
ever deeper into my mouth, as if she had been wanting to do this for a
long time and finally could.

Our faces flush with desire, we embraced each other like two lost
souls who had finally found one another after a lifetime of searching. I
gently stepped her backwards until her ass rested against the hand rail,
which wound around the elevator's walls. We leaned against the interior
of what seemed like our mini space capsule, catapulting us to new
heights. Our bodies grew firmer with purpose as the temperature of our
passion rose, until we were abruptly interrupted by the halt of the
elevator, which had reached the pinnacle of the building. We stopped
moving against gravity, and the doors slid open to reveal my private

entrance. Anissa and I moved apart a bit, almost in a daze, as I led her by the hand into my apartment.

"How does it feel to be here – just the two of us?" I asked her, as I held her hand and guided her in the direction of my bedroom.

Anissa's fingers touched her lips, as if she were asking herself whether her professor's lips really had just been there. "It feels nice," she finally said, in a bit of a daze. "Your place seems so much bigger when it's not full of party guests… And yet more intimate with just the two of us here."

Pushing the door open with my free hand, I led her into my bedroom. "This is where I sleep." Her eyes widened as she took a moment to absorb the palatial space, starting with the king-sized bed facing a huge, flat-screen TV, and then scanning her eyes across to the floor-to-ceiling window view of the Manhattan skyline. The glittering lights from the city illuminated the room like twinkling stars.

Anissa stood there, as if in a trance for a moment. "It's breathtaking… How do you ever leave this place?" she asked in awed amusement, as her thumb swished against the inside of my palm.

"There are definitely times when I'd rather just stay in bed all morning, looking out that window. But Icarus is there watching it for me when my adult responsibilities have to pull me away… Speaking of which, there he is." With my other hand, I pointed to the birdcage by the window. "It's my honor to introduce you to him."

We walked over to Icarus and Anissa's face brightened when she saw the sparrow. I took off my suit jacket and threw it onto a nearby chair.

She moved her head by the cage for a closer look. Icarus fidgeted a bit in the path of her stare. "What an adorable little bird! He seems to be healing nicely too," she noted.

"Yes. A part of me will be really torn when he's well enough to be released."

"I can see how you'd get attached to him – especially now that he shares your bedroom."

"Indeed," I admitted, pressing my hand on Anissa's mid-back. "When he's fully healed and I can set him free, it won't be easy to find a replacement." I caressed her spine downward, and then around to her hip, where I rested my hand.

"Well, if I had to be caged in a bedroom, this place would suit me just fine," she remarked, with an ironic smile.

"Good to know," I replied. "Speaking of birds in my bedroom, why don't we test out your flying skills?" I asked, looking intently into her eyes.

She gave me an amused look of curiosity. "What do you mean?"

I picked her up into my arms and held her aloft. "Well, you're heavier than my sparrow, but still light enough for me to take you flying," I observed jokingly. She seemed to enjoy resting in the air, on top of my arms, judging from her comfortable smile and the way she casually draped her arm around my neck, as if its main purpose had been to serve as an armrest.

"Do you really fly?"

"Almost. I'm still getting my pilot's license for a single-engine Cessna, but soon I'll be able to carry some precious cargo with me for weekend getaways."

"And until then?"

"Until then… This!" I spun her around twice and she released a loud giggle of surprised glee. Then I carried her over to the bed. I wanted to show her that an older man could be just as spontaneous, spirited, and physically strong as someone younger. It would be a distinct pleasure to teach her the benefits of being with a more experienced gentleman.

I kicked off my shoes. They each fell to the floor with a thud, making Anissa realize that she was still wearing hers on my bed. "Oops," she said, with an adorably guilty expression. "Don't worry, my heels are as clean as… a Manhattan sidewalk."

We shared a laugh, as I moved down to her feet and gently removed her shoes. Two more thuds. My hands moved up to her ankles and started to rub them, as I made my way up her calf. I heard her breathing grow more intense. She would be mine tonight.

I massaged her legs, gradually moving upwards, as her thighs quivered under my touch and she let out little gasps of pleasure. She placed her hand on my shoulder and then started running her fingers through my hair, as I eventually slid below the hem of her dress and delicately caressed the tender skin of her upper thighs.

As she began to quietly moan, I moved my hand over her panties, and gently explored with my fingers. The fabric felt hot and damp. I turned Anissa to her side, enough to reach the zipper on the back of her dress, easing it down slowly. Taking hold of its top, I pulled her dress downwards. She raised her hips helpfully, so that I could pull it down the length of her legs until the garment was no longer a barrier between us. She looked stunning in just her panties and bra.

Trembling a little, her hands found the top button of my dress shirt and unfastened it with slightly uncertain movements. She worked her way down as I brushed my thumbs across her pebbled nipples through the soft fabric of her bra. When she finished unbuttoning my shirt, I removed and tossed it aside. Looking deeply into her eyes, I reached around and unclasped her bra, sliding the straps gently down her arms until her chest was bare.

I let my eyes drop to appreciate the loveliness of her breasts, and remarked, almost reverently, "You're far more beautiful than I had imagined."

"Thank you… As are you," she replied, in a breathless voice, timidly taking my hand and bringing it back to her breasts.

"Well, I guess it's not the first time that you've seen – " I began, with a self-deprecating smile, referring to the shirtless photos of me that she had seen in the tabloids.

"Julien, no," she cut me off, placing her fingers lightly against my lips to quiet me. "This is infinitely better."

"Are you saying I need to work on my selfie skills?" I joked, trying to cover my embarrassment with humor. She bit her lip to hold back a smile, but with my own huge grin, I gave her permission to laugh with me about it. And when we finally did, it was liberating. I felt closer to her than ever.

"I love that we're so in tune with each other," she said with an affectionate smile, uncannily mirroring my thoughts.

I brought my lips to hers and we traded lingering kisses as my hand found her breasts once more, pleasuring her in exactly the way that I now knew she liked. Anissa's breathing grew heavier again, and I began to trail kisses along her delicate neck, moving downward to gently nip at her collarbone, eliciting an excited gasp that spurred me on. Finally reaching her beautiful breasts, now rising and falling with her rapid breathing, I began to tease her nipples with my tongue, feeling them harden even more. She moaned and reached out, blindly searching for my pants. Reluctantly, I released her from my mouth and sat up in order to help her find what she was looking for. She unfastened the button and then unzipped the fly. I took my pants off and discarded them to the side of the bed, returning my mouth to her breasts, alternating between them. My hand traveled down her stomach and near her waistline, where I eventually slipped my hand into her panties, and explored below and around her waist, until my fingers felt the raised skin of a scar shaped in a straight line. Her hand reflexively came down on mine, as if to stop me.

"That's from Syria," she said. "The car accident."

"Oh, I'm sorry." I moved my hand away from the area. It didn't seem like the kind of scar – in shape or placement – that one would get from a car accident, but I hardly wanted to dwell on such a sore topic just as we were getting so intimate.

"It's OK," she said, sounding embarrassed.

"Show me where to touch you," I urged her gently. She tentatively took my hand and guided it back to her lower abdomen.

We resumed our passionate kissing as my hands continued tracing the curves of her body, around her hips, over her breasts, and then back down to her waistline. Her breathing grew faster and heavier and I eventually slipped my hand down under her panties once more, pausing to make sure that she was comfortable with it. The way that she pushed her hips against me told me that this was a touch that she liked. I caressed her pussy delicately, until my fingers reached the wet heat of her entrance. They hovered teasingly, every now and then tickling her lips. Her thighs trembled as I found her clit, and she began to moan and writhe, as I played. Again, her hand searched around my waist area, so I took off my boxers and discarded those as well. While my hands were occupied with that task, she removed her panties. I saw her stealing glances at my hard cock and it dawned on me that she had never seen a man unclothed before. She noticed me watching her and shyly looked away.

"Don't be embarrassed," I said, in a quiet voice.

She looked back. "Will you show me?" she asked, gazing up at me uncertainly. Without a word, I took her hand and guided it to my erection, teaching her how I liked to be touched. She seemed fascinated by my every reaction, and I knew that eventually she would be empowered by her ability to please a man this way. For me, there was something especially titillating about the tentative movements of her innocent hands, knowing that this was her first time touching a man so intimately. When the pleasure became nearly excruciating, I moved until I was hovering above her, and then dipped down to lick her behind her ears and on her neck, as she wrapped her legs around my thigh and held onto my erection more firmly. I leaned closer to her, as if to kiss her, but teased her by stopping just before our lips could meet. "Do you want to do this?" I whispered.

"Yes, I do… I'm ready, Julien. I want to feel you. All of you."

"Good. Because I really want to do this with you too. But unlike you, I'm not a virgin, so we should use protection," I added, with a wry smile.

"I wasn't planning to give birth to my first child as a college sophomore." She smiled back at me.

"I'm glad to hear that," I replied in amusement. "So, except for the part where I put on a condom, I'm going to let you lead, so that you're as comfortable as possible."

"But how will I know how to lead?" she asked, her hand starting to stroke my erection in the way that I had shown her.

"Well, I'll guide you. Although I see that you're already taking matters into your own hands," I replied, to her amusement. "So now you just have to decide when you're ready."

She put her other hand on my chest, and I caressed her cheek softly before dipping to kiss her, while reaching down to pleasure her with my hands once again. I knew that, on her first time, Anissa probably wouldn't climax from intercourse alone, so I planned to help her orgasm with my fingers, but she stopped me. Her breathing became erratic and her hips more forceful as they thrust against me. She pulled back and looked into my eyes pleadingly. I couldn't deny either one of us any longer. I knelt above her and gently urged her legs apart.

"Tell me to stop, if I hurt you," I said, looking deeply into her eyes as I positioned myself above her and guided my cock to her entrance. She nodded and reached out to pull me to her, so I slowly lowered myself, using all of my self-control to hold back from thrusting into her. Bit by bit she accommodated me, her tight pussy exquisite around my cock. There was a brief moment of resistance, and then she released a gentle gasp as I filled her completely. The slightly stunned look in her eyes, already hazy with desire, is one that I will never forget. In that moment, Anissa was breathtaking.

As I slowly began to move my hips, she tossed her head back and moaned. We quickly found a rhythm, as if our bodies had always known one another, like we were meant to be joined together like this, as one. I could sense that her pleasure was as exquisite as mine, but that she was holding back somehow. I encouraged her to pleasure herself as we made love, hoping that she would feel as physically satisfied as possible. I badly wanted the two of us to travel into oblivion together. It wasn't meant to be, though, and eventually I could no longer hold back. I called out her name in a strangled voice as I came, collapsing on her and quickly rolling aside and pulling her into my arms.

Later, when her head was nestled peacefully in the crook of my arm, I became troubled by an old dilemma: in order to hide my violent nightmares from her, should I ask her to sleep in another room, as I had always done with all of the other women I've had sex with?

I couldn't bring myself to do it. Maybe I would get lucky and not have the nightmare. Or maybe I'd stay up all night thinking about it – since it takes very little to keep me awake – and then I'd try to make up for the lost sleep by napping after she leaves.

We eventually exchanged some sweet goodnights and I pulled the blanket over us. I became drowsy with Anissa still enveloped by my arm. She eventually turned to face the opposite direction, tempting me to take my limb back, if only to give it some proper circulation again. But she was holding onto it with her hands, so I just adjusted a bit until the weight of her head was almost entirely on her pillow. A few minutes later, my eyes began to feel a bit droopy, but I vaguely noticed that Anissa was whispering something. Maybe that's why she turned her back to me. I couldn't hear much of what she was saying, and didn't understand whatever I did manage to hear because it was in another language – probably Arabic. For a moment, I thought maybe she was talking in her sleep or something, but then, several minutes after the whispering stopped, she turned back towards me. I pretended to be asleep, so that she wouldn't worry about whether I had witnessed the whispering that she clearly had been trying to conceal.

As I lay there with Anissa's warm naked body cozied up next to mine, I felt myself gradually drifting towards a sleepy state. And then I was in a dream. It started off in a rather surreal way. I was in my Psychology and Markets class, delivering my lecture, when Anissa raised her hand and asked if she could analyze my nightmare for the class.

"No, that's extremely private," I replied. "No one knows about my nightmares – except my therapist, and I trusted her with that information only very recently." The class then burst into laughter as students started joking amongst themselves about how their psychology professor was himself getting psychological treatment. Anissa then very dramatically stood up and called the class to order with so much passion and presence that everyone quieted down.

"Now tell me about your nightmares, Professor Morales. It's the only way forward. For you. And for us," she said, in front of the class.

"How can I tell you about them when you're still calling me Professor Morales?" I asked her. "And in front of all these students?"

"Julien, what are you talking about? It's just the two of us," she said. "Are you feeling OK? Look around!" And sure enough, when I looked around the room, it was just she and I. "Now tell me already. Don't you trust me?"

"Yes, Anissa. I do trust you. But I forgot to shave this morning. Come with me to the bathroom and I'll tell you about it while I shave." She agreed and followed me out of the classroom and over to the nearby men's bathroom. She locked the door and it was just the two of us in the bathroom. I removed my necktie, and undid a few buttons of my dress shirt. Then I pulled out a razor from my suit jacket and began to shave.

"But Julien, don't you need to apply shaving cream first?" she asked.

"No, watch how I do it. My Latino skin doesn't mind – even without any shaving cream," I joked. I proceeded methodically and carefully to move the razor across my cheeks, converting my five o'clock shadow into a clean shave.

"Oh, I like how you did that – it looks very nice. And it really suits that image of the distinguished and successful businessman that I always associate with you," she noted flirtatiously.

But then, as I looked in the mirror, I became fixated on some hairs near my carotid artery that were still there. I pushed the blade deep against my neck to shave them off, and then blood squirted out.

"Julien, STOP – you're cutting yourself!" Anissa cried out in alarm.

"No, it's OK… I just need to get these last bristles," I replied, vigorously scraping up the different parts of my neck with the blade, until blood was pouring out of my neck, spraying all over the mirror, and filling up the sink. "Just a little more, and I can finish myself off here. Just clean up after me, will you?"

I kept slashing up my neck and face with the razor as Anissa cried out horrible shrieks until I had severed off my own head and it was bobbing up and down in the blood-filled sink.

I screamed in horror and flung the blanket off me, shooting upright and hyperventilating.

Anissa woke up, and gently put her hand on my back. "What's wrong, Julien? A nightmare?"

"Yeah... I'm... " I was still disoriented by the transition to reality, but thankful to be awake again, as I realized that I was in my bed and not the university bathroom. "I'm sorry I woke you up... I...Oh, fuck... That was such a... Such a dreadful dream... "

Her hand caressed my back. "It's OK... I have them too." She held my head and kissed it.

Chapter 3: Anissa

∞ Saturday, April 12, 2014 ∞

To My Dearest,

I'm so behind – not just because I've been too busy living life to write about it, but also because there's just so much more to tell you these days.

I barely slept last night, so I'm quite exhausted at the moment, but I need to catch you up at least a little as I try to sort things out in my head. Last night, I finally gave myself to Julien (as he insisted I now call him, unless other students are around). The lead-up to the moment was magical in every respect, but it was physically painful at times, and a part of me was – and still is – uneasy about the whole thing for many reasons. My past still haunts me when I sleep, although I saw that – much to my surprise – his does as well. There was also some guilt because of my feelings for Michael, even though he himself had requested that we keep things "light and casual." I still felt slightly unfaithful about my intimacy with Julien, and – even worse for my guilty conscience – I could hardly blame Julien for what happened; he was the perfect gentleman at every step of the way, which of course made him that much more irresistible.

At first, I thought that I would ask to sleep in a different room, so that he wouldn't overhear my nightly ritual. But I felt so warm and comfortable near him, that I decided just to wait until he fell asleep, and then turn away and whisper extra quietly. After I finished begging my parents not to enter the car that would end up crashing, I turned back towards Julien, and was relieved to see that he had been sleeping and so probably hadn't heard anything.

But I stayed up thinking about how I've been lying to him, no less than I lie to myself in my pre-sleep ritual. And I lied to him again just as we were growing more intimate than ever and he asked about my scar. I stayed up wondering if it was obvious to him that I was lying about the cicatrix being from a car crash in Syria – especially since I had earlier told him that the collision had killed my parents. I guess he might think that those were two separate accidents, but why do I even need to play this game with him? I lie to myself every night so that I can avoid nightmares, but why did I lie to him just as he was getting closer to me than any man ever has? Because there are parts of my past that I still haven't shared even with you, My Dearest. So how can I share them with him? Thus, maybe I should first tell you those unbearably painful moments, and then try to trust him with them too. He clearly suffers from some past traumas as well, so hopefully he'll understand why I was untruthful to him about mine.

All of these heavy thoughts kept me awake for nearly the entire night, and just when I felt like sheer fatigue might finally lull me into a moment of sleep, Julien violently sat up, shaken from a terrible nightmare. I tried to comfort him, and wondered what past he keeps hidden from everyone. Has he told his therapist? Or at least confided in his journal, as he would advise me to do? What dark secrets lurk deep below that elegant suit and tie, hidden from those TV interviews on financial news networks, unknown to the Columbia students feverishly taking notes at his lectures, and masked by all the trappings of his wealth and success? Who is this man, really? And how did I just give myself to him, without even knowing? I felt a mix of shame, fascination, revulsion, and confusion, as I lay awake next to him, wondering if he too was actually awake. As if that weren't enough, I also thought about how Michael would be arriving back from Syria at around midday, and I had no idea how our interactions would unfold now.

At 7 a.m., I finally had to leave. I wasn't getting any rest and I just needed to be alone to try to calm my head and make sense of things. I said goodbye to Julien, who drowsily called his driver and asked him to take me back to my dorm.

When I got home, I went for a run in the park to clear my mind. Afterwards, I took a hot shower, ate some warm oatmeal and berries, and then napped for a few hours. I needed someone to talk to, but didn't feel comfortable telling Maria – mostly because of increasing guilt about how much worse her situation is (even though it was getting better now that she had left Raqqa). Moreover, I worried that telling her about my decision to have sex outside of marriage would somehow make me feel a bit ashamed, and even regretful, on some level.

My therapist shared our cultural conservatism enough to understand my issues, but she wasn't family and was ultimately a hired professional, so it felt different with her. Originally, I had hesitated to tell Monique about the idea of selling myself, but I didn't pursue any such transaction in the end, so that was no longer a potential source of embarrassment. She might still frown on my decision to get romantically involved with my professor, but it might actually be helpful to hear her thoughts on that. So I decided to schedule a session with Monique, as soon as possible. But I wanted to talk to someone right away, besides you, My Dearest. So in the end I found Maya, who's really my best friend when it comes to this type of stuff. She's much more experienced about issues relating to men. We're very open with each other, and she's the one who encouraged me to get closer to Julien in the first place.

I met her for lunch and she immediately intuited the latest developments when I asked her, with a reddening face, "Guess who I'm no longer calling 'professor' when students aren't around?"

Maya put down the burger she was about to bite into and her lower jaw dropped for a long moment, before turning into an almost mischievous grin. "No. You didn't!" She looked away for a second and then glanced back at me to see if my expression had changed to indicate that I was maybe joking or something. But my blushing face remained the same and I just nodded in confirmation. "You didn't. I can't believe you, Anissa!" I couldn't get myself to say more and just started giggling mischievously about the whole thing. "You naughty lil' Syrian-virgin-no-more!" Maya teased me with a huge grin, her eyes expanding and head swaggering to the sides for added emphasis.

We shared a laugh. "I'm still in shock about the whole thing myself," I admitted finally.

"Well, that was a very big step you took. Good for you, girl!" She congratulated me with a high-five. I slapped her palm triumphantly. "So how was it?"

"It was good," I replied timidly. I took a small bite of my sandwich, but I knew I wasn't going to eat much – I was too focused on the conversation and the related issues.

"Oh come on! Is my Syrian sista' really gonna make me start fishin' for the details now?"

I laughed at Maya's inimitable style. Her irresistible charm always made it hard to keep anything from her. "Well, what do you want to know?"

"Um, not much… Other than *everything*!" She picked her burger back up and took a bite.

I chuckled some more and she kept prodding and charming me until I finally gave her what she insisted on getting: a detailed account of my night with Julien, from the dinner date to the sex itself. But it felt good to share the details with a trusted friend – especially because I wanted her advice on what to do about Michael, now that I had slept with Julien. "I'm just thinking about the fact that I can now never give my virginity to Michael."

"Well, it's not like he was saving his virginity for you, girlfriend! Or were you planning to pop his cherry?" Maya asked, with an exaggerated look of curiosity.

I chuckled at her suggestion and she did have a point, in a funny way. "No, that's not what I mean. Look, I gave my virginity to another man and, even worse, it's someone Michael basically dislikes. Isn't that choice something that might forever blemish our relationship – something we may never fully get past?"

"Only if you both let it."

"But is it that easy? I mean, no matter how hard you try, you can't pretend the past away or undo certain life decisions."

"Well, maybe you could get him to actually embrace the decision – you know, something that you did for him and the cause. But honestly, Anissa, I wouldn't even go there unless you really want to start dating him again. And you just got started with Julien – one dude at a time, girl!"

I laughed at her blunt style, as she took another bite of her burger. "Well, I'm supposed to meet Michael tonight – I haven't seen him in weeks because he's been in Syria the whole time."

"Well, don't you think you'll have other things to talk about? Or were you planning to greet him by saying, 'Hey Michael, it's so good to see you again after all of this time that I've been busy sleeping with Julien?'"

We shared another hearty laugh, and I felt a tad better knowing that I had some kind of plan for my meeting with Michael: just avoid all talk of Julien.

A few hours later, I met Michael for coffee. When I first saw him, waiting for me outside the entrance to Tom's Restaurant, I ran up to him and gave him a bear hug. "It's so good to see you here, back safe and sound. And thank you – thank you so much for everything you did to help my family! There are no words for how grateful I am – I'm forever in your debt for that," I said, tears starting to stream down my face.

"Look at that! I'm not even back a day and I've already made you cry," Michael joked, making me laugh, as he wiped away my tears. "Come on, let's go inside," he said, holding the door open for me.

We sat down in the first booth by the door, and for the first hour, he just caught me up on the situation in Syria and his activities there. Of course, I had a thousand questions for him – especially about my family, how they seemed to be doing, the process of relocating them, the situation in their new town of Kessab, etc.

The conversation seemed to be going great until he asked me a question that completely unraveled my plan to avoid any talk that might reveal my conflicted heart to him.

"I still can't believe that donation. Do you think he actually cares about the cause now? Or is it just some gesture to impress you?"

"Michael, you don't know anything about Julien," I replied. "I mean, *Professor Morales*," I said, softening my tone as I realized that – to Michael – I must have sounded suspiciously defensive and protective of my professor.

He put down his cup of coffee. "Oh, so now he's *Julien* to you?" Michael replied, with an expression of surprise and hurt disappointment.

"That's not the point, Michael. I'm just saying that there's a lot more to him than you realize, and I think he really has started caring about the cause," I explained, hoping I could somehow steer Michael away from his jealous suspicions.

"You now know him extremely well, it seems."

"And why are you making me feel bad about that? I mean, my getting closer to him was *your* idea originally, remember?"

"Well, I always said that I was torn about this. And I didn't think that you'd get *this* close to him."

"I'm still figuring things out, Michael. I'm confused right now. Maybe even more confused than I realized. But you were the one who said that Antioch is bigger than any jealousies that may develop along the way between us."

"Yes, I did," he said, taking out some cash to leave on the table for our coffees. "But I'm human too." He left the money on our table and got up.

"Michael, I'm sorry – please don't be upset at me, I – "

"I'm not upset. This was my fault, really. Anyway, thanks for your help with *Julien*. I'll see you around."

He walked out, without a backward glance, and I just sat there, feeling horrible and even more confused, until tears streamed down my cheeks again. And he hadn't been back even one day.

Chapter 4: Julien

Sunday, 4/13/14 at 22:15.

Saw my therapist today. Oddly, I somehow felt more powerful than usual around Lily – even though in some ways I needed her more than ever, with all of the new questions raised by the developments with Anissa. I spent the first half of our session telling her about the selfie scandal and how it brought me to a new low, but then renewed my perspective on things and maybe taught me some lessons about my own recklessness. I managed to avoid mentioning Anissa until I realized that I had to tell Lily about her or she wouldn't be able to help me with any of the related issues. Now that I was thoroughly smitten with my current student, the part of me that felt weaker around Lily also wanted her to know that her power over me had diminished a little.

After concluding that it was time to open up about my relationship with Anissa, I eased Lily into the topic: "You'll be pleased to know that I've also just decided to share something that I've been keeping from you until now," I began.

Lily's brow rose slightly, suggesting both curiosity and suspicion. "It's always nice when you open up enough for me to do my job, Julien."

I released an ironic smirk. "I never said I was an easy client. But I did triple your hourly rate, so it all works out in the end, right?"

"Is that your way of reminding me that this is all transactional?"

"Maybe. Although I've been exploring some non-transactional interactions lately. And that also has some bearing on you – in more ways than one."

She sat there, tapping her pen against her bottom lip, as if to say "I'm *still* waiting for you to reveal something useful, Julien. Stop fucking with my head."

"Remember how I was looking to hire an attractive therapist partly to help me manage my issues with women, so that I could try to understand my desires and temptations as they unfolded?"

"Yes," she replied, her eyes widening in anticipation.

"Well, that may no longer be necessary. I mean, I still find you attractive, but – as of last Saturday night – you've become sexually irrelevant. Which may actually make for more productive therapy sessions on some level."

Her eyes narrowed a bit, almost bitterly. "What happened last Saturday night, Julien?"

"The woman I've been growing increasingly obsessed with came to my place, and gave me her virginity."

"And why would that change things so much for you?" she asked, with a mixture of skepticism and curiosity.

"Because I no longer need another beautiful woman to distract me from her. She is the one I want, and the woman I will focus on. And there is a very special kind of non-transactional intimacy developing between us. In fact, if things continue to go well with her, I may not even need your services anymore."

Lily's shoulders seemed to tense up a little. "What do you mean?"

"I'm beginning to feel a unique and trusting intimacy with her that makes any kind of transactional closeness seem grossly inadequate – even artificial – by comparison."

Lily put her pen down. "But she's not a trained professional, Julien. The fact that you may open up more with her than me says nothing about her ability to analyze whatever you've shared. Although it does perhaps prepare you to reveal more to a professional who *can* help you understand yourself better."

"Oh, but you have no idea how wise and intuitive she is. Her name is Anissa, by the way. And she's as perceptive as she is whip smart."

"You know this from your dates with her?" Lily asked, with a hint of insecurity in her voice.

"Among other things."

"What do you mean?"

"Well, she's the top student in my Psychology and Markets class," I replied with a mischievous grin, as Lily's eyes popped out.

She adjusted her posture a little and recovered her composure. "Is this the first time that you've had sex with one of your students?"

"This is the first time that I've slept with a student who's currently enrolled in my class. But I've fucked plenty of former students. Although this time is different – in so many ways."

"How is it so different?"

"Because in a weird way, she feels like a kindred spirit. Like someone I could actually grow very close to – not because I'm paying her to listen to and analyze my problems, or because she's some gold digger pretending to care about me, but because we both somehow belong together on the same journey – the same road to recovery."

I could have sworn there was an undertone of jealous insecurity in Lily's reply: "Well, that's wonderful news. It sounds like you may have found someone special for yourself."

"It certainly feels that way, although we're still just getting to know each other."

"Well, maybe further sessions really aren't necessary, if she's that helpful in understanding and managing your issues."

As excited and hopeful as I was about Anissa, I wasn't quite ready to terminate therapy and clearly needed to reassure Lily of that. "Well, it's not as if all is well in paradise."

Lily barely suppressed a smug smirk. "Why is that?"

"I suspect she's been lying to me about parts of her past – probably because she doesn't trust me enough yet."

"How long have you known her?"

"About two and a half months, but we became close only recently. So, as wise and perceptive as she is for her years, and as easy as I find it to confide in her, there are still some important issues that she may *not* be able to help with – if only because they directly involve her."

"It would certainly be hard for her to give you dispassionate advice about your passion for her," she noted with a hint of sarcasm.

"Obviously. And there are still my childhood traumas. I mean, she was actually lying next to me when I awoke from one of my nightmares, but I'm not sure if I could get myself to tell her what's in my nightmares, much less the events that are probably behind them."

"You told me what's in your bad dreams – so why can't you tell her at least that much?"

"Because it might seriously disturb her – even frighten her away. Although she herself claims to have nightmares from some of the traumas she experienced during the Syrian Civil War."

"Oh, wow. On top of everything else, she's also a war refugee?" Lily shook her head slightly in disbelief. She looked at the clock on the wall in her office. "Well, our time is up, Julien. But everything you've just told me in the last half of our session makes me wonder whether you actually learned anything at all from the selfie scandal. Your sexual behavior is as reckless as ever: you're again risking your reputation – and potentially your position as a professor – by sleeping with your current student. Worse still, you may be emotionally endangering a very young woman who has undoubtedly suffered far too much in her short life, as a Syrian refugee. And you rationalize it all by claiming that you're kindred spirits." She shook her head some more and stood up, as her critique presumably continued firing away in her head.

"Well, there's obviously more to cover," I replied, as I rose to my feet. On my way out, my eyes fixed on hers for a moment. "As you can see, your services are still needed," I added with a smile and a touch of irony.

Chapter 5: Anissa

∾ Wednesday, April 16, 2014 ∾

To My Dearest,

My meeting with Michael last Saturday left me sad and confused and I mostly kept to myself, although the next day I did get a text from Julien. "I've been thinking of you, Anissa. Friday was really special – hopefully for you too. I'm here if you want to talk." I wasn't ready to talk to him but I replied: "Thanks, Julien. It was really special for me too – of course. Just been thinking about stuff and trying to study. See you soon."

Adding to my emotional dizziness on Sunday, I spoke with my sister, who kept noting how amazing Michael is, and what a brave and selfless man he is for having helped as he did. Throughout our entire call, Maria seemed so much happier, and seeing her smile so much was one of the highlights of my week. "I'm just thrilled to have some semblance of our old life back," she beamed. "I'm even playing the violin again, and I plan to see if I can volunteer at the music school here. Uncle Luke bought Antoun a football, and he started practicing again, and found some neighborhood kids to play with."

"This makes me so happy to hear," I replied. I could feel the intensity of my own smile and was dying to give Maria some kind of loving and triumphant embrace. "I told you that it would be fine. You just have to have faith," I affirmed.

"Of course, there are many challenges to our relocation, but at least here in Kessab we again have freedom, dignity, and security. It's easy to forget how important those things are, but – like good health – the minute they're gone, there's nothing you want more."

"It's so true. I always try to remind myself how lucky I am, but it really is easy to take good things for granted when you don't have to fight for them every day."

The next day (last Monday), I still hadn't talked to either Michael or Julien and was a little nervous about going to the MCA meeting scheduled for 7 p.m., knowing that there would be some tension with Michael, who would probably act cold and distant. But, like the other times I was uneasy about attending because of some spat with him, I forced myself to go on principle, reminding myself that the MCA was my cause just as much as his, and its goals and purpose were far more important than our personal quarrels.

Unfortunately, my attempt to take the higher ground and focus on the cause, rather than the man leading it, completely failed when I saw his ex-girlfriend sitting right next to him at the meeting. I could barely concentrate at the MCA gathering, as I kept thinking angrily about how Karen hadn't attended any MCA meetings while Michael was in Syria. When the meeting adjourned and everyone was leaving, I saw them interacting like a couple – holding hands and happily whispering to each other – and I felt my stomach turn a little.

As I walked back to my dorm, feeling hurt and stupid all at once, I realized that I was really in a no-win situation: had I remained perfectly faithful to Michael, the big donation from Julien might never have arrived and I might still be worried about Michael's continued feelings for Karen; on the other hand, if I became romantic with Julien for the sake of the cause (or my genuine interest in him), I could hardly expect Michael to stay faithful to me. When I called Maya to tell her about the situation, she consoled me by saying that Michael was probably acting out to hurt me because – contrary to what might be expected from his tough exterior – I had bruised his heart, and that means that he still has deep feelings for me. According to Maya, this was the fastest and most effective way for Michael to get back at me for choosing Julien over him, while trying to recover from the emotional pain and move on.

Ironically, it all seemed a bit like a self-fulfilling prophecy because until I saw Michael and Karen together, I had been genuinely torn about whether to keep seeing Julien – especially because the guilt of dating him when Michael was back in the country would have felt that much more palpable. But after witnessing how quickly Michael moved back to Karen, I had a clear conscience about continuing with Julien. In fact, he's been so wonderful that I would have felt horrible had I decided to cut him off abruptly for the sake of returning to Michael. But now I don't have to worry about hurting Julien, or making myself even more emotionally vulnerable by breaking things off with him only to discover that Michael is still attached to his ex.

Then yesterday, during my first Psychology and Markets class since having sex with Julien, I couldn't concentrate much on the lecture. For the first hour, I kept sneaking stares at our TA to see if there was anything about Elise's demeanor or expression to suggest that she was still sleeping with Julien. For the last part of class, I was too busy trying to decide whether to approach him after class. After playing through various scenarios in my head, I concluded that it would be better to give our professor the friendly look/smile that I normally did, but without going up to him after his lecture, to avoid establishing some kind of pattern that either of us might get used to or expect, or that other students might notice. So, afterwards, I shuffled out of the room with the other students, as if nothing special had ever happened between our professor and me.

About three minutes after I had left class and was heading towards my dorm room, I got a text message from Julien: "Are you going to follow me back to my driver only on UNFORGETTABLY BAD days? If that's not the case, and good-day stalking suits you as well, I haven't yet reached the car."

I felt a big and slightly naughty grin spread across my face as I sent him my reply: "I like to intervene where I have the greatest chance of significantly impacting your day."

His response came so fast it felt almost as if we were bantering in person: "So, I guess on good days, I should keep my distance. The greatest impact on a good day would be to make it horrible."

I chuckled out loud and sent him this: "How little faith you have in my powers! What if I can transform just another good day into an UNFORGETTABLY GOOD day?"

His reply text arrived a minute later and immediately charmed me into changing my route: "It sounds like your good-day stalking skills are worth waiting for. I'm on 114th & Amsterdam. Steps away from my driver."

The car ride with him was a lot happier than the previous one to the Brooklyn Bridge. This time we were headed to Julien's penthouse, where his private chef was making us a candle-light dinner of vegetarian delights as tasty as those served at the restaurants where Julien had taken me. Our table for two was set up in the corner of his living room on the sixty-fifth floor, overlooking the breathtaking view of Manhattan below.

During dinner, we talked about trust. Julien recounted more about his recent week of suicidal despair, when he had chosen to live as a homeless man, for the life lessons and perspective that the experience might offer. He told me that he had met a homeless Iraq War veteran, Craig, who had really helped him to survive "off the grid," as Julien put it. Craig was an African-American in his early thirties who had suffered from PTSD caused by some extremely painful moments from his military service in Iraq and Afghanistan.

"See that?" I joked. "Even by becoming homeless you can't escape the impact that the Middle East has on the world. Wherever you are, it will find you!"

Julien laughed. "Very true. Fortunately, I have you to help me get used to managing the inescapable consequences of the Middle East!"

"So, Craig is homeless because of his PTSD? It's so shameful that the government doesn't do more to help its veterans."

"Yes, it really is. But he's not homeless anymore."

"What do you mean?"

"Well, Craig basically saved my life a few times... Being homeless is not for the faint of heart or the uninitiated, as I quickly learned. But Craig got me through it – especially when I was physically threatened a few times. So, when I decided that I had learned enough from the experience to end it, I offered him a job at JMAT before saying goodbye."

I couldn't believe my ears. It just seemed so crazy to offer a random homeless guy a job. "You what?!"

Julien mischievously grinned in amusement, as if to acknowledge the craziness of the idea. "He's now working as a security guard at the entrance to the JMAT lobby. I figured, the man has served this country and put his life at risk for years, providing security in places far more dangerous than JMAT, so why can't he work as a security guard for my firm? Especially after he protected me without any pay at all and before he even knew who I was or that I could potentially offer him a job? He obviously still has the relevant skill set and he proved to me that he has a good, honest character. So why not?"

"Maybe because he's homeless and mentally unstable?"

"Well, he *used to be* homeless, and that obviously worsened his mental state. But my hope is that, his emotional stability and overall health will improve substantially, now that he has a job and a proper place to sleep. And from what I can tell, he's not a schizophrenic or a drug addict, or anything like that. But he hasn't been able to find employment, and he does have occasional flashbacks and other symptoms of PTSD. So there's a risk. But there's no such thing as trust without some risk."

For a moment I was just in awe of Julien's kindness and generosity. He truly was taking a risk to help a random stranger in need. "You did a really beautiful thing, and I just pray that his past never affects his behavior on the job."

"Me too," he agreed with a smile. Julien made direct eye contact with me. "Now why do you think I've shared all of this with you?"

It almost felt as if he was testing my intuition or something. I relished the challenge but my first answer was only superficially correct. "Because you trust me?"

"No. I mean, yes, I do trust you – to a degree that frankly surprises me. In fact, there's no one – not even my therapist – who knows that I chose to live as a homeless man for a week, except, of course, Craig. But that's not the reason I shared this story with you."

"Then it must be because you sense that I don't trust you," I replied, with a smile, now confident that I had the right answer.

He grinned with pride. "I love your perceptiveness. It makes me worry less about the rest of your performance in my class."

"Why would you worry about it, after my midterm?" I could feel a confident smirk on my face.

"Well, becoming romantically involved with you becomes a lot riskier if there's any controversy surrounding your final grade in the class. But if you receive and legitimately deserve an A, then there's no problem."

I looked confidently into his eyes and declared with a playful smile, "Well, as you just pointed out, there's no trust without risk. But I'll do my best to ensure that my problem sets and final exam leave you with no choice but to give me an A, so that there can be no issues for you around my grade."

He chuckled and replied, "Thanks for looking out for me too in this relationship."

I took another sip of my wine glass, in preparation for the potentially awkward question that I now had to ask. "So, why do you think I don't trust you?"

"Because of certain things you've told me."

"About what?" I asked, hoping that he was thinking of something where I actually was truthful with him but he had just misread me. My shoulders moved towards each other a little, as if that could help to hide the private facts that this conversation might expose.

"About what happened to you and your family in Syria," he replied, looking into my eyes for a moment, and then out at the view, to minimize the discomfort he must have sensed in me.

I exhaled heavily, and there was a moment of silence as I gathered my thoughts. "There are some things about my time in Syria that only my therapist knows. And there are a few details that even she doesn't know. It's something I'm still working through."

He put his hand on mine. "It's OK, Anissa. I'm not trying to pressure you into sharing things that you're still dealing with privately." His fingers began to caress my palm and wrist. "But I would like to earn more of your trust."

I felt nervous about potentially exposing myself more, but excited at the possibility of getting even closer to Julien. "And I would like to become more trusting of you."

He smiled playfully and looked straight into my eyes. "So can you trust me enough to let me help you trust me more?"

"I'll try," I replied with a simper.

After dessert, I discovered the enthralling – and sometimes scary – trust-building techniques that Julien wanted us to try. The easiest – and most sensual – one involved trusting him while I was seated and blindfolded, as he did various things that produced small pleasures or pains, and in an unpredictable sequence that drove me crazy, as I tried to guess what might come next. As I sat in the chair, without the benefit of sight, the very first thing he did was to feed me some delicious raspberries. Then, he asked me to outstretch my hand, and he put what felt like some flower petals in it. After that, a slight warmth spread below the back of my hand, but – within about ten seconds – became too hot for me to keep still. He had placed a candle far under my hand holding the petals, while gradually moving the flame closer until I moved my hand away from the intensifying heat. Then he fed me some delicious chocolates. And just as I was lost in the heavenly taste still in my mouth, he pushed the hem of my skirt up and I felt hot wax from the candle drop onto my upper thigh, making me sink my teeth into my lower lip. He asked me to stick my tongue out, and – as I was bracing for him to put some kind of sadistic clamp on it – he sprayed deliciously fluffy and sweet whipped cream onto it. I must admit, this game was surprisingly fun and even arousing at times.

The next confidence-building exercise actually seemed much easier after the blindfolded one, and I had even read about it before. Julien had me simply stretch my arms out to the side and fall straight backwards, trusting him to catch me before I hit the ground. The first three times, he caught me well before my body hit a forty-five degree angle. But the last three times he progressively tested the limits of my trust a little bit more each time, such that the very last time, he caught me only as I was just about to hit the floor.

After that, I did feel closer to him and the sex we had later that night definitely felt better – probably also because the second time wasn't quite as shocking to me as the first time was. But I still couldn't bring myself to open up and trust him as much as he had been hoping I would. When he looked searchingly into my eyes, as I lay there, with my bare breasts resting on his muscular, sweaty chest, I could sense that he knew my barriers had barely budged.

Chapter 6: Anissa

∞ Thursday, April 17, 2014 ∞

To My Dearest,

Today I spoke in my Psychology and Markets class and was careful to address Julien as "Professor Morales"; I actually found it strangely enjoyable. Addressing him so formally reminded me that I had crossed into forbidden ground and – outside of class – was getting privileged access that no other student had. As part of our pretense, I just gave our professor my usual smile when no one was looking, and left the classroom as if nothing special were happening between us. A few minutes later, even though we had never planned to meet, I made my way to where his car usually picked him up. It was totally spontaneous stalking on my part, and I couldn't be sure if he was even free to see me after class. As I approached him from about half a block behind, I think I even spotted him stopping for a moment and looking around to see if I might be in the area. When he noticed me a few moments later, he looked happily surprised – almost relieved.

"It's so nice when you read my mind like that. I don't even have to send you a text message." He opened the passenger door of his sedan for me.

While entering his car, I playfully replied, "Your hands really are too big to be typing into that phone. Telepathy is so much more efficient, right?"

During our second private dinner at his place, he returned us to the topic of trust by again mentioning the Iraq war veteran. "Craig is working out well so far," he began. "And I'm hugely relieved, because in his case there really wasn't a way to try baby steps first: either I trusted him enough to let him into the JMAT office as an employee, or I didn't."

"Couldn't you have just hired him as a part-time employee or freelance contractor, or some other arrangement like that, so that you could test him out?"

"In theory I could, but it would have only made things riskier."

"Why is that?"

"Because whatever damage he could do to my business as a full-time employee, he could do as a part-time employee. Either way, he's still an Iraq war veteran with PTSD working as a JMAT security guard."

"True. And if you brought him on board as a part-time employee, he might actually think that you don't really trust him. Or he might not feel as invested in the organization."

"Exactly. And part-time work probably wouldn't be enough to get him out of his homeless mentality, even if I still paid him enough to rent an apartment. He's much more likely to get out of his alienated state of mind and improve his overall emotional wellbeing and social connectedness, if he feels fully accepted and integrated by society. So for all of those reasons, it made more sense just to trust him all the way."

"I see what you mean," I said.

"But in your case, we can try to work up to it a bit more gradually. I have one more game for us to play."

"Is that right?" I asked, amused yet wary.

"Yes. It's actually also the scariest of all the games. So you really will have to take a leap of faith on this one. But if we can clear it together, it may just lead to a breakthrough."

"Really?" I asked, leery of his unwarranted confidence in this next "game." But I was still curious about it. "And where did you learn about this particularly scary game?"

"I didn't – I just conceived of it myself yesterday, while thinking about the other stuff we tried on Tuesday."

"I see," I responded, with a raised eyebrow. "Well, it's nice to know that I can at least serve as your guinea pig for psychological experiments in trust building!" We shared a chuckle.

An hour later, I saw just how scary his game was. He led me out onto his terrace, over sixty stories high, and walked me right over to the balcony barrier, which rose about four feet off the ground, and was all that prevented someone from falling towards instant death below.

He had his right arm wrapped around my waist, releasing butterflies in my stomach. I loved the feel of his hands on me. "Do you realize that, on Tuesday," he murmured into my ear, his hot breath almost paralyzing, "you entrusted me with your life?"

"When I fell backwards into your arms?"

"Yes. The last few times, I let you fall quite close to the ground before stopping you. Had I failed to catch you at the last second, you probably would have cracked the back of your skull on the floor, which could have killed you or left you as a vegetable. So you trusted both my judgment about how long I could wait to catch you and my ability to stop your fall."

"I hadn't really thought of it in those terms, but I guess you're right."

Julien then literally swept me off my feet with his left arm, while his right arm, which had been hugging my hip, held me up as well. Totally suspended in the air, with my fate entirely dependent on the strength of his arms, I felt a twinge of fear as I saw the vertiginous drop right next to me, over the balcony barrier high above the ground below. "Julien, what are you – "

"Now you again have to trust both my judgment and my physical strength. But this time, I'm holding you the entire time, so my arms will get tired faster. And of course, in this scenario, there's really no question that you would die almost instantly if I make a mistake." I wondered whether it was part of his game to scare me some more with those remarks.

As he held me there, just inches away from the balcony barrier, I tried to estimate how long his muscular arms could hold my 110-pound body. My voice was uneven as I admitted my anxiety about the whole idea. "I don't know about this, Julien."

"I do," he affirmed, with rock-solid conviction. "My arms are in great shape. And you should know by now that I would never do this if there were any doubt in my mind that I could." Still holding me up in the air, he leaned his head down and kissed me on the lips. I tried to enjoy the kiss but was too nervous about this "trust game" not being finished yet.

As soon as Julien lifted his head from the kiss, he walked right towards the edge, until he was pressed up against the metal balcony barrier with me suspended in the air, sixty-three floors above ground, and nothing but the power of his arms keeping me from plunging to my death below. The cool night air licked my legs and arms, and felt frighteningly windy at that height. I knew that the whole purpose of this exercise was to increase my trust in the man holding me, so the last thing I wanted to do was to express fear or ask him to stop, because he would then conclude that the whole thing had failed. But I really was scared and found myself thinking, "If his arms suddenly give out and he drops me, this would be such an absurdly stupid way to die, after all that I've somehow managed to survive!" Despite my fear, I did trust that Julien would never want me to die for any reason – least of all because of his own physical weakness or lapse in judgment. So I tried to cling to that thought, but there were a few moments when I thought that I felt his arms shaking a bit from fatigue, and it took all of my faith and willpower not to beg him to stop and bring me back to the balcony.

After about ninety seconds that felt like an eternity, I was back on solid ground. "See that? We made it," he beamed. "I'm proud of you – I was sure you'd panic at some point, but you kept your cool." He gave me a hug and I squeezed him tightly, as I let out the biggest sigh of relief for passing this latest hurdle with him, and still in one piece.

It started to feel chilly out, so he took my hand and brought me back inside. He closed the door after us and then led me up the two flights of stairs to his bedroom. As we approached the door, he said, "OK, now that my arms have recovered, I can give you a lift for the rest of the way." He picked me up again and carried me over to his bed, which was illuminated only by the city's bright lights and the giant screen TV playing silently nearby. Julien looked down at me and wryly asked, "Do you want to start calling me 'Humbert Humbert,'" referring to the older male character in *Lolita*.

"Only if we think this is an impossible love," I replied lightly.

"Well, I'm glad to see that you did the extra reading that I assigned to you. We'll have to discuss it some time," he added, as he laid me down on the bed.

Yet, despite all of our delightful banter and flirtation, and that terrifying, trust-building exercise that we successfully completed, our third time having sex together was the worst of all.

Once we were both naked, there was lots of kissing, caressing, tongue teasing, and exploring each other, steadily increasing my arousal. I knew that he wanted to try positions other than missionary, but I was most comfortable with him on top and not yet ready for something new. Thankfully, he correctly intuited my needs and gently entered me like he had before, infusing me with a burst of pleasure while our tongues became entangled in breathless kisses.

As our bodies started to move more rhythmically – even wildly – something (I think his foot) hit the unmute button of the remote control for his TV. I hadn't really noticed what was playing – it was just a bunch of random lights and moving shapes projecting away in the background – but, as luck would have it, the TV sound that was suddenly activated involved the terrified shriek of a woman. The ghastly shrill of utter horror in her voice triggered a gruesome flashback from the worst night of my life, and I froze before pushing Julien off of me. "Please stop!" I yelled, shocked and suddenly confused about what was happening.

Julien pulled out and moved to my side, with concern, confusion, and hurt overshadowing his handsome features. The horror movie that was still blasting in the background just seemed to make things worse, until he scrambled for the remote and switched off the TV.

He turned to me. "What just happened, Anissa? What's wrong?"

I looked away, embarrassed and still a bit disoriented between the past and the present. I just wanted to be alone. I felt too exposed and instinctively covered myself with the nearest blanket. "I'm... I'm sorry, Julien... I don't feel well... I need to go home."

"Was it something I did? I'm sorry about the TV turning on like that – it was an accident."

"No, it's fine. It's not your fault, I'm just – I just need to be alone for a while," I explained, as I gathered my clothes and started to get dressed. "I'm sorry, my head is all over the place right now... And... And I'm not myself... I don't want to be around anyone when I'm like this... Please try to understand."

"It's OK. I'm sorry if I pushed you too much with those trust-building games... I might have gotten carried away a little."

"No, it's not that, I'm just... I'm just still dealing with things from my past."

"I hope you'll tell me if I can help in some way. Can I have my driver take you back?"

"OK," I said, a bit disoriented, as I finished getting dressed. "I'm sorry, Julien."

I felt terrible leaving so abruptly, but I just needed to be alone, in my own space, to seek out some solace.

Chapter 7: Anissa

∞ Friday, April 18, 2014 ∞

To My Dearest,

I just got off the phone with Monique – I called her first thing this morning just to tell her that I had that terrible flashback last night. We scheduled a session for next week, and she encouraged me to try to tell you, My Dearest, about the incident, since it was something that I hadn't yet been able to talk to her about. She thought that maybe if I first discussed it in the safest possible place – with you – I would feel more comfortable opening up to her about it when we meet.

So here we go – back to January 18, 2012 in Homs, Syria.

Just hold my trembling hand again as we descend into that tenebrous cavern where humanity lost its way and evil savages took over. But before we go back there, please forgive me for misleading you a little about what happened by omitting the details I'm about to share with you now for the first time. Just as – for the sake of my sanity and the hope of avoiding horrific nightmares – I have lied to myself every night, trying to pretend that my parents died in a car accident, I have also lied to myself, and to you, about part of what happened that night in Syria. To bring us back there, I'll remind you that I was out in the front yard of our family home with our dog, Roy, for the last time before my scheduled flight out of Syria, when five Islamist intruders invaded our property. Roy immediately barked and attacked two of them but was shot dead. I screamed, my father came out firing his gun, and then he too was shot. The bloodthirsty gang of Islamists brought us into the house, at which time my mother frantically unlocked a cabinet and started taking drugs and medicines out for display.

"Here. We have so many medicines. Just tell me what you need and it's yours," she said, her voice pathetically unsteady.

"That's not necessary," said one of the armed men. "We don't need you to give these to us because this is now our pharmacy."

His leader corrected him: "No, first we give them a choice." He stroked his beard for a moment, as if he was weighing a proposal in his mind. "If they choose wisely, we don't need to take anything because they are then one of us." He looked at my father, who was sitting up in a chair with two men holding Kalashnikovs standing behind him and our housekeeper, Marisol, who was pressing a towel against his shoulder, trying to stem the bleeding. "As the man of the house, the choice is yours to make," he continued.

"What choice?" my father asked in a voice strained by the pain of his wound.

"You can renounce your faith and convert to Islam, and then you are one of us. Or you can remain a Christian dog, and you will share the fate of your dog outside. He was Christian too, right?"

The other four men snickered and laughed at their leader's joke about Roy.

"Choose wisely, Doctor. Because if you choose to stay a Christian dog, then you are not only an infidel who will get the sword, but you will get special punishment for serving the regime."

"I don't serve the regime. I serve the people of Homs. I help any patient who comes into the hospital – every religion and every political orientation."

"You don't allow Doctor Omar to give us medical supplies, so you are serving the regime, and I should just kill you now for that. But Allah is merciful and has given you the option to live by serving Islam. If you wish to accept His mercy, simply recite the Shahada and your life will be spared. The words are easy to say: There is no god but God, Muhammad is the messenger of God."

"Yes, I know these words. They are the first of the five pillars of Sunni Islam. But I am not Muslim. I am a Christian, and I believe in Jesus Christ."

"You are a brave man. It would be a shame not to have you helping the resistance against the infidel regime." He took out a cigarette and lit it.

"I condemn all atrocities against innocent Sunnis, including those committed by the *shabiha*. And when Sunni victims come to my hospital, I treat them to the best of my ability. I am a human being and a doctor before I am a Syrian. And I am a Syrian before I am a Christian."

"If you become a Muslim, you can continue to work as a doctor for Muslims fighting in the resistance."

"When a bleeding man comes to the hospital, I ask which wounds to suture – not what God he prays to, or whose war he fights. And when a pregnant woman arrives, I ask whether a natural birth or a C-section is preferable, not who her prophet is."

"By embracing Islam, you save your life now, and will heal holy warriors fighting jihad."

"I am a Christian. And as a doctor, I heal everyone. And nothing you can do will change that."

"So you have made your choice and you will die tonight," he replied, resting his cigarette on a piece of furniture nearby. "But first – because you fired Doctor Omar and cut off our medical supplies – we have a special treat for you. Ahmad has fought bravely against infidels in recent weeks and deserves a reward. Especially because he has been looking for a wife."

The two men standing behind my father and Marisol took the Kalashnikovs they were holding and hung them from their shoulders using the strap, so that their hands were now free. They each took out combat knives. One put his blade to my father's throat, and the other started to walk towards me.

"So Ahmad will take your daughter now as his wife and Osama will make sure that you are a witness to this act. Then, if he wants to keep your daughter as his wife and she embraces Islam, then her life will be spared. Otherwise, she will share your fate. The same for your housekeeper and your wife – Osama will choose which one he wants as his wife. But we start with your daughter."

My father and mother screamed out in horror as Ahmad rushed closer, grabbed me, and threw me down on to the nearby sofa. Hovering above me with his knife, he said, "Pull down your pants, or I'll cut them off." Whimpering in terror, I struggled to comply with his command, somewhat constrained by the winter coat that was still on me. Trembling with fear, I willed my fingers to settle on the waistband of my pants, yet fought their movement simultaneously. Thoughts of what I was about to experience had seized my ability to cooperate any further. I froze up. Furious at my noncompliance, Ahmad's eyes flared with an anger that terrorized me even more.

Ahmad mercilessly took hold of my waistline and yanked everything – my pants, along with my underwear – down to below my knees. He released a sadistic smile as he saw my forced nakedness. I heard my parents' cries wailing in the background, as the monster invaded me with his vileness. I experienced a brutally abrupt tear, an irrevocable rip of pain and defilement, as I screamed in absolute horror. After what seemed like an eternity but was maybe just a minute, I felt drops of my own blood crawling down my inner thigh. But the pain down there was strangely offset by the pain from the knife that he had been pressing against my body the whole time, just below my waistline, to ensure I didn't resist his attack. The blade cut into my flesh a little, and the pain from that wound apparently distracted my mind a little from the far greater harm that was being inflicted upon the rest of my body. And just as I thought that I might faint from all of the emotional and physical trauma, I heard a noise that I will never forget – the loud bang of a gunshot piercing the icy, dread-filled night. The unbearable weight of my satanic attacker fell limply onto me, crushing my chest as he collapsed on top of me, blood from the wound to his skull splattering all over my face. His weight rested on me and I couldn't endure his imprisonment any longer. I pushed the devilish thing off of me, finding that my older brother had arrived with a security guard.

I had to survive this nightmare, I told myself. I somehow had to make a difference, from a position of power and strength – not like this. I realized that I had to flee, however I could, in whatever minutes of fighting remained. I dropped to the floor, getting on my hands and knees to stay below the gunfire, as I scrambled further into our house, until I reached the corner, where I turned left towards the stairs. With the sound of fighting and shots still raging on the other side of the wall now protecting me, I stood and sprinted up the stairs as fast as I could to my room, until I reached my bags. Trying to ensure that nothing got lost in my frenzied escape, I stopped to zip my purse shut, sling it across my chest over my coat, and then put my backpack on.

In a breathless panic, I ran back down the stairs while praying to God that none of the attackers had moved deeper into the house. When I reached the bottom step, a temporary and uneasy relief washed over me as I found no intruders there. I turned left to move towards the doorway leading to the backyard. Just as I was about to leave the area and make my escape, I heard an intense volley of gunfire and several different voices yelling "Allahu Akbar! Allahu Akbar!" I shuddered profusely, horrified at the thought of what must have just happened as I flew through the backdoor, sprinting as fast as I could to the six-foot fence separating Mohammed's yard from our own.

Antoun and I had climbed it many times to fetch his football, but a moment of doubt emerged when I realized that I had never tried to do so with my backpack, purse, and winter coat on me. But then my father's powerful words returned to me, and scaling the fence while encumbered suddenly seemed like a small feat. Nothing would stop me. I would climb that fence, and I would survive this nightmare.

I banged on my neighbor's door until it opened just slightly, revealing an armed man with a concerned look, as he assessed my identity for a moment. He ushered me inside, shutting and locking the door behind me. As he led me through the house to the living room, I used my sleeve to wipe the blood off my face.

Moments later, Mohammed arrived looking distraught. "Inās, I'm so sorry I couldn't do more to help. Samir and I together have just two guns and only he is skilled at using one. If we went in to help, we could have easily been killed there or targeted here the day after, and then I couldn't possibly keep my promise to your father to take you to the airport in two days."

* * *

I've been shaking and crying, but there you have it, My Dearest. Now you know everything. There are no more secrets or lies between us. Now you know that, in reality, I haven't been a virgin since I was sixteen – long before I met Julien. Now you have all of the details of that hellish last time that I saw my parents alive. I had to shed many trembling tears to share everything with you, so I hope that I can now more easily talk about all of this with Monique on Wednesday.

With absurd timing – as if to remind me of the lies that I've been telling to Julien – I just got a text from him saying, "Worried about you. So sorry about last night. Can't talk now during market trading hours, but I can give you priority at my office hours on campus later, if you want to talk." Should I just be honest with him, even before I've spoken to Monique, so that I don't have to keep him in limbo for almost a week – especially since I'll definitely see him again this Tuesday, if not sooner?

As if this hasn't been enough of an emotional tribulation, I just received an email from the MCA asking all members to attend an emergency meeting today at 12 p.m. So I have about three hours to recover from what I just shared with you, and prepare myself to walk into what will probably be another psychological tempest. Not only will I have to see Michael and Karen together (which will hopefully sting less because I've continued my relationship with Julien), but I will also be exposed to all of the bad news from Syria that warranted this "emergency meeting." I'm going to go for a run and take a shower, and hopefully that will calm me enough to handle whatever awaits me at this meeting. I'll write to you more after the meeting.

* * *

Unfortunately, my worst fears about the MCA meeting materialized. But my resentment at seeing Michael and Karen next to each other was quickly overshadowed by the horrific news that prompted the sudden gathering. Michael informed us that Kessab had been the target of three days of brutal, cross-border attacks from Turkey by al-Qaeda-linked fighters, with at least one report claiming about eighty dead in the attacks.[1]

According to news reports, the ground assault was reportedly preceded by an artillery bombardment of Kessab launched from inside Turkey. The armed incursion began in the early morning, with Islamist rebels crossing the Syrian-Turkish border and attacking the civilian population. The assailants immediately seized two guard posts overlooking the village, including a strategic hill known as Observatory 45 and later took control of the border crossing point. Snipers targeted civilians and launched mortar attacks on the town and the surrounding villages.

According to eyewitness accounts, the attackers crossed the international border by openly passing through Turkish military barracks and even carried their injured back to Turkey for medical treatment. Thus, it appeared that Turkey was backing the aggressors. Michael noted that this marked the third time in the last century that Turks were directly or indirectly involved in the displacement of the Armenian Christians in Kessab. In 1909, Turkish armed forces entered and pillaged the town, killing almost 200 people. In 1915, during the Ottoman-era genocide of about two million Armenians, the entire population of Kessab was deported to the deserts of Deir al-Zour, near the Iraqi border, and Jordan. Close to 5,000 people reportedly died. Only a fraction survived to make their way back to the historical town by the 1920s.

In this latest outrage, Michael noted that about 2,000 residents were

---

[1] Note that all of the background events from the Syrian Civil War depicted in *The Syrian Virgin* and *Anissa's Redemption* are based on extensive research and news reports that are believed to be accurate. However, to accommodate the chronology of the fictional story, the date of one major incident – the Islamist invasion of Kessab (the Christian-Armenian village in northern Syria) – was moved by a few weeks (from March 21, 2014 to April 18, 2014). The death toll from the attack on Kessab is disputed. *Asbarez Armenian News* and *International Business Times* cite a figure of 80 killed. But reports from the *Christian Science Monitor* and *Al-Monitor* paint a less violent picture while still confirming significant population displacement.

forced to flee their homes, and there were reports that some families were taken hostage, the town's three Armenian churches were desecrated, and some residences were pillaged. Kessab residents feared that armed bandits overrunning their town would impose strict Islamist doctrine, with public beheadings of "infidels" and the levy of a *jizya* (protection tax) on Christians.

All I could think about was my family members, who had sought refuge in Kessab barely a week ago, and now were again forced to uproot themselves because of Islamist invaders. That awful feeling of vulnerability and helplessness started to creep back into me as I felt myself vicariously fleeing the same evil forces that again endangered my last relatives in Syria. I realized that they'd probably all be unreachable now and, sure enough, as soon as I got back to my dorm (and just before writing this to you) I tried to contact them but couldn't reach anyone. I had no idea when I'd be able to speak to any of them again.

But Michael's urgent plea, after he shared this deeply unsettling news, reminded me that my family wasn't as helpless as it had been before I came to the USA. Michael called on every MCA member to do his or her best to raise more money for the organization.

"I'm trying to create a well-armed Christian militia to protect our houses of worship and communities in Syria and Iraq. We're also trying to repair desecrated churches, feed and shelter displaced families, and raise awareness among Western media and governments. But this effort is going to take many millions."

Not once during the emergency meeting did Michael look at me. And he very clearly avoided asking me for any help with another donation from Julien. Of course, he's very discreet and would have never publicly asked that of me, but – if things were normal between us – he would have certainly made the request privately, either before or after the meeting, in person or via email. But he didn't. He just made a general plea to the whole group.

But I don't care – these games are all so petty. I'm going to do my best to get another donation anyway – not for him, but for my family and all of the other vulnerable Christians suffering terribly at the hands of these barbaric Islamists.

Speaking of Julien, he actually invited me to see him at his office hours later this evening, so I can try to get his help when I meet with him. It's an emergency, after all. My only worry is that if I ask for another five-million-dollar donation, I may be cheapening my whole relationship with him by transforming it back into that transaction that we had half-jokingly discussed (where he was supposed to donate five million before I had sex with him, and five million after). As it turns out, we've actually followed those terms rather closely, even though he asked me never to mention them again: he donated five million, I had sex with him, and now I'm thinking about asking him for another five million.

Further complicating things, after that terrible flashback I had last night while we were having sex for the third time, he probably doubts whether we're even sexually compatible – especially after all of those trust-building exercises we did together. I could see how, from his perspective, it might seem as if those games actually made things worse, which might make him think that achieving real intimacy with me may just be too difficult. Oh, and then on top of that, if there's to be any hope of him understanding what happened, I'd need to admit that I've been lying to him this whole time (which he vaguely suspects anyway) and that I wasn't even a virgin and there was no car accident.

But I have no choice – this is an emergency. I have to do whatever I can to help, which means opening up to him completely – even well before I was planning to, or even had a chance to discuss it with Monique. I'm just thankful that I took a moment at least to tell you, My Dearest. That will hopefully make it a little easier when I meet with Julien later. I'll write more afterwards to let you know how it went.

* * *

I wasn't sure how much time I would need with Julien, so I went to his office a little early, and was pleased to see that, when he arrived at 6 pm., I was the first to see him and there was no other student there waiting after me, which would make our time together feel less rushed and more private. When he greeted me, his face released a subdued smile – like he was delighted to see me but was hiding it from anyone in the university who might happen to pass by. We entered his office and he locked the door behind us.

"Hi Anissa. It's nice to see you again. Have a seat," he said, as he went behind his desk and I sat in the chair nearby. "Does this mean you read my mind or you just saw my text?" he asked with a smile, trying to lighten the mood a bit. He turned on his computer and took a seat, facing me attentively.

"Maybe a little of both," I replied coyly. Julien looked down at my fidgeting hands, and we both became more aware of my increasing nervousness, as my tone adjusted to my more serious reason for coming to his office hours. "Julien, I want to apologize for last night – it really wasn't your fault."

"Actually, I'm the one who should apologize – I swear to you that I don't normally try to have sex to the sound of horror movies blasting in the background," he added, with an endearingly self-deprecating tone and embarrassed frown.

I released a much needed chuckle and the tension in my throat diminished a little. "I know – that was just a remote-control mishap." I looked at the door nearby and wondered how much of our conversation could be heard, if a student were to arrive and wait outside for Julien's next opening. There was no way I could get myself to open up in this environment.

"You're not comfortable talking here, are you?" he asked. I shook my head meekly. Julien reached for a nearby sticker sign, adjusted the time on it to "30" so that the placard said "Back in 30 minutes." He got up out of his chair, walked around his desk, and opened the door for me. "Come on. Let's find a place where students won't be looking for me." I stepped back into the hallway as he attached the sign to his office door.

We put our coats back on as we headed to the elevator. Once we had left the building, we walked for about five minutes to a secluded part of campus nearby, where there was an empty bench and we could easily see if anyone was approaching. "Better?" he asked, as we sat down.

"Yes. Thank you… What I'm about to tell you is extremely personal and private – I haven't even told my therapist about it yet. But I really do feel very close to you, and you've been such an angel that you deserve to know about the barriers that still stand between us when it comes to our intimacy."

He gently put his hand on mine. "I'm not such an angel. But if anyone can help me to reconnect with my angelic side, it would be you. I just wish there were more that I could do to relieve some of your internal suffering."

"Well, maybe talking about it with you now will help a little. You were right when you said that you sensed that I wasn't being truthful with you about what happened to me and my family in Syria."

"It's funny, but at one point, after I realized that I didn't have the real story about your trauma in Syria, I recalled that time in class when you tried to claim that people who convince themselves that a falsehood is true and repeat it to others are not lying because they genuinely believe in its truth. I wondered whether you were thinking of yourself when you gave that answer."

My eyes widened at his almost frightening perspicacity – nothing seemed to escape him. "That's exactly what I was thinking of," I admitted. "I made up a lie about my parents dying in a car crash, and my therapist actually encouraged me to embrace that narrative because it normalized their death, since countless people die in road accidents every year. So that's what I started telling everyone. The more I repeated it, the more convincingly I told the story, and the more I started to believe it myself."

"I knew something wasn't right when you mentioned that the scar on your hip was from that accident."

I nodded. "The problem with lying to others is that you eventually say something that contradicts your story. But when you lie to yourself because you prefer your fabrication over the truth, you don't notice the inconsistencies." I looked away for a moment. Was I really ready to tell him? Maybe it was enough just to admit that I had lied without actually telling him the truth.

"It's OK, Anissa," he began, rubbing my arm reassuringly. "Your therapist's advice makes perfect sense, and I probably would have suggested the same thing. You really don't need to tell me what happened, if you're not ready."

But I had to tell him. I had worked up to this moment now, and the emergency of Kessab was looming in the background, waiting for me to help however I could. And helping meant gaining additional support through more intimacy and trust with Julien. "No, I think I'm ready. I really do trust you, Julien."

"So, dangling you from my balcony, did help a bit," he joked, trying to put me at ease a little.

I chuckled. "I suppose it did. But I had a good feeling about you long before that, or you would have never gotten me to try that with you."

"That's a fair point. I doubt I could get any of my investors to do that with me, even if they do trust me with their money," he added lightly.

My hand squeezed his in nervous anticipation, as I told him the truth, with tears starting to stream down my face. "Julien, my parents never got into any car. Islamist gunmen invaded our house and

murdered them, my older brother, our housekeeper, and our dog." I
looked away for a moment, wiping away my tears and struggling to
continue, because the next confession seemed to expose the greatest
deception of all, where Julien was considered. "And one of them raped
me before I managed to escape. So, I also lied about being a virgin. I lied
to you, and to everyone else – including, above all, myself." I cried some
more, shaking, as a great weight was finally lifted off of me.

Julien's face tightened empathetically. He pulled me into his chest,
hugging me tightly, his reassuring arms easing my dread just slightly.
"I'm so sorry, Anissa. So sorry. My heart breaks for you!" He held me
for a few minutes, as I sobbed into his neck. His lips kissed my forehead
every so often while his hand caressed my cheek.

I eventually composed myself, wiping away my tears and sitting
back up to look at him. "What's even worse is that this whole nightmare
continues. The little that's left of my family in Syria – my younger
brother and older sister, my uncle, and his family all managed to leave
the unbearably oppressive city of Raqqa, which is barbarically ruled by
ISIS. Thanks to your help, they recently managed to resettle safely in
Kessab about a week ago, as I mentioned during one of our recent
dinners. And then just this morning, I learned that Kessab has been
attacked by Islamists and up to eighty people may have been killed, with
another 2,000 residents forced to flee. I tried to contact my relatives
there, but can't get through to anyone, so I don't know if they've been
killed or are on the run now. Michael asked every member of the MCA
to try to help raise funds for an adequately-armed Christian militia that
can defend our vulnerable communities. And the MCA needs money to
provide food and shelter to all of these displaced Christians. I feel
terrible even mentioning this to you, because you've already been so
generous – and I'm already eternally grateful to you – your help directly
enabled my family to escape Raqqa in the first place. But I just had to –
"

He cut me off with a smile. "You can stop now, Anissa."

I cringed a little, thinking that I had gone too far this time. "I'm…
I'm sorry, Julien… I just get so emotional – I got a little carried away.
Forget I mentioned this last thing I told you."

Julien gently put his hand on my cheek and turned me so that I was
facing him enough to make eye contact. "No, Anissa. You can stop now,
because I've already sent the money."

I looked at him with a mix of hope and confusion. "What do you mean?"

"Well, I gave my assistant the wire transfer instructions a few hours ago, but it was after the market closed, so the funds probably won't reach the MCA bank account before banks open on Monday."

"Wire transfer?" I repeated, still confused and doubtful.

"Yes. I caught the horrible news about Kessab after markets closed. I subscribed to one of the news sources listed in that presentation you gave me about the work that MCA is doing. They send out a lot of news alerts, so I don't pay attention to most of them, but I remembered that you had mentioned your family relocating to Kessab, and that detail in the email subject line caught my eye."

My mouth was agape, as I tried to process everything he was saying. I just couldn't believe what a good man he was. All I could bring myself to say was one word: "Really?"

"Yes, really. I sent six million dollars."

An enormous smile spread across my face and happy tears fell to my cheeks as I felt overwhelming appreciation for him. "What?"

A surprised expression formed on his face. "I know – I can hardly believe it myself."

I laughed. "But why *six* million?"

"Well, the deal that we had jokingly discussed involved five million before, and five million after."

"Yes, but you said that you wanted us never again to mention anything about an arrangement."

"And I don't. Which is precisely why I had to do something other than what we had arranged," he explained with a mischievous smirk.

"Either that, or you wanted to make sure that I still owed you something after this second donation," I replied teasingly.

"You mean you're still not addicted enough to come to me without owing me anything?" he quipped. "Clearly, I need to work on my technique a bit."

I laughed, and threw my arms around him. What started as countless kisses of gratitude quickly became more, as my lips pressed up against his neck and clean-shaven cheek. His alluring aftershave moved me towards his mouth, and I had just begun to caress his tongue with my own when he pulled away a little. "I think we just lost our privacy," he noted lightly, with a slight nod of his head. I looked in the direction of his gaze and saw a small group of students talking amongst themselves but walking towards us.

Chapter 8: Julien

Sunday, 4/20/14 at 23:50.

I've been regularly thinking about Anissa since Thursday night, when she freaked out while we were having sex. In fact, I focused my entire therapy session with Lily on the related issues.

"There's trouble in paradise," I began. "My prediction that my student lover could soon address all my needs and make therapy no longer necessary was wildly premature."

Lily scoffed slightly, looking vindicated. "Surely you must have sensed that it was premature when you shared it with me."

"I did," I conceded.

She uncrossed her legs, switching the one on top, before fixing her eyes on mine. "Why are you so eager to diminish my power in this situation?"

"Because I've given you far more power than I have to anyone else – other than Anissa. And I'm not used to that – it makes me uncomfortable at times."

Lily's eyes narrowed suspiciously. "In what way have you given her more power?"

"Well, for starters, I donated eleven million dollars to her cause. I let her share my bed, where she saw my nightmare first hand. And I think about her even more than I used to think about you."

She made a few notes on her yellow pad, and then looked up at me with a raised eyebrow. "I didn't realize that you used to think about me."

"Now you know. I'm not even sure why I told you that. But this session isn't about you. It's about Anissa."

Lily seemed reluctant to refocus. "Right. Anissa… So why is there now trouble in paradise, as you put it?"

"Many reasons. I'm not sure if we're even sexually compatible. At first, I thought it might be because she was a virgin when we met and just not very comfortable with her own sexuality. But on Friday, I discovered more about her horrible past that explains her sexual difficulties and other issues. She was raped. And when you add that to the fact that her parents and older brother were murdered by Islamist extremists when she was sixteen, this is one extremely traumatized woman."

Lily's face softened with empathy. "That is a lot for any person to handle. But I think you like the challenge of nurturing broken creatures – like your bird, Icarus." She looked down and flipped through some pages of notes until she found what she was looking for. "During one of our very first sessions, you said that 'nursing Icarus back to health gives me some sort of answer when I'm peering down the nihilistic abyss.' And when I asked you to explain that, you said that 'there's something very simple and decent about nursing him back to health – especially because I accidentally broke his wing.'"

"Yes, but I never broke Anissa's wing. And I have serious doubts as to whether I can really fix it. In many ways, her needs are a bottomless pit. Even if I somehow truly healed her, I could easily go bankrupt trying to support her cause. The extent of suffering in Syria is well beyond the capacity of entire donor countries and humanitarian organizations. Even the more limited goal of protecting the Christians of Syria and Iraq is way beyond the scope of what any one person can do."

"And you feel like she expects that of you?"

"Well, she's about as sweet and grateful as someone can be, and she's never once pressured me into giving anything – she's just educated me a little about the need and what her organization is doing to meet it. But that actually makes me feel even guiltier about not doing more, because I know how much she and those she's trying to help need the support of people like me. But, as good and innocent as she may be, how do I know if my wealth isn't a big part of her attraction to me? After all, she's known me only when I had billions."

Lily stopped taking notes and looked up. "But isn't that true of any woman you met for the first time in the last fifteen years or so? You can't be sure with any of them that your wealth isn't partly responsible for their attraction to you, unless of course you lose all of your money and they still like you just as much."

"Very true. Like power, money has a frightening capacity to distort people's behavior: it can change those who have it or those around them who need it – usually both. And just as she doesn't know whether I'd be as generous with her cause if I were less wealthy, I don't know if she'd be as interested in me."

Lily tapped her pen on her lower lip for a moment. "True, but you could always stop your financial support of her cause, just to see whether her behavior towards you changes."

I nodded in agreement, leaned back, and cupped the back of my head in my hands. "That's exactly what I'm planning to do. The problem is that we've already established this image of me as this magnanimous philanthropist. So altering that is a bit like Anissa altering her image as this exceptionally innocent woman."

"Well, she clearly isn't as innocent as you thought: she was literally robbed of her innocence."

"Exactly. And a part of me was perversely excited by the privileged and exclusive status of being the very first man inside of her, which I clearly wasn't in the end. But that's obviously a stupidly superficial distinction for me to care about. And I don't. I certainly don't blame her for lying to me about her virginity – for her own comfort, or even to increase my perception of her uniqueness in the hope that I'd help her cause."

"Julien, it sounds to me like this relationship is simply maturing. You both need to see each other for who you really are, rather than for the idealized and misleading image that was projected for courtship purposes."

I rubbed the scruff on my cheek. "One of the things that I find most intriguing about Anissa is that she apparently can bring out the best in me, and gives me perspective like no one else ever has… I'm probably *not* as generous as I want her to think I am. The truth is that I would have never made any donations to her cause without her. But she does make me strive towards something better, and I genuinely like that. Unfortunately, the biggest issue – my past – will still end this relationship. And that's why there is trouble in paradise."

Lily gave me that annoyed look that she always produced whenever I failed to reveal something obviously important to the topic at hand. "And why is your past the biggest issue?"

"Because it's not something that I can ever reveal to *anyone* – especially not her. But it haunts me, and she will always want to know about it, just as you do, and my refusal to discuss it will drive a wedge between us. Whereas you would just view me as a difficult or uncooperative therapy client, she would view me as a closed life-partner who purposely prevents true intimacy from forming."

"You don't think she would understand your wish not to discuss it, given that Anissa herself survived traumas that she didn't readily reveal to you?"

"Well, that's precisely the problem. We've known each other for just a few months and she's already revealed the details of her traumas, so it's only natural for her to expect me to reciprocate in the near future. And I can't. So, ultimately, even if we can get past all of the other questions – about sexual compatibility, money and motives, my womanizing ways, etc. – this issue will create distance between us, and I'll end up breaking her heart, which breaks my heart. Because this woman – at the age of eighteen – has already suffered more than a lifetime of pain, and the last thing I'd want to do is cause her any more grief."

By the time I left Lily's office, I had practically talked myself into never seeing Anissa again outside of the classroom. But God clearly wanted to toy with me a bit longer, because on the way back to my place I got this text from her: "Can't stop thinking about you. I want to give you something very special. When can I see you?"

Two hours later, she was in my bedroom. The air was thick with sexual tension, perhaps because of her pent-up gratitude for my six-million-dollar donation, and maybe an eagerness to assure me that the way our sexual intimacy unraveled the last time was an anomaly. Needless to say, our fourth time having sex was the best yet for me (and, as far as I could tell, for her as well). So, maybe my doubts about sexual compatibility were premature.

As she lay naked with her breasts resting atop my chest, we basked in the relaxed afterglow of our closeness for a few precious moments, as I caressed the curve of her spine. She rose from my chest to look at me more intently, as a lock of her hair fell and blocked part of her eye. "Are you sure that you forgive me for lying to you?" she began. "I can see how it might really disturb someone. Virginity means so much in my culture. And Jihadists exploit that by raping women – which basically marks them as damaged goods."

Reaching forward, I brushed the fallen lock of hair behind her ear, so that both of her exquisite eyes were visible. "Of course I forgive you, Anissa. In my mind, you really were still a virgin, at least as far as consensual sex was concerned. And that's the only kind that counts in my book. Coerced sex isn't something that anyone should experience even once." I gently caressed her cheek with the back of my hand. "Losing one's virginity is all about the conscious decision to have sex for the first time, and with rape there is no such decision. So, that special moment didn't really happen in your life until you chose to give yourself to me. So it's just as much of an honor, as far as I'm concerned. And compared to my sexual history, you're about as virginal as they get!" I added, trying to add some levity into the discussion.

She smiled and then offered a joke of her own: "And it's only fitting that there be a Syrian virgin behind the virgin state that she's trying to support, right?"

"Exactly," I agreed lightheartedly.

"So you forgive me for misleading you?" Her eyes searched mine for reassurance, their plea piercing my heart.

"Of course I do," I said, holding her intense stare with my own. "I can certainly understand why you'd need to lie to yourself and others about it."

"Well, in preparation to tell you the truth and maybe to try to start living with it more honestly, I thought a lot about whether there was any way to see some good in it. And, in a way, it's actually what saved my life."

I furrowed my brow. "How so?"

"Well, the rape delayed things long enough for my older brother to show up with his security guard, and I was able to escape only thanks to the shootout that ensued. Had the Islamists not wanted to rape the women, starting with me, they would have just slaughtered us all well before my brother arrived with security."

I shook my head in disbelief. "I just can't believe what you've lived through. It really breaks my heart to hear your stories."

"Sometimes I can't believe it either. But I have faith that it's all somehow part of God's master plan, and I do my best to transform the painful past into a present guided by purpose and goodness. And you've been a huge part of that," she said with a shining, grateful smile.

A part of me was dying to share with her the concerns that I had mentioned to Lily, about wanting to know that Anissa likes me for who I am and not for my wealth or what I can do for her cause. But it wasn't the right time – especially not after she just mentioned her family history. So I focused on the other side of the coin: "It's been my honor to help such a worthy cause. You really do give me perspective, and help me to be a better person, Anissa."

She dipped down to give me a deep kiss, and then sprang off of me, wrapping herself in a sheet before getting off the bed. "There's something really special that I want to give you." She went over to her purse and rummaged through it for a moment, as I suddenly recalled her last text message and wondered what her gift could be.

She came back and sat beside me with her hand concealing whatever it was that she wanted to give me. "The help you've given is way beyond anything that I could have ever done myself; even in several lifetimes of working and saving, I probably couldn't give what you donated – at least not at my age, and even if all of my relatives were pitching in. You literally made it possible for my family to leave the hell that was Raqqa. Of course, Islamists attacked them again, and I don't even know what their current fate is. I'm really worried and concerned about them – this war is so miserable and unpredictable… In this kind of situation, you need good friends who can help. And it's only because you've been that kind of friend to my family and community, and to such an extraordinary extent, that I could even think of giving you something so valuable to me."

I sat up, with no clue how to respond to such a momentous introduction before whatever honor she was about to bestow upon me. I almost preferred not to know. "You're too kind, Anissa. But no thanks are needed – and certainly not such personal, precious gifts. Really."

"I know, but I truly want to give this to you. It's the only other thing I could give you, besides my first time, to show you how grateful I am and how important what you've done is."

"Well, now you've overwhelmed me with curiosity, so I at least have to ask what this gift is that you want to offer me," I replied with a smile.

Anissa turned her hand over and opened her fist, revealing a silver cross on a necklace in her palm. "This is the last thing that my mother gave me, on the last night that I saw her alive. It's been in our family for generations, starting with my mother's grandmother. My mother gave it to me for my trip to the USA, as a reminder of my roots. But – as a token of my eternal gratitude to you – I want you to have it, as a reminder of the community that you've so helped."

I held her hand and peered at the family keepsake she wanted to transfer to me. It really did look beautiful, with its budding flower shapes on each end of the crucifix. There was something ancient and mystical about it – perhaps because I knew that it had traveled generations and continents before reaching my bedroom. I looked up at Anissa. "I'm incredibly touched by the symbolism of your gesture." I gently used my hand to fold her fingers back over the necklace. "But there's no way that I could take something like this from you. It's far too important to your family history, your identity, and your personal story.

Really. Just the fact that you even thought of giving it to me is already unforgettably special. But I couldn't live with the guilt of being the reason that you're not wearing it."

"You and your Mexican-Catholic guilt," she joked, with a half-smile that suggested a touch of disappointment.

"I have a much better idea," I said, getting up to fetch my phone. "Put that on your neck, where it belongs, and let me take some photos of it, with your beautiful chest, but also some close-ups of the cross itself."

"You want to do this with me topless?"

"I promise you – this will not lead to another selfie scandal," he joked.

I chuckled. "Well, I've just never been photographed nude before."

"Would you consider it as an alternative to giving away your necklace to someone outside of your family – something that you've also never done before?"

She smiled. "Fair enough. I trusted you not to drop me from your balcony. So I suppose I can trust you never to show these to anyone."

"Yes, you can," I assured her.

We then had a fifteen-minute amateur photography session of sorts, during which I snapped some beautiful and very sexy photos of her, and some close-ups of the cross on her neck.

By around 11 p.m., we thought it would be best for her to sleep in one of my guest bedrooms, given that we both had to wake up early the next day, and that neither of us was a very good sleeper even alone, much less with a fellow insomniac in the bed.

Chapter 9: Anissa

∞ Monday, April 21, 2014 ∞

To My Dearest,

I still haven't been able to reach my family in Syria. I never see Maria or Uncle Luke available on Skype, and whenever I try their cell phones, the call goes straight to voicemail. I looked for some updates about the situation in and near Kessab online, and I found stories of residents fleeing to neighboring towns. Other reports indicated that some refugees were robbed and murdered by Islamists in the area, and in other cases, kidnapped for ransom.

We held a campus rally for Kessab and about fifty people showed up, but they were mostly members of the MCA and the campus organization for Armenian students. Placards held up in the crowd tried to raise awareness about the current situation and the horrible prospect of history repeating itself: "Third Expulsion of Kessab's Christians," "Turkey: Your Past & Present Shame Humanity," "Freedom & Security for Mideast Christians Now," and "Has the Armenian Genocide Taught Us Nothing?"

At one point, when Michael addressed the crowd about the attack on Kessab and what was happening, I hoped that he might have more information that offered some clues about the fate of my family. But, unfortunately, his speech to the group contained no additional details beyond what I had already read on the Internet.

After he handed his megaphone to the next speaker, I saw him walk over to Karen, who stood by his side for the rest of the demonstration. But about fifteen minutes later, his eyes crossed mine through the crowd assembled there, and I saw him say something to Karen, presumably excusing himself for a moment because he then walked through the various people standing between them and me, until he reached me.

"Hi, Inās. I'm so sorry about everything that's happened." His lips pursed in genuine empathy. "I wish I had news for you about your family, but I don't."

"It's OK," I replied, looking away for a moment to relieve the tension. "Hopefully my sister will contact me soon."

"I wish we had a bigger turnout for this protest, but it's always hard with last-minute rallies on campus."

"I know."

"Sometimes I wonder how much these protests even help when it's the facts on the ground over there that really matter."

"Of course they matter," I corrected his moment of defeatism. "The more awareness there is about these issues, the more likely it is that world powers, or even individuals, will try to help."

"I know – I just don't want our members getting discouraged by the apathy that's all around us. What really matters is trying to change the concrete reality in Syria however we can, because if we wait for the world to wake up, there won't be any Christians left there. I'm going to spend the next forty-eight hours arranging for weapons procurements and delivery. That's the most urgent task – to get our people some armed security."

I looked over at Karen, who was watching us. "So you got the money?"

"That's why I wanted to talk to you briefly," he began awkwardly. "So that I could thank you for your help getting the latest donation from your professor so fast. It's beyond anything I could have hoped for, and it should really help with security and avoiding more situations like Kessab, if we can mobilize Christian militia members fast enough – and to enough critical locations."

"You don't need to thank me, Michael. First of all, he gave that money before I even had a chance to ask him for it. He read about Kessab while he was at his office and decided to donate on his own. So it really came from the goodness of his heart, contrary to what you think about him. And secondly, even if I did have to ask him for it, I would have done so for the cause, not for you. So no need to thank me either way," I noted, somewhat bitterly.

Michael winced at the tense awkwardness between us. "Right. Well, I'm still grateful and just felt the need to tell you." He looked down for a moment, as if he wasn't quite sure how to end the conversation. "Sorry again, about your family. I'll let you know if I hear anything," he added, before turning around and walking back towards Karen.

Ugh. I have so many mixed feelings about how things have unfolded between us – a mixture of regret, bitterness, confusion, and questions about what might have been…

And I'm also torn about Julien. I think I'm falling in love with him, even though I really don't know anything about him, except that he's incredibly smart and successful and has horrible nightmares. But I know nothing about his family, his childhood, his past loves, or anything else for that matter. And every time I've tried to ask about even the most basic details of his childhood, he manages to change the subject or turn the focus to me. All he has ever told me is that he grew up in Mexico, and was extremely close with his mother, who died of cancer shortly after he graduated from high school. That's literally all I know about a man who is becoming an obsession – a man I want to love even more than I realized I could love.

My relationship with him is so important – not only because he seems like a potential soul mate (if I could just get him to open up more), but also because of what he has done, and can continue to do, to help my family and community. Last night I tried to bring us even closer by offering him a priceless token of my love and gratitude, but he refused to accept it from me, which left me feeling strangely rejected and unsure about him again. I've been wondering whether he wouldn't take my necklace because he's afraid he won't stay with me over the long term.

I just wish that I didn't feel so much weaker and more vulnerable than Julien. Will there always be a giant power disparity between us because I need his help so much? And I know nothing about him... Am I really falling for a man who is almost a complete stranger?

There seems to be a gross imbalance in everything about my relationship with Julien. He has far more wealth and power, and I need him infinitely more than he needs me. He is the only one I've ever completely given myself to, but he's probably lost count of his prior sexual encounters. I've trusted him with my deepest and darkest secrets, while he avoids sharing his.

All of these thoughts made it impossible for me to concentrate on anything, and I finally called him on his cell, in the evening. Our call began with our usual, light banter, but he thankfully sensed that something was bothering me, so I didn't have to make that potentially abrupt and awkward transition from badinage to candid concerns. "What's wrong, Anissa?" he asked.

"I've just been thinking... about us." I was a little nervous about sharing my worries, as this could potentially lead to our first official quarrel, but I had to press on. "I just feel like things are very imbalanced between us – especially when it comes to trust."

"Is this your way of telling me that you'd like to try holding me up over my balcony?" he joked, trying to lighten the mood.

I chuckled. "Do students who accidentally kill their professor generally still pass the class?"

He laughed a bit. "I guess I probably shouldn't explore this scenario too much, right?" He laughed a bit and a brief pause followed, as he shifted back to a more serious tone. "I'm sorry, Anissa, I shouldn't make light of your concerns so much. How would you like me to trust you more?"

"Well, that's just it. You seem to block me everywhere I try to gain your trust." I looked out of my small dorm window, and wondered if Julien was looking out of his giant window.

"You don't think the fact that I'm dating you while you're still my student involves a huge amount of trust on my part? By doing that, I'm quite literally trusting you not to get me fired from Columbia University for a scandal that would surely end up all over the tabloids."

I rolled my eyes a little, glad that he couldn't see me. "Well, I'm also risking my reputation by dating my professor. Maybe I'm even violating some official university rule that I'm blissfully unaware of."

"Anissa, I can assure you that any risk to you is far smaller than the potential peril I accept by dating a current student."

"Is that the best you can come up with for an example of how you are trusting me?"

There was a silent pause and I could practically hear Julien running his fingers through his hair as he was thinking. "How about if I give you six hours to control my Twitter account? If you wanted to, you could very quickly destroy my online reputation with about half a million followers."

"You know I would never do something like that. And even if I were that crazy and careless, it's in my interest to see your influence enhanced, not diminished – if only for the sake of the cause I'm so happy to see you supporting. And you should know all of that, so that's not really showing me how you trust me."

I heard him exhale in slight frustration. "So what would satisfy you?"

"How about trusting me with the very basics – like some details about your father, your childhood, etc."

"I told you that he was a butcher, and that seeing him at work upset me so much that I became a vegetarian."

"There's obviously far more to tell me than that. Maybe then I'd also have some insight into your nightmares."

"Those are details that I haven't even brought myself to share with my shrink."

"Well, I told you about my rape before I told my therapist. She won't find out until I see her this Wednesday."

"I know, and I appreciate that you confide in me so much. But I didn't ask for that information or pressure you to disclose it before you felt ready. And I'm not ready to share what you want to know. I'm sorry."

I shook my head in frustration. "OK. Well, can we come up with some other way for you to show me how much you trust me?"

"Why don't we think about it some more, and see if we can come up with something by the end of class tomorrow?"

"OK," I replied, hopeful that we would soon make progress on the issue. We said goodbye on good terms.

Today, a few hours before Julien's class, I decided to consult with Maya, since she has known him for much longer, and is more socially savvy than I am. I was curious to see if she had any suggestions, but she nearly spit out her coffee when I asked her.

"Sometimes I think you're almost too precious, Anissa," she said in thorough amusement. "Most women in your shoes would be ecstatic just to have Julien as a friend, much less getting to sleep with him. But you're now trying to get all up in his business!"

I chuckled, as Maya reminded me that I had lost sight of the bigger picture and what a quasi-celebrity Julien is. "I guess you're right," I conceded. "But don't you think it's weird to sleep with someone and know so little about him? The basics of his personal life and family history, whether there are other women in his life – you know, that sort of thing."

"My Syrian sista', let me tell you right now: Julien has other women in his life. Many. That's just who he is, and everyone who sleeps with him knows that. I'm actually a bit surprised if any of this is coming to you as news. The man is a rock star of finance. He's on TV – as in, random people often recognize him on the street. He's an Ivy League Professor. Latino magazines regularly profile him. He's a billionaire. You can't expect him to act like some house-trained husband."

"I hadn't really thought of it that way," I admitted, trying to hide my deep disappointment, if any of this was true. Julien had led me to believe that I was different for him – that he viewed me as special and would treat me accordingly. Thus, instead of somehow reassuring me, or giving me some concrete ideas for how to test Julien's trust, or just get to know him better, Maya actually increased my general pessimism and anxiety.

A few hours later, I was in Julien's class, where he and I maintained our usual feigned indifference to each other, and then I discreetly met him by the intersection where his driver usually picked him up. By that time, I had thought of a good test of his trust – especially in light of my conversation with Maya – and was wondering if Julien had come up with anything better as I joined him in the back seat of his dark sedan.

He offered to show me his bank accounts – something that very few people have seen – but I didn't actually care about that (to his surprised amusement) and I didn't feel like it would help me to know him any better. His other ideas were no better, so I finally told him mine. I wanted temporary access to his Facebook account, which then prompted a negotiation of sorts.

"Nobody has access to my account. Not even Raegan."

"Well, that's all the more reason to give it to me temporarily – so that you've actually trusted me more than anyone else with something personal."

"How about if I let you browse my Timeline and photos?"

"I can do that without your trust or permission – that's public."

"There's much more stuff that isn't public and that you haven't seen because we're not connected on there."

"OK, that's a start," I agreed with a smile.

About an hour later, I was lying tummy down on his bed, logged into his Facebook account, with him hovering over me in the background. I rolled over to look at him and remarked, "It's not really trusting me if you're going to look over my shoulder every second that I'm looking at your account."

He tightened his lips a bit in reluctant defeat. "Fine. I will have total faith in you regarding my account, which means you are not to post any status updates or comments, or go into my inbox. Can I trust you to respect those boundaries without me standing here to make sure?" I nodded as convincingly as I could, even though I knew that curiosity would probably overwhelm me as soon as he left me alone. "OK, so I'm going to take a quick shower, while you browse my account within the limitations we agreed upon." He sounded a little frustrated and uneasy about the whole thing, as if he didn't actually trust me with this at all but had been cornered into proving that he did.

In the end, his gut was right: I wasn't trustworthy when it came to this. I had to know. It wasn't just idle curiosity – I needed to understand the hidden risks of giving my heart to Julien, especially after Maya's warning. I worried that his genuine interest in me was causing him to hide facts that he feared would turn me away from him. And what I saw wasn't pretty.

As I violated the very boundaries that we had established and went straight into his inbox, I found an endless stream of messages from beautiful women. I saw that Julien responded only to about ten percent of those messages. But when he did respond, he did so in a way that always playfully left his options open, and never in a way that indicated he was now seeing someone or even just unavailable for some unspecified reason. Worse still, I saw that during the time we had started dating – but before we had slept together – he was having sex with several women (judging from the "before" and "after" messages). Those women included: his TA for my class (Elise), Raegan, and some other woman I had never heard of.

But the worst surprise of going through his inbox was discovering that Maya – yes, Maya! – was also among those women with whom Julien had still been sleeping after he and I had started dating! I felt so betrayed. Here I was stupidly thinking that she was some close and reliable friend. And of course I felt cheated on by Julien, even though I tried my hardest to find some principle that would exonerate him – his fame and stature, the fact that there were no indications that he was cheating on me once we had started having sex, the fact that he's been so kind and generous, etc. But the angry and pessimistic thoughts kept crowding out the forgiving and loving ones, as I wondered what other secrets he was keeping from me – about his past, his father, and just in general.

My disturbed and anxious thoughts were interrupted by his voice calling out from the master bathroom nearby. "Find anything interesting?" he asked, as he emerged with a white towel wrapped around his waist. I clicked out of his inbox, still unsure how I would confront him.

As he walked over, I handed him his laptop. "Here you go. I don't want to see any more." As he took his computer from me, he could tell that I was upset.

Then his expression hardened into the suspicious and angry look of someone who's just discovered that he's been deceived. "Does that mean that you didn't respect the guidelines that I trusted you to follow?"

I looked away in a moment of shame at so openly betraying his confidence. "No, I didn't. You can't expect me to trust you with my deepest and darkest secrets, while you keep everything hidden from me. I could live with that kind of imbalance for a while, as we get closer. But how can we truly get closer when you're still keeping your options open with other women?"

His look of outrage grew steadily worse, as he raised his voice. "So that gives you license to deceive me into invading my privacy?"

I felt a tear streaming down my cheek. "You've already invaded mine by deception," I retorted. "By making me think that you were more committed to me than you really are. I'm just one of many to you."

"I haven't slept with anyone since you and I had sex."

"You say that as if it's some heroic accomplishment," I quipped mockingly. "But you also haven't ruled out the possibility – you're keeping your options open."

"And have you ruled out the possibility of sleeping with Michael?"

"Yes, as a matter of fact. He and I were very much finished as a couple – although now I don't know any more if I made the right decision."

"Look, it's not as if we ever discussed exclusivity – something I haven't had with a woman in well over a decade."

"Well, maybe that tells me everything I need to know about you and our prospects. And your evasive secrecy is super sketchy. I share my deepest, darkest secrets with you – stuff that I've told no one else, and you won't tell me a single thing about your childhood or your father," I pointed out, as I started to gather my things in preparation to leave. I looked up at him. "What are you hiding from me? I can only imagine, now that I've seen what you've been concealing, as far as your infidelity to the trust, intimacy, and love that I gave you before anyone else."

Julien looked upset and bewildered by our conversation. "This is how you thank me for trusting you as I've never trusted anyone else? I've never given anyone access to my Facebook account – not even Raegan. You then violate that trust, but I'm the bad guy in this story?"

"I'm sorry, Julien. But I can't seem to get you to open up to me about some really important things, and I can't be the only one who trusts so much in this relationship. And I needed to know what I was getting myself into. And now I know. And I can promise you that I won't be invading your privacy anymore," I added, wiping away some tears, and putting the last of my things into my bag.

I walked out of his bedroom and towards the elevator at the entrance to his apartment. He followed me there as he responded: "The sad irony is that your abuse of my trust just now will powerfully reinforce all of the mistrust that I thought you might help me to overcome."

I pushed the elevator button and turned slightly, so that I was closer to facing him but still ready to enter the elevator as soon as it opened. "I'm the sucker who finally trusted a man, only to see it backfire. I gave myself to the wrong man," I said, feeling a lump of regret in my throat and then burying my head in my hands for a moment, shaking it.

Julien's voice softened slightly. "Anissa, how can you say something like that?"

I finally looked back up, feeling even more upset and regretful. "Michael doesn't need the charms of a much younger woman to get him to do the right thing. He regularly risks his life to do so because that's what's in his nature – it's his natural impulse. When was the last time you risked everything – your very life – to help others? When?" I repeated, defying him to answer. But he was silent.

The elevator arrived. As the doors opened, I turned to look at Julien and give him one last, parting statement. "And you may be some big shot celebrity of sorts, but I need someone who doesn't sleep with half of Manhattan." I stepped into the elevator, and hit the button for the ground floor. "Goodbye, Julien."

makes you think that's not the case?"

"Because I snuck into his Facebook inbox, that's why. And I saw the messages between the two of you joking about how, right after that first date he took me on, you were helping him to release his pent-up urges so that he could take things slow and play it cool with me."

Maya looked away, embarrassed. "I can't believe you went into his private business like that," she finally said.

"And I can't believe that you were sleeping with him this whole time… When did you start having sex with him?"

"Last September."

"But why would you even try to encourage me to get closer to Julien if you were with him?"

Maya shook her head again and regained her usual swagger. "You are still precious, my Syrian sista'. Even if you're a bit inexperienced about the ways of the world."

"What do you mean?"

"Because the smart way to date someone like Julien is to find out what you can do for him – find out what he wants. It's nice to have a guy like Julien owing you favors."

"So you brought me to his party to keep yourself in his good graces?"

"I was trying to *hook you up*, Anissa. Like I've told you, I have girlfriends that don't talk to me anymore because I haven't brought them to one of his VIP parties."

"But why didn't you at least tell me that you were sleeping with him this whole time?"

"Girl, that's *private* – between him and me. That was part of our deal – that we'd never discuss it with anyone."

"But I told you that I slept with him, so – at that point – why couldn't you at least tell me the same thing? I thought you were my friend."

"I *am* your friend. But just because you broke confidence with him, doesn't mean I should."

I was speechless and appalled, and could only shake my head in amazement.

Maya stooped down to pick up her bag, apparently concluding that our talk was coming to an end. "You think you own him just because he slept with you? Do you know how many supermodels he's slept with, Anissa? Nobody owns him – it's just not possible. And everyone who sleeps with him knows that. But I guess you're a bit naïve."

"If loyalty among friends and fidelity among lovers is naïve, then yes, I am proudly naïve. I'm just glad I finally found out who shares my values, and who doesn't."

I turned around and walked away, angry and disappointed in yet another person I thought I could trust.

Chapter 11: Anissa

ᘌ Sunday, April 27, 2014 ᘍ

To My Dearest,

The last few days I mostly kept to myself, trying to get out of the doldrums by focusing more on my studies and my physical fitness training. I actually skipped the Psychology and Markets lecture last Thursday – it was my first time missing any college lecture. I just wasn't ready to see Julien again – actually, I should probably go back to referring to him as "Professor Morales" again. It would have been really awkward to see him, and I didn't want to give him even the chance to try to talk to me afterwards. I also might have been unable to suppress the temptation to call out our TA for sleeping with our professor, and I knew that I just needed a bit more time to cool off. So I had to get the notes for that lecture from one of my classmates.

On Friday, I also skipped my Economics study group to avoid seeing Maya. Instead, I went to the campus Jiu-jitsu class that I had been wanting to try out, and actually saw Michael training there. We smiled at each other politely, and I could sense that he wanted to talk to me afterwards, but he kept his distance out of respect for whatever boundaries we had implicitly established. I was happy just to try to clear my head and be with myself in whatever Zen moment of concentration I could find while training.

By the end of yesterday, Professor Morales still hadn't tried to contact me to apologize or anything else, so I was quite sure that it was over between us, and was feeling better about moving on. I also got the email that Michael sent to all MCA members, asking everyone to show up to today's vigil, organized by the main Jewish student group on campus, in honor of Holocaust Remembrance Day. His email emphasized the importance of showing solidarity and building bridges with others who have suffered from genocide.

It was a last-minute request, so I doubted many MCA members would make it, but I decided to go, if only for the renewed perspective it would give me on whatever small life problems and disappointments I was experiencing at the moment.

It was a nice, early-spring day. I arrived at the campus sundial about ten minutes early, and was surprised to see that Michael was also there early, among the few other students already gathered at the site of the event. None of them looked familiar, so I assumed they were all from the Jewish organization. This time, when Michael and I saw each other, I went up to him with a meek smile and we exchanged greetings.

"How's your doctoral work coming along?" I asked him.

"I convinced the department to give me another three months because of the work I'm doing in Syria."

"That's great news – I'm glad they were willing to accommodate the cause," I added with a wink. I kept looking around to see if his girlfriend would appear, and then I finally just asked him about her: "Where's Karen?"

"I don't know, but I don't think she'll be coming." Michael looked down for a moment. "In fact, I'd be surprised if she shows up to any more MCA meetings."

As he raised his head again, I noticed that Michael's stubble was a bit longer than usual. "Why is that?"

"We started having some problems after she scored that $100,000 donation that she was working on."

"I didn't realize that she'd raised that money."

"Yes, she did. And I was naturally thrilled, but then she started asking me if I could envision her and me as an engaged couple soon. I think she assumed that if she just impressed me with her help for the MCA, the rest would fall into place."

"Ha. Well if $11 million wasn't going to do it for me, I don't see how $100,000 could do it for her," I remarked, with a bit of guilt at my snarky cattiness. "I'm sorry, I shouldn't have said that."

Michael chuckled. "Yeah, well, of course I didn't mention your numbers to her. There was enough drama without me adding any fuel to the fire. And I wanted to respect your privacy – if word got out that you brought in that kind of money, who knows what rumors would start, or how many people would start approaching you with random requests for help?"

I smiled gratefully. "That was very considerate of you."

"But it wasn't just the sudden pressure that I felt from her… I think there were just too many cultural differences between us – which became much clearer after I finally met her family for dinner."

"What kind of differences?"

"Well, I just didn't feel as comfortable around them as I had hoped I would. And I always imagined myself having in-laws who share my culture."

"You mean like Middle Eastern hospitality? Or more the language and history?"

"All of that – and the smaller everyday things like food, music, etc. I just realized that those things are all too much a part of my identity for my life partner and her family not to share them with me," he explained.

I repressed the impulse to say, "I had a feeling that would happen!" and tried to look as blasé as possible about the best news I had heard all week. "Well, I'm glad Karen was able to raise that money from her donor because we're not getting any more from Professor Morales – I'm done with him."

Michael looked surprised but also seemed to be repressing his delight at the good news. "Really? What happened?"

I noticed that the area began to fill up with other students who were arriving. "Oh, it's a long story – not for when this vigil is about to start."

"Good point," he conceded with a smile. He put his hand lightly on my shoulder. "Well, for what it's worth, I'm really sorry about the way we did things."

"Me too."

"But if we look at the bright side, you helped in a huge way. Thanks to your efforts, I'm in the process of creating half a dozen militias, totaling hundreds of armed men, to protect Christian populations in Syria. My deputies and various local leaders are managing the logistics and have told me that weapons and training should be arriving in two days. And we've found several contractors and construction companies that can help to repair damaged churches. We're also bringing in special medical personnel and equipment to care for any of our security forces or civilians who get hurt... Now you see why I had to get more time before defending my dissertation?" he asked lightly.

As more students arrived, the crowd gathering around the sundial pushed me closer to Michael. "You do sound a tad busy these days," I noted ironically. "If I didn't know better, I'd think you were trying to build a new country or something," I added playfully.

Michael chuckled, as he looked down at me. "Yes, well, considering how fast eleven million dollars gets gobbled up for this basic stuff, the cost of founding a country is still a long way off. We'll need some heavyweight lobbyists for that project... But you know by now what we say to any challenge, right?" he asked with a wink.

"If you will it, it is no dream," I affirmed.

"Exactly."

Our conversation was cut short as the event organizer began to speak. We turned our attention to him, but somehow the whole thing brought me closer to Michael – maybe because it indirectly reminded me that he deeply cares about important issues. And it made Julien and his whole lifestyle of luxuriously pampered living, frivolous fun, and womanizing seem trivial and embarrassingly different from my own values and concerns. I was so glad that I hadn't given him my family necklace in the end.

The memorial event was very moving, but the part that will probably stay with me forever was when one of the speakers recited aloud a poem by an Israeli Holocaust survivor, Dan Pagis, about a woman and her son on a train transporting them to the Nazi death camps. I shed a tear as I listened, but its powerful symbolism haunted me long after, as the poem poignantly summed up – in so few words – how short humanity has fallen at times. The sudden ending sends a chill down my spine every time I read the laconic poem – the vanquished voice of the innocent abruptly cut off by the evil that the world has countenanced.

When I got back to my dorm after the event, I had to print out a copy for myself. Here it is.

Written in Pencil in the Sealed Railway Car

Here in this carload
I, Eve,
with my son Abel.
If you see my older boy,
Cain, the son of man,
tell him that I

Chapter 12: Julien

Sunday, 4/27/14 at 22:06.

Anissa was absent from my lecture last Thursday, and I seriously doubt that she was out sick. I'm surprised at how much I miss her and regret the way things unfolded between us. I obviously didn't handle it well. The minute I sensed that she was a different kind of woman, I should have gone to greater lengths to treat her accordingly. But old habits die hard and I wanted to avoid seeming overly interested in her, which meant getting my usual releases along the way. I think a part of me was also scared that I might actually fall for her, which would have meant losing what I've grown so used to having: complete control.

Even though she was absent on Thursday, I assume that she'll attend class this Tuesday and I've been feeling a bit anxious about the whole thing. It's obviously not the venue for me to make any sort of conciliatory overture to her, and in some sense it feels as if I should have already made one, if I was going to make one at all. But it will also feel strange for us to play it cool, as we did when we were dating, because this time there will be no stolen glances or smiles – just a cold indifference to each other. Yet, trying to create a better energy could itself produce some kind of awkwardness in front of the other students.

I'm going to go see my therapist now, and I'll probably end up discussing this issue for most of the time with her, but I'll write more when I come back.

* * *

Back from my psychological sparring session with Lily. In the hope of getting over Anissa by now focusing on my therapist, I toyed with the leggy redhead a little along the way.

"Dating Anissa certainly falls into that reckless pattern we've discussed," I conceded. "But I haven't felt as close to a woman in a very long time. You gave me that feeling almost as much, even if I always dismissed it."

Lily gently rubbed her pen between her open palms, and I imagined that she was doing that to my cock instead. "What do you mean, you dismissed that feeling?" she asked.

"Well, I knew that it was the ultimate illusion. You obviously don't actually care for me the way Anissa did, so it made no sense for me to feel like I was getting closer to you."

Lily took a hard swallow. She clearly wanted to object to this claim more vociferously, but managed to subdue the impulse. "Julien, that's an apples-to-oranges comparison. She was your girlfriend. I am your therapist."

"Exactly. She genuinely cared about me. You're just paid to care about me. If I stop paying, you stop caring."

"You don't know that," she replied. "And you're not paying me to care for you. You're paying me to treat you as best I can, using my professional skills and background."

"So if I told you that I now want to start seeing you in a non-professional way or not at all, what would you choose?"

Lily adjusted her posture for a moment before uncrossing her legs and switching the thigh on top. "You mean if you asked me to date you while you're still my client?"

"Yes."

There was an awkward silence, as she struggled with the question for a moment. "Well, I… " Then she abruptly regained her control. "Julien, how did this become about me again? I've never dated an existing client and I'm not planning on starting now. That's a breach of my professional ethics."

"And if we terminated therapy?"

"Well, the APA's code of ethics requires that at least two years pass before a therapist can enter into a sexual relationship with a former client."

"And you're worried that I'd report you? You don't trust me?"

Lily exhaled and rolled her eyes. "I'm not your rebound obsession, Julien. But I can help you to manage what you're going through."

"I'm not so sure – especially if you can't answer my question."

"It's not relevant to your treatment."

"Maybe it is. Maybe if I knew that you actually cared about me and were drawn to me enough that you'd want to date me, I'd feel more comfortable opening up to you in therapy. Because then maybe the whole thing would seem more authentic to me."

I felt some intellectually sadistic satisfaction in seeing her struggle with the dilemma I had foisted on her, like a chess player who has just cornered his opponent's queen. If she admitted that she had any feelings for me, she might already be getting dangerously close to transgressing her professional duties. If she refused, she might lose me as a client and possibly feel like a failure on some level.

She finally caved, and let me peel away a small layer of the cold and distant façade that she had been maintaining. "I think I would trust you not to report me," she began, fixing her eyes on mine and then looking away. "But I'm not sure I could handle the conflict internally."

Chapter 13: Anissa

∾ Tuesday, April 29, 2014 ∾

To My Dearest,

I saw Michael again yesterday and was left in tears. But not because of him – he was an angel. Michael asked to see me because he had some important news that he preferred to share in person.

Anxious to hear what he had to say, I waited for him on the steps of Low Library, where he said he would meet me, by the Alma Mater statue. A few minutes later, he showed up with his book bag slung over one of his broad shoulders. We hugged briefly and then we sat down on the steps, in a secluded spot nearby, and he told me the terrible news: one of his rebel contacts told him that he thinks my sister was kidnapped after she and the rest of my family in Syria were assaulted while fleeing the Islamist onslaught on Kessab.

"My source isn't completely sure and needs to look into it more. But I wanted to tell you as soon as I heard, because it's really not something that you'd be able to find out very easily on your own, and I can't even imagine how much you've been thinking about your relatives."

I put my head on his shoulder and started to cry. "I try to call them on Skype or their cell at least twice a day. And there's never an answer." He wrapped his arm around my back to comfort me.

"Inās, look at me," he said, cupping my cheek gently with his palm and turning me towards his eyes. "I promise you, I will get you whatever information I can, as fast as I can. And if Maria has indeed been kidnapped, then I will do everything in my power to secure her release. Even if I have to go get her myself."

Some more tears flowed from my eyes, both at Maria's possible plight and at Michael's beautifully selfless heroism. "Thank you, Michael," I said, wiping some tears away.

He kissed my forehead and held me for a while on the steps as I cried. With so many emotions stirring me, I ended up speaking far more freely and openly than I would have otherwise planned to, but he was very kind and understanding, so I didn't have any regrets in the end.

"Michael, I can't hide things from you anymore. You mean too much to me, and you deserve to know before anything more happens between us, so you can decide what you think is best. But the truth is that I gave myself to Professor Morales, and – believe it or not – I did it largely to secure a big donation, both to impress you and to help the cause. I was really torn about it because I wasn't sure if you'd ever forgive me, even though we agreed to keep things casual and light. I still had feelings for you and felt torn about the whole thing. But we also really needed the money for MCA and I wanted to do whatever I could to help."

"I know, Inās," he said gently, running his fingers through my hair. "I pushed you in that direction, out of desperation for the cause, so I can hardly blame you for going there, even if it tore me apart to think about it."

"And there's something else that you should know. I lied to you about my past. There was no car accident. My parents were massacred by a group of Islamists who nearly murdered me too. I got away only because one of them raped me, and that slowed down their slaughter long enough for my older brother to arrive with an armed guard. I escaped in the gun battle that followed. But the next day I saw – in a horrific YouTube video – that they were all beheaded," I burst into tears. "So all that's left of my family in Syria is what you can manage to find."

Michael held me tighter. "Oh God, Inās. I'm so sorry. So terribly sorry to hear what you and your family have been through."

"It's a trauma that I've been struggling to live with for the last two years. I've tried lying to myself and to everyone else, including you. But I ended up finally coming to terms with it, and – as someone I feel so close to – you deserve to have the truth, so I finally had to tell you."

It was excruciating to recount all of those details, but I had to tell him, and a great weight felt as if it had been lifted, now that I no longer had to lie to him about my past or try to hide that I had slept with Professor Morales. And I was so relieved that Michael still accepted me.

Despite my confession, I felt some lingering guilt for having made Professor Morales "first" on the biggest steps of trust and intimacy: I shared my body and my personal story with him before Michael. But so much of that happened when I was swept up in countless emotions, a student-professor crush, and the desire to help as much, and as fast, as I could.

By the end of that hour-long chat on the steps, Michael and I ended up in a really long and passionate kiss. As our lips were pressed together, and our tongues endlessly explored each other's mouths, it felt as if we were both relieved and happy finally to be "home" – as if we had each realized the folly of trying to date outside of our community and were grateful for this second chance to be together.

Then, today, at my request, Michael showed up at Hamilton Hall to pick me up from my Psychology and Markets class. I asked him to pick me up there for a few reasons: I wanted to feel more comfortable in an intrinsically uncomfortable situation, I intended to show Michael that I was very much choosing him over my professor now, and I hoped to deter Professor Morales from even trying to talk to me after his lecture while also showing him that I was proud, strong, attractive, and had already successfully moved on from him. This was my first time seeing Professor Morales since breaking things off with him, so it felt tense and awkward for me, and I avoided his gaze for the entire time that I was in the room with him. But I'm pretty sure he saw Michael standing just outside the entrance, as other students were leaving after the class adjourned, and my professor probably also noticed me moving excitedly towards Michael and taking his hand as we both left the area together.

Chapter 14: Julien

Sunday, 5/4/14 at 23:46.

The last week has been psychologically challenging for me, as the rupture in relations with Anissa became increasingly complete and final. Not only has neither of us tried to contact the other, but at the end of class last Tuesday, she showed up with Michael, the man to whom I've apparently been sending all of my disposable income (mostly to please her, even if it is for a good cause). Seeing her excitedly run up to him after class and take his hand as they left together was a low blow that only added insult to injury. I feel completely played – as if everything that happened with Anissa was just part of some elaborate scheme of theirs to suck me dry. Of course, if I'm honest with myself, I know that my personal issues are the main cause for my breakup with her, but the way she so quickly moved on to another man makes me second-guess my impressions of her – especially because his organization was the main beneficiary of the generosity that Anissa inspired in me... Maybe she's not quite the angel I thought she was.

On the other hand, perhaps this is actually an indication of how much she still feels for me. There is no quick cure for heartbreak – only the cruel but palliative satisfaction of knowing that the other suffers too. Indeed, wounded love can make for fierce vengeance. And, from what I know of Anissa, it does seem a bit out of character for her to behave so spitefully, so I'd like to think that she really is just deeply hurt, angry, and looking for some way to injure me back... I hope she knows how well she's succeeded.

Last Thursday, our interactions mirrored those of Tuesday: cold indifference between us during class, with Michael picking her up at the end of my lecture. But Thursday's slights felt particularly painful because that was the last day of the course, marking the final time that I would definitely see her again without some kind of conscious effort by both of us to meet. Any spontaneity made possible by the college environment officially ended with that lecture, unless I happen to see her at another campus demonstration – but that obviously wouldn't involve the same feeling or dynamic as having her as a student in my class. Of course, if she were to work at JMAT, as an intern, then it could continue to some extent. But she already feels like a stranger and has started dating Michael again, so having her around the office would only frustrate me – I'd rather just try to forget Anissa than regularly see her and recall how I lost her to another man.

In my attempt to forget – or at least not obsess about – Anissa, I've been burying my head in work. The fund on the whole is doing well again, and the JMAT research division uncovered an exciting opportunity: a small portfolio of distressed real estate assets that an all-cash buyer can pick up for about $300 million, and probably flip for a quick profit of $200-400 million. So I've been spending most of my time analyzing the fundamentals of the deal and confirming that this trade makes sense for JMAT's overall strategy and risk profile.

But yesterday, after the market closed, I returned to my doldrums as I went back to Columbia for my last office hours of the semester, and found myself pathetically hoping that Anissa might show up for some reason. But she didn't. Nor was she anywhere near my car when I was about to head home. As I sat back against the passenger seat of my sedan, leaving the university, my throat hardened and it felt as if a mason were methodically etching the words "you lost her" into my stone heart.

I felt myself getting increasingly depressed about the whole thing, and realized that I shouldn't go back home to an empty apartment on a Friday night, where I would just brood in my bedroom next to Icarus. I had to do something randomly different – if only to distract my mind, and knock it off its otherwise certain collision course with melancholy. When I saw that we were approaching the Gramercy area, I asked my driver to keep heading downtown, past my residence, to the nearest movie theater.

When we arrived at the movie theater, I went up to the cashier and bought a ticket to whatever movie was starting next; it turned out to be a new release titled *Walk of Shame*. I didn't even know what the film was about, but was glad to hear that it was a comedy, which seemed like the most appropriate genre to escape my current gloominess. The previews had just started when I bought the ticket, so I got some popcorn and went into the theater to find an empty seat. There weren't many spots available but I noticed, about one-third of the way towards the back, that there were three empty seats in a row. I picked the middle seat and sat down. About ten minutes later, just as the last preview was ending, an unaccompanied woman sat next to me. At first, I didn't really notice her because it was dark. But something about her smell – especially her perfume – was strangely familiar. At the risk of oddly and blatantly staring at a total stranger, I turned to face her and – to my delighted and amused surprise – it was my therapist!

"Lily!" I exclaimed, my face lighting up. The trailer beaming onto the screen beyond us illuminated her face just enough for me to see how pleasantly surprised she looked.

"Julien! What – how random! What are you doing here?"

For a moment I just shrugged in speechless disbelief at the curious serendipity of it all. "I could ask the same of you! And of all the seats in the theater, how did you happen to pick the one right next to me?"

"Well, there actually weren't that many options – that's what happens when you arrive just as the trailers are ending for a new release," she noted in amusement.

"Shhhhh!!" Some annoyed moviegoers nearby reminded us that they could hear us just as the movie was about to start.

We ended up sharing my popcorn and napkins, and plenty of laughs at the movie (which was a comedy of misadventures about a news anchor who finds herself in the wrong part of LA following a night of partying). After one particularly funny scene, my hands came together as if to clap, and then as I went to put them down, my right hand gradually came down over Lily's side of the armrest between us, and gently and subtly found her hand. We both kept watching the screen, almost as if to deny that anything was happening, even as our hands began to caress each other.

The fact that we were meeting for the first time in a totally different context – as two single people in a dark theater that brings them together in laughter – apparently made us forget for a moment that we had any sort of professional relationship. We were clearly eager to experience each other in a different setting, but proposing that we do so had always been a line that no one had ever tried to cross. However, now that happenstance had thrown us into those circumstances, neither of us seemed too intent on resisting the charms of chance.

We held hands for almost the rest of the movie, and our fingers took turns caressing the other's palm in a suggestive, affectionate, or sensual way. It was exactly the escape that I needed – far more effective than even the movie itself, which was also entertaining. In fact, towards the end of the film, I began to worry a bit about what to do once the lights came on. Invite her for dinner and drinks somewhere? Suggest a neighborhood stroll that leads to my apartment? The glare of the theater lights turning back on would produce a rude and abrupt reminder that we had just ventured into new and unknown territory with our hands and now had to decide whether to move deeper into that foreign land or retreat back to our comfort zones, as if nothing had just happened.

As I wrestled with these questions in my head, dreading the moment that the lights returned, I was actually relieved when I felt my phone vibrate with a new message, just as the film credits started rolling. It was the lead manager on the distressed real estate deal that JMAT was considering, informing me that the lawyers for the seller had just notified us that a competitive bid had come in, and that we had to act fast if we wanted to secure the deal. I would need to get on my laptop at home as soon as possible and analyze some documents for discussion with my deal team, so that we could reach a decision in the coming hours. The potential risk and awkwardness of encouraging Lily to breach her professional duties had been narrowly avoided thanks to my own professional duties.

As the lights finally came on, Lily took her time standing up, stretching, straightening out her clothes, and gathering her things, as if to extend for as long as possible the time available for someone to propose what we do next. Her face had that flexible but expectant look, like someone who had time on her hands and was waiting for direction.

"It was great to see you again... Outside of your office for a change," I said, making it clear that we were about to say goodbye.

"Yes, it was," she agreed reluctantly, with an affectionate smile. "A pleasant surprise indeed." She seemed almost frozen in place, awkwardly standing by her seat, as if she still hadn't decided what to do next, or was wrestling with the idea of proposing that we extend the evening together somehow.

I held up my phone with a frown. "Unfortunately, work calls, so I have to run back home to take care of this deal that just went into overdrive." I nodded with my head to indicate that I was going to walk towards the end of the aisle, and Lily finally took the hint and started to walk in that direction ahead of me. "How'd you like the movie?" I asked, as we made our way to the theater lobby.

"It was very funny."

"I thought so too," I agreed, as we approached the exit. "Well, sorry I have to run like this, but I'll see you in two days – not in the theater unfortunately," I added with a smile.

"Right," she chuckled. "Good luck with your deal, and see you on Sunday."

When I got home, I spent the next four hours focused on the

potential acquisition, and we decided to make a bid. The next morning, the lawyers for the seller informed us that our offer had been accepted, and I was excited about the deal, knowing that it would improve the fund's overall returns with a quick infusion of cash.

By this morning, my head was back to women – but fortunately I was focused more on Lily than on Anissa. I wasn't sure how I would relate to Lily when I saw her again in the therapy context. I wondered whether she also had struggled with that question, and whether she might even abruptly cancel our session. Luckily, she didn't.

In the end, amusingly enough, we spent most of our time together analyzing the very situation in which we had found ourselves just a few days earlier. There was something a bit surreal about how clinically we could dissect a moment that we had both shared, as we went from subjectively experiencing it to dispassionately observing it.

"Why do you think you chose not to take things any further?" she asked me at one point, playing with a lock of her hair.

My eyebrow rose in interest. Was she asking this as my therapist, or as a woman who wanted me to take her back to my place and fuck her? "Would you have been willing to follow me down that road?"

She leaned back in her chair a little, crossing her legs. "Maybe. I was clearly lost in that experience and susceptible to you on some very basic level. But for me it was also a major, threshold moment, as it may have been for you – albeit for very different reasons."

"Yes. For you, it was a threshold moment because you hadn't yet embarked on actions that would produce an insurmountable internal conflict, in terms of your professional duties. A little hand touching might cause you some brief qualms but can ultimately be dismissed as trivially minor, or rationalized away as casual contact. You were well on the safe side of the spectrum of sexual contact. But the moment when our mouths might have met for a kiss, or I would have fondled your breast, or you would have come back to my place, you would have more clearly crossed that line. And – even if you trusted me never to report you – it would still be a technical violation that your conscience would forever have to live with."

Lily nodded her head slightly in reluctant agreement, her eyebrows raised with an impressed look. "Very good, Julien. And now tell me why it was still a threshold moment for you, even though you had no professional ethics at risk."

"Well, there's a funny parallel in our reasons for holding back. My reluctance also stemmed from the desire to avoid a technical violation that my conscience would forever have to live with."

She scrunched her eyebrows a bit in confusion. "How so?"

"I realized that I'm still so attached to Anissa that I worried about a technical violation of my fidelity to her. While I wasn't perfectly faithful to her at the very beginning of our relationship, once we had sex for the first time, I didn't go on any more dates or sleep with anyone else – perhaps out of some idyllic fantasy that maybe Anissa *was* the one. And if she was indeed my soul mate and future life partner, then I wanted to have a perfect record of fidelity with her, so that I'd have nothing to hide or later confess to her."

Lily dropped her gaze from my eyes for a moment. "But you said that your relationship with her had definitely ended."

"It did. But I guess I'm still harboring the hope that we'll find some way to get back together, and me sleeping with you would only complicate those prospects and sully an otherwise pristine record. So, as tempted as I was to explore and indulge more with you, I suppressed those desires."

She forced a silver-lining smile on her lips. "And, in so doing, you proved to yourself that you have self-control."

"See that? You validated my decision to find a therapist to whom I was physically attracted – so that we could together study and better understand my sexual behavior in ways that might help me to control it. You've fulfilled your purpose!"

Lily tried to continue smiling as she looked at the clock on the wall and noticed that our time had expired. "Well, I'm glad I could be part of this breakthrough for you," she said dryly, standing up to give me her cue that our session was over. "Maybe you don't actually need my services any more now."

I followed her to the door, which she held open for me whenever our sessions came to an end.

I looked intently into her eyes for a moment. "Don't worry, Lily. We're not done with each other just yet." I gave her a playful wink as I walked out the door.

Chapter 15: Anissa

∽ Thursday, May 8, 2014 ∾

To My Dearest,

Now that classes have officially ended, I've been super busy cramming for my finals, and my first one, in Masterpieces of Western Literature and Philosophy, is actually tomorrow afternoon. Nevertheless, I'm taking a study break to write to you because there's so much weighing on my mind, and a lot to catch you up on. Michael and I have been back together for about a week, and – while we've enjoyed plenty of make-out sessions – I told him yesterday that I wasn't ready to take things much further. I explained that my academic focus had completely deteriorated because of so many personal developments – from the breakup with my professor to the horrible news about my family in Kessab – and that I desperately needed to catch up in time for exams. I also noted that my head was still a bit confused so soon after leaving Professor Morales, and I just needed some time to adjust – ideally with minimal emotional drama in my life until I was done with finals.

Michael was totally understanding and a complete gentleman about the whole thing, noting that he himself was rather behind on his own academics and just about everything else, because of how much the MCA had taken over his life. He also mentioned that he was doing his best to find Syrian rebel contacts who could track down the details of the kidnapper who held my sister – a situation that was now confirmed, unfortunately. I can't even imagine what poor Maria must be enduring these days and my heart aches every time I think of her.

Michael already sent money to many potential informants, after allocating the last $50,000 in the MCA's bank account to get precise information on Maria's whereabouts and to pay any ransom that might be involved in releasing her. He is even offering the captors some initial money in exchange for allowing a Skype call between her and me, so that I could at least see that she's still alive. He said that our call may happen even later today, so I've been full of anxious anticipation to talk with my sister again.

Michael decided that he would also be making a trip to Syria soon, both to help with the release of my sister, if and when that could be arranged, and to manage the countless details that he was having trouble overseeing from afar: coordination among different Christian militia groups, ensuring their proper military and related training, developing and communicating policies for sharing certain emergency resources that MCA had purchased, church repair projects, etc.

I told Michael that as soon as I was done with my exams, I wanted to work for the MCA on a full-time basis during my summer break, helping however I could in New York. Michael was of course delighted, and offered to pay me a decent salary for the summer, as soon as more funds came in. My duties would include fundraising (but from sources other than Professor Morales, whom Michael and I both wanted to avoid), new member recruitment, managing MCA's social media accounts, and helping with the organization of political activism (rallies, letter-writing campaigns, etc.). Most students were trying to get summer internships at prestigious companies, law firms, investment banks, management consulting companies, or working for members of Congress, but I decided that helping the MCA would be the most personally rewarding thing I could do, and it would still offer plenty of high-level experience to sound impressive on my resume.

I have to leave now for the Psychology and Markets final exam review session being offered by our TA. I really don't want to see her but I'm behind in the class and skipping this session would only disadvantage me relative to all of the students who attend it. I should also try to be more indifferent about her – I'm over Professor Morales and could really care less who else he was sleeping with or which women may be in his bed these days. I'll try to find the time to write a bit more when I return.

* * *

My review session made me realize just how behind I am in Psychology and Markets, but something far more important came up soon after I got back to my dorm room: I was able to see Maria on Skype, along with Michael, who had arranged the video conference call! Her captors, standing behind her wearing masks and holding Kalashnikovs, don't speak English, so that's what she used to talk to me for the five minutes that they allowed her to communicate with me. From the moment that I saw her appear on my laptop, I was crying tears of relief and sorrow for all that she had been through, which I could only imagine from her sad, weary eyes. But there was no time for her to give me the whole story, so she just rushed to the most important updates.

"Inās, please listen carefully because you must know what happened, in case this is the last time we speak," she said, breaking down in tears. "Because there's no one else who can tell you what happened."

"No, Maria, you mustn't say that." I started sobbing even harder. "This isn't the last time. I will see you again soon – in person. You mustn't give up hope!"

"Inās, hope has not helped us. Because Antoun, Uncle Luke, and his whole family," she choked up again. "They were all gunned down by Islamic State fighters who stopped us as we were fleeing Kessab from the attacks."

My face shriveled up in horror. "Oh no! What are you saying, Maria?"

"I… I survived only because, after they robbed us all of our money and possessions, including the two minivans we were traveling in, one of the attackers decided… He decided that he wanted to take me as his wife. So he pulled me aside and then his men murdered everyone else in our family."

We were both in tears when I saw one of the two masked men take her away, her arm flailing back towards the laptop she had been talking to me through, as my hand reached out and touched my computer screen. The other abductor appeared where my sister had been sitting and spoke to me in Arabic, informing me that the deal was five minutes for $5,000, and that we had already spoken for five minutes. He then warned Michael and me that he would kill her by the end of the month if we didn't pay their $100,000 ransom. The captor ominously suggested that Maria's suffering would be minimized if, within the next forty-eight hours, Michael confirms through his intermediary that he can make the payment so that they can agree on an exchange mechanism.

Chapter 16: Julien

Sunday, 5/11/14 at 19:27.

Today in therapy, Lily wanted to focus on my issues of trust, which became that much more interesting to explore because she and I have established that there's some tempting chemistry between us, even if we have both decided – at least for now – not to succumb to it.

"Are you ready finally to delve into our favorite topic?" she asked, with an ironic smile.

"You mean my childhood?"

She nodded with a look that seemed braced for my usual refusal.

"Did you finally visit a slaughterhouse?" I rejoined. "Can you show me some photos of your visit?"

"I may just call your bluff, Julien. What will you do then?"

"I will honor the promise implicit in my original challenge: if you show me some photos of your first visit to a slaughterhouse, then I'll tell you more about my childhood."

Her lip rose slightly, as if with defiant determination. "OK. We may be testing that promise sooner than you think. But in the meantime, you should realize that you're just cheating yourself by linking our discussion of your childhood to your evangelism about the virtues of vegetarianism."

"It's not really about vegetarianism. As I've told you before, you can't really fully understand my childhood trauma without witnessing the horrors of animal butchery."

"And that's the *only* reason I plan to visit a slaughterhouse soon. But I really hope you'll keep your end of the bargain, because you'll never be able to get close to any woman – whether it's Anissa or anyone else – until you confront your past."

"I know. But, believe it or not, I have pushed myself to be more trusting, even though the selfie scandal seriously damaged the little faith that I did have in others. And I'm worried that my decision to be more trusting – even if it was for a much nobler cause this time – is going to come back to bite me again."

Preparing for some new disclosures, Lily picked up her pen and positioned it above her yellow pad. "What do you mean?"

She began noting things about my account as I relayed it to her. "Last Friday, the homeless Iraq War veteran, Craig, who had really

helped me during the week after the selfie scandal, had a violent flashback at my office – not even a month after I had hired him as a security guard for the JMAT lobby area."

"What exactly happened?"

"A courier arrived at the JMAT lobby with a big, red pouch of documents. I guess something about the man's face or uniform, or maybe the appearance and size of his parcel triggered a flashback in Craig, transporting him back to some traumatic event involving a bomb in a package."

Lily looked up from her note-taking. "This is based on some discussion with him that you had afterwards?"

"Yes. And he also told me about that bomb incident when we first became acquainted."

"How did Craig's flashback manifest itself?"

"He reportedly started telling everyone in the lobby to clear the area because of a bomb threat, before seizing the pouch, hurling it to the side, and tackling the poor courier to the ground, where he proceeded to beat him. The people in the lobby were obviously very confused and alarmed, but they soon realized that there was no bomb and that Craig had gone out of his mind. Some people rushed to pull him off the battered courier, and managed to restrain him until the police arrived to take Craig into custody."

Lily put down her pen and gave me an empathetic look. "I'm sorry things turned out that way... What sort of consequences are you expecting?"

"Oh, I'm sure there will be lawsuits against my fund and even me personally, for hiring someone who was obviously a risk. But much worse than any legal damages I'll have to pay is the headline risk."

"You think he would disclose details that might embarrass you when talking to the police?"

"Not intentionally. And I got him a lawyer. But who knows what he might have said to the cops before the lawyer showed up? Even if he revealed nothing, reporters always have a way of digging up whatever details you'd rather keep private. So they'll have a field day with this one."

"Well, you should know not to take it personally. Exposing the flaws of the rich and powerful sells more newspapers."

I shook my head, disappointed at myself. "It was really stupid of me. We have one of the most rigorous background checks and hiring processes on Wall Street, and I basically gave this guy a pass because I felt sorry for him and he had helped me at my lowest and weakest moment. Sometimes I think trust is just the triumph of emotion over reason."

She exhaled and shook her head a little. "Julien, you can't let one very unusual incident turn you into a complete cynic. That sounds more like a lapse in your judgment than a good reason to trust people less."

"But when it comes to decisions involving people, isn't every case of bad judgment basically an instance of misplaced trust?"

"I suppose. But I suspect that your real fear of trust began with your father – someone who should have been safe for you, but wasn't."

"That's true," I conceded.

Later, after our time together had ended, when she was holding the door open for me, we again entered the most awkward moment of each session – the farewell, after which we had technically left the therapist-client context. The physical space between us was at its narrowest point then, and our self-control was more tested than ever.

As I looked down into Lily's radiant blue eyes, passing her close enough to stop for an embrace that would bring me into contact with her gorgeous breasts, I thought to myself, "We proved that we can control ourselves after touching hands… Do you think we could handle a hug?"

She smiled, with a look that almost dared me to say it. "Goodbye, Julien. See you next week."

"Until next time, Lily."

Chapter 17: Anissa

∽ Monday, May 12, 2014 ∽

To My Dearest,

I just woke up from a desperately needed, four-hour nap. I literally crashed into my bed, after staying up for nearly thirty consecutive hours, catching up and studying for, and then finally taking my Psychology and Markets final, which certainly lived up to its reputation for difficulty. I was originally planning to sleep for at least a few hours before the exam, but I was too worried and nervous about it to relax enough for sleep, so I just kept studying the whole time. Ever since breaking things off with my professor, I was no longer so sure I could feel comfortable working at JMAT, so the pressure I had placed on myself to remain his star student faded a bit. And after everything that has happened with Maria (I'll get to that soon), it became that much harder to care about my finals or give them the necessary priority. But I was still nervous about doing well enough to avoid a bad grade, and I have to make one last effort to stay focused, because I still have my Economics final in four days. I think my first final, in Masterpieces of Western Literature and Philosophy, went reasonably well, and hope the same is true of Introduction to American Government and Politics, but I won't know for sure until I get my final grades for those courses.

Now to the more urgent news. My sister's abductors had menacingly suggested that Michael confirm – within forty-eight hours – that he can make the $100,000 ransom payment to minimize Maria's suffering between now and her eventual release. Right after that call, Michael and I met to discuss how to get the necessary funds in time, since at that point the MCA had only about $45,000 left in its account and it was clear to both of us that there was no way I would be going to Professor Morales for help with this. Michael offered to pitch in his personal savings of about $20,000, but that still left a $25,000 shortfall. I called Uncle Tony, feeling guilty that I hadn't been in touch in over a month, and explained the situation to him, asking him to contribute whatever remained of the $10,000 my father had wired him for my stay.

He sounded upset. "Inās, before we get to the matter of money, how is that you're telling me only now that Maria has been kidnapped in Syria?"

I took a hard swallow as I spoke into my cell phone. "I'm so sorry, Uncle Tony. I found out myself only recently, and I've been trying to figure out what to do. And I know that I really should have stayed in touch more over the last month, but finals have been incredibly stressful and sort of took over my life."

I could tell from Uncle Tony's silence – which contrasted starkly from his typically jovial manner – that he was upset by the news.

I eventually continued. "I'm just hoping that I still have some of the money my father sent you that I can contribute towards her ransom."

"That money was all used up, Inās."

"Really?"

"Yes. I should send you a bill for the shortfall, but we'll leave that for another time, when there's no one around to mow the lawn or do the laundry," he added, trying to lighten the mood a little. "But, fortunately for Maria, she has an uncle in New York who has no idea what else to do with the $25,000 sitting in his bank account."

I let out a much needed laugh. "So you can help with the money we still need?"

"Did you really think I was going to say no?"

"Well, I just wasn't sure if you'd have the money available."

"Inās, when it comes to family, there's always a way. Besides, if Maria isn't released, who's going to call me when you have your final exams?" I laughed again at his teasing ways and remembered how much I missed his company.

After we discussed the banking logistics of getting Uncle Tony's funds to the MCA, he naturally asked about Antoun, and I had to tell him that he and all of Uncle Luke's family were murdered after fleeing Kessab. It was a gut-wrenching conversation that I was hoping to avoid until after finals, but we stayed on the phone for another hour, crying together about our loss and exchanging memories of my younger brother – whose prankster ways and obsession with football had often led my parents to compare him to Uncle Tony.

Chapter 18: Anissa

∞ Monday, May 19, 2014 ∞

To My Dearest,

Sorry that I haven't written to you in a while – I've been working nonstop trying to help Michael with countless projects in Syria, including the most important one of all: securing the release of my sister. We learned that she is being held by Jabhat Al-Nusra fighters in Salma, a small village in northwest Syria whose control was split between moderate and jihadi rebels. For what it's worth, I neglected myself as much as you – my birthday was exactly one week ago and I literally did nothing for it, although Michael did remember to call me and sing me a happy birthday over Skype, which was very sweet of him.

He actually left the U.S. three days before my birthday, after finalizing all of the details of the transaction with Maria's captors, which exchange he was personally going to oversee. Michael determined that it was far safer to get to Salma via Lebanon than from Damascus, so his flight was from New York to Beirut. From there, Michael spent several days gathering intelligence from his operatives in the area, and eventually arranged his careful transit to Salma, along with a rather complicated set of security procedures and guarantees, to minimize the chances that these kidnappers might try to harm him or my sister, when he brought them the money for her release.

Michael arrived with the $100,000 ransom in a convoy of three SUVs full of twenty armed men, including mostly fighters from his Christian militia, and some moderate Sunni rebels with ties to various Islamist rebels. He also arranged for a "deterrent" force of snipers and men armed with rocket-propelled grenades who would lie in wait, with the ability – in the event of any sudden betrayal – to kill several Jabhat Al-Nusra fighters manning checkpoints.

In the end, the exchange was executed without a hitch, and Michael escorted Maria to his secure convoy, which then transported both of them back over the Lebanese border and south to Beirut. While the sectarianism of Syria's Civil war has crept into Lebanon – particularly in the city of Tripoli – the capital is still relatively safe. Nevertheless, Michael wanted Maria to feel as safe and comfortable as possible, after everything that she had been through, so he arranged for her to stay with some of his trusted Christian contacts while I tried to get her a visa to Canada. During that time, Michael went back to Syria to tend to the many projects and issues demanding his attention.

The plan was for Uncle Tony to bring Maria across the border the same way that he had brought me into the U.S. a little over two years ago, and I would of course travel with him to greet her at the Montreal airport. Michael would try to fly with her, if the timing of his return to the U.S. (which depended on his duties in Syria) was close enough to the issuance of her visa.

Fortunately, I had maintained some contact with my father's connections in Canada, and promised that I would try to visit them with my sister, once Uncle Tony and I drove to Montreal to pick her up, or as soon as possible if it couldn't be arranged on that trip. I even offered to pay them something for their assistance, but they were unbelievably kind and refused to accept anything except a promise that we would try to meet them in person someday.

I just finished a three-hour video call with Maria, going over all of these details, catching up with her in general, and giving her a virtual hug and shoulder to cry on, after all that she's been through. During our talk, I also heard more details about her awful ordeal and riveting escape before being recaptured.

The group that murdered our family members fleeing Kessab was Ahrar al-Sham, one of the founding members of the Islamic Front, and mainly active in northern Syria. I looked up the group online and read about how Ahrar al-Sham, like other Islamic Front factions, is largely financed and supported by Qatar and Turkey. The Islamic Front rejects democracy and secularism, and seeks to implement a strict interpretation of Sharia law.

Maria told me that a man named Osama, who seemed about fifty years old to her, took her captive. He was one of the senior members of the armed gunmen and planned to use her as his concubine. She was tied up and put in the backseat of a car with a gunman next to her in a ride that lasted for a few hours, although my sister had no idea which town she ended up in. The gunman who was in the backseat with her took her to a private home, where he locked her in a bedroom, after tying her leg to the bed post. Maria said that a few hours later, Osama returned and tried to rape her but she managed to block each of his attempts, until he gave up and just beat her. Osama also tried multiple times to convert her to Islam, but she refused, which only brought more physical abuse. This pattern continued for about a week and Maria was fed just one meal per day, on the same ceramic plate that was usually left in her room without being cleaned properly.

Then, a sixteen-year-old girl from Idlib named Jamila was brought into the same bedroom and tied to a different bed post. She had been driving with her parents, who had taken a wrong turn and ended up at a rebel checkpoint. When they checked her father's ID and saw that he belonged to the same Alawite sect as the regime, the Islamic Front rebels shot him dead on the spot and took his wife and daughter captive. Jamila was separated from her mother and brought to the same house where my sister was held.

Maria warned Jamila that Osama would try to rape and convert her, but if she showed resistance, Osama would just hit her. She told Jamila not to be afraid and that they would find a way to free themselves, explaining that Osama and his guard always left after sunset to go to the mosque, and sometimes Osama came back alone. Luckily, the Alawite girl still had her cell phone on her and her older cousin was close with a Sunni friend who could help, which emboldened Maria to pursue an escape plan. The bedroom window had a slight view of the area where Osama's car was parked, so my sister knew roughly when they were away for about two hours. The next time Osama and his guard had left, Maria broke her plate on the floor, and tossed one of the sharp, blade-like shards across the floor to Jamila, and kept another one for herself. They each used it to cut through the rope that was tying them to a different bedpost. But because the rope was relatively thick, it would take them several hours to cut through it, so they didn't have enough time to attempt an escape the same night that they began trying to sever the rope. They also needed Osama to unlock the bedroom door, which couldn't be unlocked from inside the bedroom, so they had to plan their escape for a night when he came back from the mosque alone.

The night when the two captives began sawing away at the cords restraining them, Osama came back with his guard. A few hours later, he tried for the second time to rape Jamila, but she again resisted and was beaten. Luckily, Osama didn't notice that the rope connecting her ankle to the bedpost was nearly torn through.

The next night, soon after Osama and his guard left to pray, Maria and Jamila nearly freed themselves but the plan was to leave their binds still slightly intact to avoid arousing suspicion, in the event that Osama came back with the guard and they would have to wait for another night when he came back alone. Fortunately, Osama returned from the mosque by himself that night. Maria called him into the bedroom (effectively unlocking the door with his arrival). When Osama entered the room, Maria told him that she didn't want him to abuse Jamila anymore and would willingly give herself to him, if he would spare her. My sister was supine on the bed mattress, near the bedpost to which her ankle was tied, with her legs spread somewhat invitingly. There were no sheets or pillows that could facilitate her plan, so she hid the ceramic plate shard just behind the mattress, on the bedframe, leaning against the nearby wall.

Osama was all too happy finally to have sex with a woman he hadn't been able to force himself upon yet, and hardly noticed my sister's right hand hiding slightly over the edge of the mattress, where it lay in wait, holding the sharp plate fragment. He closed the door with a perverse smile and removed the belt from his pants as he made his way towards Maria, with Jamila looking on, also holding a sharp plate fragment by her arm that was hidden under the mattress nearby.

The bearded fifty-something man arrived at the edge of the bed, leaned over my sister's body, and started yanking down her jeans and panties, until she was exposed, while Jamila finished cutting the rope that had restricted her leg. He then dropped his pants and leaned in to violate her. But just as his face looked as if he was starting to relax and enjoy his own wickedness, Maria's hand, holding her makeshift dagger behind the mattress, rammed the sharp plate fragment directly into Osama's neck, where she stabbed him repeatedly, as Jamila joined the effort, stabbing him with her plate fragment as well.

Despite all of the stab wounds and flowing blood, Osama managed to resist a little, but eventually went down and stopped moving. My sister and Jamila's hands were shaking as they scrambled for their next move. The bedroom hadn't been relocked from the outside, so they were finally able to exit their prison. The two found a nearby bathroom, where they washed off the blood that was on them. Then they scoured the house looking for anything that might be useful and found some traditional, long black *abayas* and *hijabs*, the modest garb worn by Muslim women, which they donned as the best possible disguise to flee what was presumably a Sunni area.

There was no point in trying to steal Osama's car because they had no idea where they were and would ultimately run into a checkpoint where their IDs would endanger them. They walked for about twenty minutes until they reached a market, where they learned from the store clerk that they were in the town of Aziz. Jamila called her cousin in Idlib, who sent his Sunni friend, Awwad, to pick them up. They had to wait about two hours for Awwad to drive there from Idlib.

Jamila wanted to be taken to her cousin's house and my sister, after thinking about the issue for about a month of captivity, wanted to leave Syria and try to join me in New York. She had no more close family in the country and was tired of living in constant fear as a vulnerable religious minority. Her best hope was to get to Beirut and then try to get a visa from there to Canada. So she asked Awwad to take her to the Idlib bus station, where she would buy a ride to Lattakia, and from there take a bus to Beirut. Awwad was extremely kind to her and gave her enough money to cover both bus tickets and a few days of food, because Maria literally had nothing on her except the *hijab* and black *abaya* that she wore.

Unfortunately, the bus that my sister eventually took to get to Lattakia was stopped by Jabhat Al-Nusra fighters who demanded to see the ID of every passenger. When they saw Maria's Christian name and ID, they realized that her traditional Muslim garb was a subterfuge and they pulled her off the bus. The Islamist gunmen took her to the house in Salma from which she called me a little over a week ago, after Michael paid off her captors for some proof that she was alive. Tired of fighting and with no hope of fleeing the much better guarded house where she was kept, Maria told her abductors that she had relatives in the U.S. who could pay for her release. They didn't trust her to make any phone calls or get on the Internet, so she told them that they could contact me through Michael Kassab, who is known among certain moderate rebel groups. And that's how she eventually came to be freed.

It was a riveting but emotionally exhausting story for me to hear. There was, however, a silver lining in it that related directly to my work for the MCA.

One of my summer internship duties has been to cultivate press contacts and try to get sympathetic coverage for our cause. Thanks to Maria's incredible story of survival, I think I'll be able to secure two major news stories that will help our nonprofit – especially as we try to raise more funds. The first article will be all about my sister's ordeal and the MCA's role in freeing her. The second article will be about what the MCA has accomplished thus far, and what its ambitious objectives are going forward, if the organization is able to raise more funds.

Before we said goodbye, I explained to Maria the value that her story could have to the cause, and asked if she would be OK with its publication now that she was safely in Beirut and on her way to join me in North America. "If the publication of my experience might somehow save others from similar horrors, then I'm all for it," she confirmed. "Just make sure they don't reveal my name because I still need to clear border controls in a few countries, and I don't want the details of my escape from Osama to complicate things in some unexpected way."

Chapter 19: Julien

Sunday, 5/25/14 at 19:27.

It's been about a month since I had sex (the last time was with Anissa). I can't seem to get myself to fuck someone else, because I'm still hooked on the pipe dream that Anissa and I might somehow get back together. But a month is a very long time for me, and probably explains why I've been so horny lately. A few hours ago, as Lily and I were saying goodbye at the end of our therapy session, I was breathtakingly close to pulling her in for a hug. Her breasts seemed particularly perky at that moment – maybe because she was pushing them out a little (I couldn't tell for sure) – and there was something powerfully inviting about her twinkling blue eyes and pouty lips. Somehow I continued resisting the temptation, but when I got home, I just couldn't stop thinking about sex, imagining the two of us stepping back into her office, closing the door, and ravenously flouting whatever taboos or ethical concerns had been holding us back all this time as we stripped each other and fucked.

To relieve my pent-up desire, I was extremely tempted to call one of my standbys – Elise, Raegan, Maya, or one of the others. It's been only about a month since I stopped responding to their regular Facebook and text messages, inquiring about my availability to see them, so it would probably still be easy to have one of them come over, even on the spur of the moment.

But I'll hold out a bit longer, until I can check in with Anissa. I've been so tempted to text or email her, but had to stop myself each time, out of an abundance of caution. After all, if she didn't answer, or if the conversation didn't go well, she could later claim that I retaliated against her with a lower grade, unless I give her an A. That was prudent planning on my part because, given how she did on her final exam, unfortunately I can't in good conscience give her that grade. While the final exam is graded anonymously, I still prefer to err on the side of caution and avoid any possible accusation or appearance of impropriety. And that means that I can't contact her at all until she has her grade.

I do wonder if she still thinks of me and whether she's really with Michael now, or if she purposely had him pick her up from the last two lectures of my course just to get back at me somehow. Both of them (and their political efforts) have been on my mind quite a lot lately –

probably because of two major news stories that I recently read.

The first was a captivating story about a young woman's gripping ordeal – watching her relatives gunned down, killing and fleeing her kidnapper, only to be abducted again before finally being released when her ransom was paid by the MCA. The article didn't state the poor woman's name, for her security, but it did mention that she had moved from Raqqa to Kessab, only to have to flee that Armenian village when it came under attack by Islamists, so I'm almost positive that she is Anissa's sister. I felt terrible for the woman, and the fact that she might be the sister of Anissa, who herself has suffered so much, made it that much worse: "how much misfortune can a single family sustain?" I thought to myself, shaking my head in pity.

The second article, an in-depth feature about the MCA, Michael, and some of those working closely with him (including Anissa), provided extensive details about all of their important efforts in Syria, and what they've managed to accomplish thanks to the generous support of an anonymous donor. I couldn't help smiling when I read that, as if this whole thing was our little secret. I also felt genuinely glad to have made such a difference to so many people who desperately needed some help and support but weren't getting it from a world that has been shamefully indifferent.

Then, I thought about how this distressed asset deal just earned JMAT a few hundred million dollars, which means that, after the fund gets its share of that profit, and after the tax that I'll have to pay on my personal gain, I'm probably about twenty million dollars richer than I was yesterday. So why not give half of that to a good cause? What else would I do with the money? The economic law of diminishing marginal returns applies as much to wealth as anything else – which is why very wealthy people need to make vastly greater sums of additional money for the gains to feel good.

The more I think about my psychology as it relates to this particular scenario, the more I'm convinced that I would probably derive greater psychic benefit out of keeping ten million dollars and giving away the other ten million to such a good cause, than I would get out of keeping all twenty million for myself. And, on the off-chance that Anissa might forgive me, I'd be transmitting a very positive message, and the ultimate sign of strength and confidence: I'm so comfortable with who I am that I can be generous even to those who spite me, out of heartbreak, jealousy, or any other reason.

Whether Anissa and Michael have been playing me for my money or that's just some paranoid notion that I've conjured up in my own head, they'll be very grateful for this. More importantly, by being above any sort of petty grudges, maybe I can reintroduce some good karma into the air. And if nothing comes of it in terms of Anissa and me, I'll still have done a good thing. If nothing else, maybe it'll make Anissa feel a little better about the grade I unfortunately have to give her, based on her final exam.

Chapter 20: Anissa

∽ Tuesday, June 3, 2014 ∾

To My Dearest,

I've been busier than ever helping the MCA on a full-time basis, and it's as hectic as what I imagine running a company must feel like. Michael even suggested that, on my resume, I more accurately reflect the depth of the work experience with a title like "Deputy Head of North American Operations" or something else a bit more impressive-sounding than just "Summer Intern."

Most exciting of all, the Canadian friends of my father came through for our family again and were able to expedite a visa for Maria today. It was a bitter sweet moment to think about how my father – if only in spirit – is still looking after us. The personal connections that he made when he was alive are still strong enough – thanks to his blessed memory – to help his eldest daughter in her time of need.

I spoke to Michael and he thinks he'll be able to wrap up his work in Syria and come back to Beirut to fly back with my sister, so that she's accompanied for her whole trip to Montreal and then New York. So even though she could actually fly back today, we're booking her flight for June 5th so that Michael can return with her. "There's endless work on the ground in Syria, which means I'm never really done," he noted. "But there are things that I need to take care of in New York, including my dissertation. So I might as well time my return so that Maria doesn't have to travel alone to a foreign country for the first time. She's been through enough as it is."

"I can't thank you enough for everything you've done, Michael," I said, moved by how considerate and giving he was. I extended my hand towards the laptop screen and touched the video image of him.

He smiled humbly and extended his hand, as if to virtually touch mine back. "I'm really the one who should thank you," he replied. "Although I thought we decided that you weren't going to ask your professor for any more donations."

My eyes looked away in a moment of confusion. "What do you mean? I haven't been in touch with Professor Morales in over a month."

Michael's expression then mirrored my confused look. "Oh. That's odd."

"Why? What happened?"

"The MCA received a wire for ten million dollars yesterday."

My eyes practically popped out of their sockets and I couldn't get my mouth to close. "What?!"

"I know, I couldn't believe it either. The funds came from that same foundation that sent us the first two wires totaling eleven million dollars."

My faith in the universe suddenly felt restored a little. "That's amazing news!"

Michael released a big grin. "Yes, it really is. I guess now you can pay back your Uncle Tony the $25,000 he contributed, I can restore my meager personal savings that were chipped in to release Maria, and we can definitely pay you a nice salary for all of your great work this summer," he added with a wink.

I was so elated after hearing about the huge, and totally unexpected, donation from Professor Morales that it more than made up for the disappointing news about my overall performance in his class. I actually got my grade yesterday (so I now have all of the results from my second semester) and I've been trying not to think about it. Actually, I don't really want to tell you about my latest grades because they were nothing like what I received in my fall semester, and maybe that's just a reflection of a more mature, well-rounded approach to my spring term. Indeed, during these last months, countless other aspects of my life took over and crowded out my academic focus. I'll mention the B that I received in Psychology and Markets only because that class meant so much to me up until I stopped dating Professor Morales. For most of this semester, that course fueled my fantasy of a high-paying job at JMAT, but after Professor Morales and I had a falling out, and I got a B in his course, that dream is gone, it seems.

Nevertheless, after just learning about his unbelievably magnanimous contribution to the MCA, I'm again confused about him, thinking that maybe I judged him too harshly or with too little information. Also, if I'm being totally honest with you, My Dearest, I should tell you that I did still think about him a lot over the last month, even though I tried to forget about him and that's why I barely mentioned his name to you anymore. But I couldn't help wondering if he was seeing anyone – Maya, our TA, or someone else – after we stopped dating. I also worried about whether our breakup might impact my grade somehow. And now that I got a B in his class, I am curious as to whether the breakdown of our personal relationship might have somehow influenced the outcome for the worse, although a part of me seriously doubts that possibility, in light of his generous donation. Yes, I'm very confused. I'm even tempted to discuss everything with him, although I'm not sure that I'm ready for that.

To muddle my mind and heart even more, yesterday I read a story in the paper about another scandal that just hit Professor Morales. Someone from my Psychology and Markets class emailed a bunch of students, including me, the following article, from the same tabloid that had reported, with gleeful sarcasm, on his selfie scandal. Under the headline, "Office Attack After Psych Expert Hires Homeless Man," the article read as follows:

"Last month, Craig Walkenford, a homeless man hired as a security guard at JM Analytics & Trading (JMAT), the twenty-billion-dollar hedge fund owned and run by Julien Morales, allegedly attacked a Lightfoot Express Courier (LEC) deliveryman, who had arrived at the office with a package. The police report states that Mr. Walkenford, who had worked at JMAT for just a few weeks, suddenly screamed, tackled the unsuspecting courier, and proceeded to pummel him on the ground until those nearby could stop the attack by restraining the new hire. According to sources, the violent outburst shook up the employees and potential investors who were waiting in the lobby of the prestigious Midtown hedge fund. Mr. Walkenford was taken into police custody on May 9th, but details of the incident emerged when LEC and its injured employee today announced that they intend to sue JMAT and Mr. Morales for negligently hiring an emotionally unstable person for an office security role. According to the police report, Mr. Walkenford, 31, is a veteran who was deployed in a U.S. infantry unit in the 2003 Iraq War, and subsequently served in three tours of duty in Iraq and Afghanistan before being honorably discharged in 2007. Due to chronic and often violent bouts of PTSD that Mr. Walkenford (in the police report) attributes to his military service, he was unable to hold a job and ended up living as a vagabond in the New York area for the last few years. Mr. Morales, a thirty-nine-year-old psychology professor at Columbia University, took the unusual step of personally clearing the homeless man to work at his hedge fund, rather than requiring him to pass through the firm's notoriously rigorous hiring procedures. The billionaire finance tycoon apparently befriended him while "trying out" homelessness for a few days. The bizarre incident comes after a similarly erratic moment, last April, when Mr. Morales, who is known for his playboy lifestyle and swanky VIP parties, was revealed in shirtless selfies that he had sent to a socialite about half his age. Repeated calls to JMAT with a request for comment, were not returned."

The article boiled my blood because it misleadingly made Professor Morales look like a man plagued by poor judgment and reckless behavior. But, unlike the last scandal, I personally knew just how unfair the press was being towards him and I even felt partly responsible for the incident – since the whole "trying out homelessness" thing was my idea, even if it was suggested half in jest. My professor clearly tried to do a good thing by helping this poor veteran and the paper put the worst possible spin on the incident.

Chapter 21: Julien

Wednesday, 6/4/14 at 21:13.

Ah, the beauty of karma: put some good energy into the universe, and you may just bless your own life with it. To my delighted surprise, Raegan called me at around 5 p.m. to inform me that Anissa was in the reception area and had requested to meet with me, even though she had no appointment. I didn't want to signal even to my most trusted assistant that there was anything special about Anissa that allowed her to meet with me unannounced like this — mainly to avoid setting a precedent or encouraging any speculation.

"Ah yes. I asked her to see me about her final grade. Send her up, and please hold all of my calls."

"Will do."

A few minutes later, Anissa appeared at the doorway to my office, dressed casually in a light, spring skirt, as if she were going to class. Raegan was standing next to her, awaiting my next instructions.

I looked up from my computer. "Thank you, Raegan," I said with a smile. "Hi, Anissa. Please, come inside and have a seat," I said, pointing to the comfortable chair by the window.

Raegan nodded, and shut the door behind her as Anissa entered and took the seat I had suggested. Slowly, I left my desk and casually walked over to the chair beside her. I couldn't allow her to see my unease and simultaneous excitement that she was here, in my office.

But my palms grew clammy as we avoided each other's eyes. I had thought of her so much during our month apart and was curious if I, too, had stayed in her thoughts. I also wasn't sure how to interact with her: with a cold formalism, or a more familiar playfulness? Was she here to complain about her grade, or to thank me for my donation? Or did she want to discuss our relationship? I assumed it was about her grade or my donation, since she had chosen to meet me in my office rather than a more casual setting.

"Hi, Professor Morales," she began, instantly telling me where things were at that moment between us: cold and distant. I almost cringed at the distance and immediately wanted to find some way for us to return to our freer and more comfortable way of interacting before our last night together.

"Technically, I'm not your professor anymore," I gently corrected her with a smile. "Unless you're here to challenge your grade, in which case – for the purposes of this conversation – I would still be your professor."

One side of her mouth reluctantly rose into a half smile. "I'm not here about my grade, although it's obviously not what I would have wanted to get in your class."

"I know. It pained me to give it to you, because I know you can do so much better. But that's also why I insist on anonymous grading. Fairness demands that every exam be evaluated without letting any prior performance or interactions color the results. Honestly, I was very surprised to discover that the answers belonged to you. I even rescored your exam to make sure that I hadn't made some error, but unfortunately the result was the same. I figured there was probably some external factor that impacted your performance… I even worried for a moment that maybe I had something to do with it."

Anissa exhaled in frustration. "Yes, there was an external factor, but it wasn't you. I mean, I'm sure that the way things happened between us didn't help. But that wasn't what ruined my performance on your exam. I didn't do very well on any of my finals this semester. And unfortunately, my academic transcript can't include a footnote that says, 'Anissa's spring term grades were affected by the kidnapping of her sister during final exams.' So it feels unfair on some level. But I'm grateful that I was at least able to help my last surviving relative in Syria. I learned many things this semester that aren't reflected by my GPA."

"Well, I'm glad that you had the wisdom to remember what really matters. Some students are so competitive or driven that they forget the bigger picture. Speaking of which, I'm very sorry to hear about your sister and everything that's happened to your family in Syria. I actually read a story in the paper about a kidnapped woman who was released thanks to the efforts of the MCA, and I immediately thought that she might be your sister."

Anissa nodded her head sadly, looking out the window. "Yes, that was my sister, Maria, you read about. And that actually brings me to the main reason for coming to your office today." She turned slightly, so that her gaze held mine. "I wanted to thank you for your incredibly generous donation."

I smiled and couldn't resist making a joke. "If it's going to cost me ten million dollars every time I want to chat with you, I'm going to go broke very quickly."

"You've wanted to talk to me that much?" she asked, with a nervous chuckle, as her cheeks flushed a little.

"Well, I guess that's what happens after not seeing you for a month." I looked down for a moment and then out the window at the fiftieth floor view of Manhattan. "I realize that I probably brought that on myself, and I actually was meaning to talk to you about things."

"So, why didn't you?"

I continued gazing out the window but saw her looking at me in the reflection of the glass. "Well, I thought maybe it was best if we both just had some time to think. And I also didn't want you to feel pressured to respond in a certain way just as finals were on the horizon. I thought it would be best for us to talk after you have your grade in my class and are no longer my student."

"I was very upset. I still am, a little. But after your amazing donation to the MCA and what I read in the papers – "

I turned to look back at Anissa. "You mean the incident here with Craig?"

"Yes. I was so angry that you were being misrepresented like that in the media."

"No good deed goes unpunished, as the saying goes," I noted wryly. "But it is funny how when we weren't talking, we sort of stayed in touch through newspaper articles."

Her expression lightened in amusement. "True – as if the universe had conspired to keep each of us in the other's thoughts."

"I guess the universe knew that I owed you an apology," I conceded with a smile, reaching out and lightly placing my hand on hers. "You really are unlike any woman I've ever met, and it just took a while for my bad habits to catch up with that realization."

She looked down, as if to conceal her emotions. "I guess I should also apologize to you for invading your privacy the way I did."

"Well, I can't really blame you," I said, taking my hand back. "And, for what it's worth, I haven't been physically intimate with another woman – or even gone on any dates with anyone – since the last time we slept together. And I'll go one step further than that: if you'll have me back, I promise that I'll be faithful to you and inform anyone who tries to get close to me that I'm seriously dating you – and I haven't been that monogamous in over a decade, so I hope you recognize what a big deal that would be."

Her lips pursed together empathetically for a moment, and then her eyebrow rose skeptically. "You know that's not the only issue, Julien," she replied. But just the fact that she chose to call me by my first name again lifted me with some inner joy – as if I was making progress and there was hope here.

I put my hand on her wrist. "I know, Anissa. I'm working on the other issue with my therapist, trying to build up to it. But you, of all people, should know how hard it is. And since you apparently overcame it, maybe you'll end up helping me to deal with it even better than she can."

Anissa smiled warmly. "Well, I'm glad to hear that you're at least trying."

"I really am. And if you'll give us another chance, I promise you that – within three months of when we're back together – I'll share all of the details of my childhood with you. Everything you want to know. And if I refuse to reveal any details that you ask about, then you can leave me for good."

Her face lit up into a radiant smile, and for a moment I thought Anissa might reach over and try to hug or kiss me, but she still seemed to be restraining herself. "Julien, a part of me wants nothing more than to get back together with you and give us another try… But things happened since we stopped seeing each other…"

I took a hard swallow. "I wasn't sure if you had asked Michael to pick you up from my class the last two lectures mainly to get back at me in some way, or because – "

"Well, it was definitely that too. I just needed his support during a very emotional time for me. And I was mad at you. But he and I really are very close, and have become a lot closer over the last month – because of how much we've been working together for the MCA and because of all the help that he's provided to my family in Syria, often at great risk to himself. He's actually due back the day after tomorrow, when my uncle and I will drive to Montreal to pick up my sister and him from the airport."

"Wow – well, that's certainly understandable," I remarked, unsure of what to say, as I reluctantly concluded that my prospects for having her back were apparently much worse than I had hoped.

"Yes, he's been amazing… It's hard to believe that he's already been in Syria for nearly a month," she added.

"Well, I'm glad you found someone who's worthy of you, Anissa. And you won't have to see me in class anymore, so at least there won't be that awkwardness now." I smiled ironically at her. "We can truly have a clean break, which is, in many ways, much healthier." I rose from my chair to signal that our meeting was over. She stood up and followed me to the door, where I held it open for her. "But I'm glad we could at least have this chat, so thank you for coming by."

"Thank *you*, Julien. For everything. You're an incredibly special man."

Chapter 22: Anissa

∽ Saturday, June 7, 2014 ∾

To My Dearest,

Yesterday I joined Uncle Tony for the six-hour drive north to Montreal to pick up my sister and Michael from the airport. I felt bad not being able to pitch in with the driving, but I had never learned, because of a certain phobia I had developed ever since the last time I rode in a car in Syria (which fear just grew worse thanks to the lie I constantly told myself and others about my parents dying in a car crash). Fortunately, my uncle didn't seem to mind, and we used the time to catch up on everything that I hadn't been able to talk to him about during my stressful exam period. I also gave him more details about my work for the MCA, all of which impressed him – especially the part about having raised enough money to pay him back the $25,000 he had kindly contributed towards the ransom we paid for Maria's release.

When we finally reached Montreal, parked the car, and made our way to the international arrivals area, I felt as if at least a decade had passed since I first came through the same airport a little over two years ago. I was in such a different place now – more confident, more secure about being in the United States, and more knowledgeable about myself and the world. I had been through so many new experiences and finally confronted past ones that I had hid from for so long. Just the fact that Maria was now the refugee and I was the New York resident picking her up made me think about how, thanks to the unfairness of chance, I was effectively "ahead" of my sister, even though she was older than me. Here she was, starting over in a new country, arriving with basically nothing to rebuild her life, other than me and our uncle. I had planned to offer her the option to share my small dorm room with me, although, as I expected, she ultimately opted for the greater space and privacy of staying with Uncle Tony.

As we stood in the busy arrivals area, with lots of expectant faces and a few hired drivers holding signs with the names of the travelers they were supposed to pick up, I suddenly thought about one important respect in which Maria's arrival was easier than mine: she was more of a mature and confident adult – twenty-two rather than sixteen – and, above all, she was traveling with a strong male escort. On a few occasions, I had actually been wondering about how she and Michael would relate, but I never bothered to ask Maria about such details, because she had enough to worry about and I didn't want her to think that I was getting jealously possessive or somehow more focused on relatively petty details. So I really had no idea how the two of them had gotten along – from the time he had helped to relocate her and our family from Raqqa to Kessab, to his involvement in her release from captivity, and then to escorting her to Beirut and finally Montreal. But I caught my first uncensored glimpse of their interpersonal dynamic when I spotted the two of them turning the corner into the arrivals area. Apparently neither knew that I could see them, because they looked at each other in the most happy and comfortable way possible, until they realized that they were now visible to the people waiting for travelers in the arrivals area, and then their facial expressions quickly switched to the focused task of scanning the crowd for me and Uncle Tony.

Maria's eyes soon met mine and I felt my face light up with the widest grin as I ran towards her, while she hurried in my direction until we collided in a joyous embrace. It was our first physical contact since Christmas 2011, when she had left with Uncle Luke and our younger brother for Raqqa, back when Islamists hadn't yet invaded the city and turned it into a living hell. With tears of joy streaming down our faces, we hugged so tightly it felt as if we might never let go, for fear of being separated for too long again. Eventually, we stepped back from our embrace briefly just to look each other over – as if to confirm that we were in fact experiencing this moment together and it wasn't some dream. It had been so long that I had somehow forgotten that she's actually a few inches taller than me. She looked exhausted from the international flight, and the countless ordeals suffered before it, but she was still as beautiful as ever: above circles of fatigue were her bright hazel eyes; her black, wavy hair draped over her shoulders; and her lovely figure was somehow accentuated by the backpack hanging from both of her shoulders, although she was clearly still regaining some of the weight she had lost in captivity. After our brief, mutual inspection, we resumed our hugging.

For a moment, it felt as if Maria and I were the only two people in the airport. But Uncle Tony eventually approached our endless, vice-like embrace and gave us a mopey face, as if he were being purposely excluded from all of the fun.

"Excuse me, but what's an uncle gotta do to get a hug around here?" he asked in Arabic, placing his palms gently on each of our shoulders. "I was told that I'm on the welcoming committee too," he protested, in his inimitable, jocular way. We laughed as we wiped away our tears and broke apart so that Uncle Tony could embrace Maria too.

I then ran up to Michael and wrapped my arms snugly around his. Uncle Tony eventually came over to Michael and said, "So, you must be the famous Michael Kassab – I've heard a lot about you."

"Uncle Tony, you're looking at the future president of Antioch," I beamed, as the two shook hands warmly.

"Look, I'm just thankful that the guy got me back my niece. After that, he can run for president of any country he wants, and I'll vote for him!"

We all shared a much-needed, hearty laugh, and then headed to Uncle Tony's car.

Chapter 23: Julien

Sunday, 6/8/14 at 23:49.

Today I spent nearly all of my time with Lily grieving over the final loss of Anissa.

"I forgot what this feels like," I confessed at one point. "I think I've experienced it only one other time, many years ago, before I became wealthy."

Lily leaned back in her seat. "What?"

"Heartbreak. I think that's what this is – that terrible, dull ache that you just sit with, knowing that the person you felt inexplicably close to, who often even seemed like an extension of you, is suddenly gone. Out of reach. That human being who completed you and made you better is suddenly paired up with someone else for a different destiny, leaving you alone to search out yours just when you thought you had found it. That same person is now so completely tied to someone else that your messages and phone calls now produce a dreaded awkwardness rather than an exciting joy. It's a terrible emptiness. The only consolation is maybe the realization that you can feel that way about someone, but it's always drowned out by the knowledge that it could take years to find someone else who makes you feel that way, if you're even lucky enough to get a second chance."

Lily looked genuinely empathetic. "I'm sorry to hear that this has been so hard on you."

"Me too. The emotional impact really took me by surprise – another indication of how rare it is for me to feel this way about someone. And, absurdly enough, there's a kind of butterfly effect from all of this that's causing me to act selfishly towards another living creature."

She furrowed her brow at my admittedly cryptic confession. "What do you mean?"

"Well, four days ago, right after Anissa had come to my office, my veterinarian for Icarus told me that he's well enough to fly and fend for himself in the wild again. But I just can't bring myself to set him free. I've grown used to sharing my bedroom with the little guy and, now that Anissa is definitely out of the picture, I feel all the more attached to this small bird for some reason… I know that I'm being terribly selfish by keeping him in that cage, now that I've nursed him back to health. And I feel awful about it, but I just can't let him go."

"Maybe that's because Anissa was a kind of Icarus for you."

"She definitely was."

"What about the other aspects of your life, Julien? Doesn't the success of that distressed asset deal you mentioned help to balance out your mood a little?"

"No, it doesn't. On the contrary – thinking about that only reminds me of what I've lost because it was thoughts of Anissa that had prompted me to give away half of my personal profit from that deal."

"Oh, I didn't realize that you had done that," she replied. "That was very nice of you."

"After you get past that level of comfort that lots of money can buy, wealth has the fading appeal of beauty – to others and even to yourself."

"What do you mean?"

"As the cliché goes, find me a stunningly beautiful woman, and I'll find you a guy who's bored of fucking her. In the same way, if you find me an obscenely wealthy husband, I'll find you a wife who thinks he doesn't have enough money. And that probably makes him feel the same way in the end. But not Anissa – she was remarkably and genuinely different, and would never fall into that pattern."

"I thought you worried at times that she was using you for your wealth."

"Yes, but even when I thought that, I never suspected that she was attracted to my money for her own personal benefit. She's not some gold-digging materialist who insatiably chases brand names and luxurious comforts. Any pressure I ever felt from Anissa to spend money only made me a better person – because it was always for a good cause."

"And you don't think you'll find someone else with her values?"

"I might. But I don't know if she'll hold my interest in the same way."

Lily gave me a playful but genuine smile. "Well, for what it's worth, I couldn't care less about brand names and luxurious comforts, and would choose philanthropy over consumerism any day of the week."

Lily didn't have to use herself as an example. And yet she did. Sometimes the subtext screams louder than spoken words. I felt tempted to take her right there and then, in her office, maybe on her desk – if only just to get over Anissa and finally confirm, in a very definitive and assertive way, that Lily and I *were* going to go there, whatever the consequences might be to her license or our professional relationship. It would be therapeutic in a way that no amount of therapy could be: it would make me realize that Anissa was replaceable and not some impossibly unique angel whose loss I was doomed to mourn for the rest of my life. But *something* held me back. All I could bring myself to do was flirt a little. "I knew there was a reason I liked you," I remarked with a wink, feeling very unsatisfied with the results of my self-control. "But let's not overstate your asceticism when I tripled your hourly rate to see me on Sundays."

She smiled at the invitation to banter a little. "That's not a measure of my materialism, Julien – that's just how much I value my days off. This is not exactly play time for me."

My mouth formed an exaggerated frown. "It's not? You mean I'm a pain in the ass for you – a job that you have to tolerate to pay the bills?"

"Well, you are a pain in the ass when it comes to extracting anything about your childhood."

"I guess you should be paid extra just for the patience involved in that thankless process. It's almost as hard as the job of a dentist trying to perform a root canal on a cat surrounded by moving mice."

She nodded in knowing amusement. "Actually, I think giving that cat a root canal would be easier."

"Unfortunately, that's probably truer than ever, because my motivation to tackle my past has now fallen significantly. Of course, I still care about resolving the issue someday, and I'm aware that it's something that I need to do at some point, but there's no urgency now."

"Even if I prove to you with photos that I visited a slaughterhouse?"

"Well, a deal is a deal. So I will honor the terms of my challenge to you, but I just don't know how deeply I'll be prepared to explore the related issues with you. It's really something that I try to think about as little as possible."

"I can certainly understand that. And I guess you'll have to understand if we end up reaching an impasse and therapy is no longer productive."

Lily looked up at the clock on the wall, and I knew from her expression that our time was up. "Yes, I know that's a possibility," I conceded, tilting my head to the side a little and raising an eyebrow. "Look, if there were a love interest at stake, my motivation to plunge into the darkness would probably be a lot greater."

My sexy therapist stood up and I followed her to the door, which she opened.

"We always end up here, don't we, Julien?" she noted, staring into my eyes.

I looked back into her blue irises, and had to summon all of my willpower not to take her into my arms and ravish her mouth. The temptation was all the more powerful because of how cleverly she had timed her rhetorical question: "We always end up here, don't we?" That question literally referred to the exact physical spot where we awkwardly and reluctantly said goodbye at the end of every session together. And "*here*" also referred to our ongoing dilemma about whether *she* could be that love interest for me – a dilemma that made ending up *here*, at the door, all the more electrifying.

Chapter 24: Anissa

∽ Thursday, June 12, 2014 ∾

To My Dearest,

The last six days since my trip with Uncle Tony to Montreal have felt a bit disoriented as far as where my heart is. After I broke up with Julien, I had only about two weeks with Michael before he left for Syria. And when I saw him again for the first time at the Montreal airport, it felt too awkward to kiss him there, in front of my relatives and also after being apart for so long.

I'm guessing he must also feel a bit uncomfortable because he hasn't really tried to see me since his return. On the other hand, he's insanely behind on his life after being gone for about a month, on top of the ongoing pressures from the MCA's activities in Syria, so it's understandable that he would need a while to adjust to the time zone change, catch his breath, and work through the endless to-do list that has been impatiently awaiting his return.

Seeing Julien just before going to Montreal probably added to my confusion. I still feel a strong pull towards him and – for all of his faults – he has a core goodness that still shines through. I was reminded of that after reading the awful article about the incident at JMAT involving the homeless war veteran and, of course, learning of his incredible generosity towards the MCA. In addition, everything he said to me in his office has stayed with me, and I keep wondering if I'm making a terrible mistake by not giving him a second chance. Even worse, maybe I'm being unfair to him, since I know him so much better than those who don't seem open to his potential goodness (like the journalists who delight in every chance to portray him in a negative light).

On the bright side, I've been spending a lot of time with Maria, trying to help her get acclimated to life in New York. She said that she plans to reconnect with her love of music in a city that offers so many unique opportunities for her to do that. I also talked to her about how helpful it was for me to see a therapist after escaping Syria and offered to introduce her to Monique. Maria seemed open to the idea, and I'm hopeful that she'll decide to start seeing her.

I actually have to leave now for an MCA meeting – the first that Michael is running since leaving for Syria last month. I'm excited that

Maria will be attending as well – if only so that she can see that there is a growing group of activists trying to help our community. That should lift her spirits a bit, and maybe she'll even make some new friends there. I think it would also be fun for us to work together on an issue that matters so much to us both, so hopefully she'll decide to become actively involved in the MCA. I'll write you more when I get back.

* * *

I just returned from the MCA meeting and most of it was spent discussing how the threat of ISIS is metastasizing across Syria and into Iraq, because world powers have failed to stop this cancer. Michael drew our attention to news reports about a week ago that ISIS had attacked Mosul with only about 1,500 fighters and had apparently scared away Iraqi soldiers, who were at least fifteen times more numerous. Then he mentioned reports from yesterday that ISIS had seized large quantities of US-supplied military equipment and had looted over four hundred million dollars' worth of Iraqi currency from the banks in Mosul, Iraq's second largest city. The terrorist group had also freed thousands of prisoners, many of whom are likely to join the insurgency. I just couldn't believe how the world was letting these monsters take over so easily.

As I expected, Maria found some strength and solace in the group solidarity provided by the MCA, and was also grateful that she could now do something to help, rather than passively watch our community get victimized by armed and violent Islamists. My sister is not allowed to have a paying job while seeking political asylum in the United States, but she can certainly volunteer her time.

"Thank you so much for bringing me here," Maria whispered to me at one point during the meeting.

"You mean the United States or this MCA meeting?" I asked with a knowing smile.

"Both!" she beamed. "You'll be seeing even more of me now because I'd like to become an active member in this organization."

At one point in the meeting, someone who was new to the MCA posed a question to the thirty people there. "Why doesn't the West show more concern over the plight of Christians in Syria and Iraq?"

To my surprise, Maria raised her hand and offered her explanation: "To the jihadists, we are *kafirs*, or infidels. But to the West we are just Arabs."

"That's exactly right!" I affirmed, impressed with my sister's insight. Many of the Middle East Christian members present nodded their heads and talked amongst themselves in agreement.

At the end of the meeting, my sister and I went up to Michael to speak with him and a surprising level of awkwardness ensued. He and Maria seemed to stiffen up a little, and I myself felt uneasy, not sure how I was supposed to behave around him – especially with my sister next to me. Michael managed to ease the weirdness a little by focusing our chat on developments in Syria and Iraq, but then he abruptly excused himself, saying that he had to rush back home to take care of some things. I didn't know what to make of the whole thing.

Maria accompanied me back to my dorm room and, at that point, I couldn't resist asking her more explicitly about Michael. There was *something* that was making it uncomfortable for the three of us to be together, and my curiosity to find the explanation wouldn't go away. To get the most candid and natural response out of Maria, I decided that I would ask her in Arabic, even though I had been insisting – to help her linguistic adjustment – that she start using only English when she spoke to me, Uncle Tony, or any other Arabic speakers she met in New York.

I broached the topic in a fairly direct but friendly way – as if it were just a light observation for us to muse over: "Did you notice how awkward it seemed when the three of us were talking just now?"

She smiled in surprise, as she responded in Arabic: "Why did you suddenly switch to Arabic for this question?"

"Well, I figured that trying to explain this awkwardness could involve a lot of subtle observations or carefully worded statements, so I thought it would be easier and more natural for you to discuss it in Arabic."

"Yes, definitely," she confirmed with a smile, as we entered my dorm room and each took a seat on my twin-sized bed. "And I agree that Michael seemed a bit stiff or unsure of himself when it was just the three of us, but I think he was just eager to return to his work because he's so busy these days."

"I agree… Except that he also seemed that way to me at the airport, when I came to pick you up… So that's why I thought maybe there's something else going on."

Maria's arms crossed her chest and she seemed to crouch inward a little. "I think maybe we're all just not used to being around each other – I mean, you and I aren't even used to being around each other, after so much time."

Her answer felt like a diplomatic evasion. "True, but it seems less weird when it's just the two of us, don't you think?" I persisted.

"I guess."

"Tell me honestly, Maria. How do you feel about Michael?"

My sister suddenly leaned back with her elbows on the bed, almost as if to avoid direct eye contact with me. "Well, he's a wonderful man," she said almost wistfully, looking up through the corner of her eyes. "And I'm really happy that you found him." She looked away for a moment, and then looking back at me with a forced smile, added, "He'd make for a great brother-in-law, so you certainly have my blessing."

"Well, it's just nice to have your blessing for anything," I said with a grateful smile. "I'm so happy to have you here, and safely back in my life!"

"Me too," she replied with a smile that shared in my appreciation but was still hiding something.

I had to put my sister at ease a bit more about the subtext surrounding this topic, if I was going to get any real information out of her. So I opened to Maria a little more. "Believe it or not, I'm actually very torn about things with Michael."

Her expression morphed into one of complete surprise, almost relief. "Why? What do you mean?"

"Well, we never talked about this, but I was actually dating my professor for a while."

Maria's face lit up in amusement at my naughty confession. "Really?!"

"Yes. His name is Julien, and I still think about him a lot."

"Oh. Does Michael know this?"

"No. Since the two of you arrived, he and I haven't even had a chance to talk much. In fact, I hardly even saw him after I had stopped dating Julien because I had to focus on my final exams."

"Oh," she said, as if she wanted to avoid taking any position on the issue. "Well, I'm sure that God will steer your heart wherever it's meant to go."

I gently put my hand on my sister's shoulder. "Tell me honestly, Maria. If I weren't in any way involved with Michael, how would you feel towards him?

She still wasn't ready to go there. "What do you mean?"

"I mean, if I weren't in the picture at all, could you see yourself getting romantically involved with Michael?"

"Why are you asking me such a question?"

"I just have a feeling about this and want to know. Please be honest with me, Maria. I promise I won't be upset with you, whatever your answer is, as long as it's honest. Could you see yourself with him?"

A smile that she could hardly repress gradually crept onto her face, and then she nodded silently while looking down, as if slightly ashamed.

Chapter 25: Julien

Sunday, 6/15/14 at 21:45.

My therapy session today began with me updating Lily about the aftermath of the incident involving Craig Walkenford. I told her how my lawyers amicably resolved the defendants' claims out of court with a settlement payment of about half a million dollars. But I explained that the bigger, related cost was the set of redemptions and lost investors attributable to the bad press about Craig's violent flashback at JMAT.

"The investors who were in the lobby when it happened all decided against working with our fund, but that was to be expected, and a relatively small loss. The bigger problem was that some of my long-term investors began to doubt my judgment and emotional stability, and a few of them even emailed me directly, asking me if I really had chosen to be temporarily homeless."

Lily's expression seemed to be one of pity. "And how did you answer those questions?"

"I tried to explain that I was under a lot of stress at the time and had simply taken a brief break from work and fell asleep in the park from exhaustion, and that's how the rumors started. But doubt can be a hard thing to remove once it settles into someone's mind. And I think confirmation bias is probably strengthened when money is at risk."

"As a defense mechanism?" Lily clarified.

"Yes. To protect their capital, I think investors have an even stronger tendency to search for, interpret, or recall information in a way that confirms their beliefs or hypotheses. And if something calls into question the integrity or emotional stability of the person in charge of their money, investors will feel a strong motivation either to doubt the reports and seek out information that confirms their faith in the fund manager, or to panic and seek out more proof that they should withdraw their funds from that manager before they suffer a major loss."

"So how did most of your investors react?"

"Predictably, those whose investments have performed relatively well over the last quarter tended to dismiss the reports as rumors or distorted mudslinging. But those who were disappointed with their returns over the same period generally believed the reports and questioned the safety of keeping their money with me. On the whole, our total assets under management fell by about ten percent as a result of this mess."

"But you're confident that your firm can recover from that?"

"Yes. We've come back from worse. And I have no regrets about helping Craig. In fact, after karma paid me the nicest possible visit yesterday, I decided to pay for him to get treated at a live-in facility that will hopefully get him back on his feet someday."

Lily looked impressed by the gesture. "Well, that was very kind of you." She then squinted a little. "What visit from karma do you mean?"

I released a smile. "Anissa called me yesterday, asking if we could meet. I took her out to dinner last night, so we could talk."

"And what happened?"

"She told me that she hadn't been able to stop thinking about me and was increasingly doubtful about whether she should still date Michael, whom she had barely seen after she and I broke up, because of his lengthy trip to Syria. She admitted that – out of her own inexperience and emotional frailty – she might have judged me too harshly."

Lily tapped her pen against her lower lip, and her eyes narrowed a bit. "And what do you think was her motive for these confessions?"

I stroked the small scruff that was building up on my face. "I'm not sure there was a specific motive – it all felt very natural. Basically, we just opened up to each other more about how we felt."

"About each other as individuals or about your relationship?"

"Both. We each admitted what we found so special in the other, acknowledged the major mistakes that we thought we had made, and ultimately exchanged apologies. By the time we said goodnight, we had agreed to give ourselves a second chance."

There was an unmistakable look of disappointment on Lily's face. "You think that's a good idea?" she asked, in the most detached and clinical tone she could summon.

"Yes. I feel like I've been on cloud nine ever since," I admitted with a grin. "And this is actually good news for *you* as well," I added ironically, knowing that it would annoy her.

She did her best to look unfazed by my comment. "How is this good news for me, Julien?"

"Well, we won't have any more of those awkward goodbyes at the end of therapy. Now that my attentions are again fully focused on Anissa, it should be a lot easier to respect your professional boundaries."

"I see," she replied with an expression that seemed to say, "It's not as if anyone was really suffering from those awkward goodbyes."

"Oh, and my motivation to tackle my past is now greater than ever. I repeated my promise to Anissa that I would be completely open about it with her within three months or she could terminate our relationship for that failure alone."

Lily brushed aside a lock of her red hair that had fallen in front of her and placed it behind her ear. "Well, as your therapist, I think that's probably the only good thing that will come of this."

I couldn't resist the temptation to toy with her. "Why are you being such a party pooper, Lily?"

"I've told you before all of the reasons why this relationship seems unhealthy for you and her."

"Perhaps I have a selective memory, but the only reason that comes to mind is no longer relevant now that my class is over and I'm no longer her professor."

Lily rolled her eyes slightly and shook her head. "Julien, you've got deep and severe traumas that have prevented you from being truly intimate with anyone and you have yet to tackle them even in therapy. As if that weren't enough, you're more than twice her age, she's a victim of rape and the trauma of seeing her family butchered, and you're now making her your guinea pig as you try out this new thing called a serious and faithful relationship."

Maybe Lily had a point.

Chapter 26: Anissa

∽ Saturday, June 21, 2014 ಲಿ

To My Dearest,

It's been a week since I met Julien for dinner, when we agreed to give our relationship a second chance. So much has happened since then, but I've been too busy living these things to write about them. I'll try to catch you up now as fast as I can.

Before that dinner with Julien, I had thought long and hard about my relationship with Michael, and my sister's interest in him – something I had sensed from the moment I saw the two of them in the Montreal airport. I could tell that they were really happy together and unusually comfortable around each other. I also thought about how Maria had suffered so much during the last two years, when I was living a much safer and happier life in the U.S., and I wanted her at least to have some joy and a beginning of hope. And Michael was exactly what she needed – a source of strength and pride for Middle East Christians in general, and especially one who was a refugee like her, who had fought hard for her freedom and dignity.

To my own nerdy amusement, I even analyzed how my romantic decision had the potential to produce, in economic terms, a Pareto optimal outcome. If I chose Michael, then I might or might not end up as happy as would be the case if I chose Julien, but my sister would definitely lose Michael; on the other hand, if I chose Julien, then she would gain Michael, and our collective happiness would thus be optimized.

Of course, I still cringed at the thought of explaining all of this to Michael, and couldn't really imagine a more awkward conversation. But we had to have that talk, and I was finally able to sit down with him for coffee on June 13th (the day after the MCA meeting that Maria attended with me, and the day before my dinner with Julien).

"Judging from how hard it is to get a private meeting with you these days, I'd say you're already the president of a new country," I teased him, after we had settled into our seats with our coffees.

He winced in embarrassment as his hands fidgeted around his coffee cup. "I'm really sorry, Inās. It's been more hectic than ever, especially after such a long absence."

I gave him an understanding smile. "I know, I'm just giving you a hard time." I paused for a moment until his eyes met mine. "But I am also wondering if that's the only reason it's been so hard for us to meet."

"What do you mean?"

"Well, my woman's intuition tells me that something might have changed for you during your time in Syria."

He looked away for a moment. "It was just a really stressful time, but you were a tremendous help, and I'm extremely grateful for it." His face lightened up in amusement at what he was about to say. "Believe it or not, I'm even starting to like your professor, after everything he's done for the MCA."

"He's not so bad, right?" I asked with an ironic half-smile. "It's funny how you've effectively been partners in so many MCA-related projects – including the liberation of my sister."

He chuckled at my surprising but true observation.

"You do have a point."

"And as thankful as I am, she must have been totally awed by your help."

"It was a pleasure to come to her assistance – she's a very special woman. I guess it runs in the family," he added with a wink.

"You certainly made an impression on her." I raised my eyebrows suggestively, before taking a sip of my coffee.

"Well, I'm sure that every captive feels that way about anyone involved in liberating him or her."

"So you don't think there's any special connection between the two of you?" I asked.

His feet shuffled below the table and lightly bumped mine. "What do you mean? What are you getting at, Inās?" His tone sounded both evasive and defensive.

"It's OK, Michael. I sensed it from the moment I saw the two of you together at the airport – before you knew that anyone might see how the two of you were interacting."

Michael's eyebrows rose in surprise, as he tried to dance around the facts. "We had just been traveling together for over fourteen hours. It's only natural that we'd get to know each other a bit during that time."

"On top of the time that you spent with her in Beirut."

Michael took a sip of his coffee, and then put his cup down. "Yes, but we obviously respected certain boundaries, Inās. We slept in different rooms – I was there only as the man in charge of her safety and to help her get by in Beirut until her visa was approved."

I realized that I needed to approach the issue more theoretically, as I had done with my sister. "I don't doubt that, Michael. But tell me honestly: if I didn't exist, would you be interested in Maria?"

He looked away for a moment, uncomfortable with being put on the spot – almost as if I had asked him whether, in the abstract, he was prepared to cheat on me with my sister. I had to make it even more acceptable for him to speak frankly, so that his response would be clearly beyond reproach. "OK, let's take it one step further. Suppose that I never broke up with Julien – imagine that he and I have been happily dating since the first time he took me out to dinner a few months ago. You then liberate Maria from her captivity and spend all of this time with her. Would you want something more with her? Or would you always just think of her as a friend?"

Michael's face lightened up, almost as if a burden had been lifted. "Well, if that were the case, I'm quite sure that she and I would be exploring much more than friendship by now."

Relieved that I finally got him to confirm what my gut had told me all along, I couldn't resist making a joke. "If you can't have one Toma sister, there's always another one you can try for, right?"

He chuckled. "Well, I wouldn't put it that way. Maria is hardly just a consolation prize. But I would never want to disrespect you like that – especially after we were trying to turn a new leaf. So I just never even let my mind go there."

I put my hand on his arm for emphasis. "I know, Michael, and I really appreciate it. But I need to be completely honest with you about something… "

His shoulders stiffened a little. I took my hand away and put it back on my coffee cup. "I still thought about Julien a lot after he and I broke up. Nothing happened between us while you were away, but I kept wondering whether I had been too quick to leave him. And it's not really fair to you that I'm still attached to him on some level."

Michael raised his eyebrows for a moment and then looked down. I couldn't tell if he was hurt or relieved, but he was definitely surprised and gathering his thoughts. With a self-deprecating smirk, he finally reacted: "Well, I'm the last guy to judge you for still feeling attached to your last relationship."

I chuckled. "It's funny how life happens sometimes. Reality is always so much messier than the neat fantasies of life that we nurture in our minds."

"Very true."

"So when are you asking Maria out on a date?" I asked lightly, with a mischievous smile.

Michael laughed. "How about we set it up right now?" he quipped with exaggerated enthusiasm, clearly meant to mock my hasty transition.

I was so relieved that we had made it out of that heavy conversation without too many feelings being hurt that I couldn't resist some more comic relief and whipped out my cell phone. "You don't think I'll take you up on that offer, do you?"

"No, I don't!" he replied, practically daring me.

I dialed Maria's number and put her on speaker phone.

"Hello?" she answered.

"Hi, Maria, how's it going?" I began. Michael shook his head in amused disbelief.

"Good, how are you, Inās?"

"I'm doing great, actually. I'm just super excited because there's this really great guy that I want you to meet. I think the two of you would get along fantastically well!"

Maria's voice sounded cautiously curious. "Oh really? Wow, that's quite a recommendation. So who is this guy and where did you meet him?"

"I met him on Facebook actually."

Maria's voice suddenly became more skeptical. "Really? But isn't that kind of random?" she added. Michael was clearly trying to restrain himself from bursting into laughs and spoiling the prank.

"It was kind of random, but I then met him in person, so I can vouch for him – he's really a good guy."

Her voice sounded more trusting again. "Well, if you met him and you think we would be good together, then I'll be happy to meet him."

"Oh, well I'm very glad to hear that because he's actually right here next to me, waiting to ask you out on your first date."

Maria's tone went back to sounding confused and skeptical. "What do you mean? Really?"

"Yes, you've actually met him before. His name is Michael Kassab. Here, why don't you talk to him directly," I added pushing my phone closer to Michael with a huge grin on my face.

"What?! Are you playing some kind of joke on me?"

I nudged Michael with my hand and urged him with my eyes to say something, but he was still in shock from the whole thing.

"No, I'm not! I swear to you he's right here – I'm not used to seeing him so speechless, but I think he gets shy just thinking about you."

Michael finally released a laugh and spoke. "Hi, Maria… Was your sister this much of a troublemaker back when you were living together in Homs?"

Maria sounded totally shocked and amused. "Oh hi, Michael… Wow, what a surprise! No, she was much better behaved back then. Clearly she's making up for lost time now!"

We all shared a laugh.

* * *

The next evening, I had dinner with my former professor and, by the end of the night, it was as if we had never stopped dating. I told him about how I had set up Michael with my sister, and that seemed to bring Julien and me even closer to one another. We had each removed all rival suitors from the playing field, we were no longer worried about a professor-student scandal, and he had committed to revealing his childhood traumas within three months. With all of those issues behind us, every time I've seen him since that dinner has been absolutely magical.

Last Thursday, after two more dinner dates, we also had sex again, and I actually enjoyed it more than any of the previous times. I decided to stay and try to sleep in his bed that night, despite the possibility that one of us might wake up the other because of a nightmare. To try to avoid my own nightmares, I went through my usual ritual of whispering to my parents not to enter the car, and didn't even mind that Julien might overhear me. In the end, it was he who woke us up with his nightmare. I just tried to hold and soothe him, until he fell back asleep in my arms.

Today, he took me on our most extravagant date yet, treating me to a private helicopter tour of Manhattan, starting in Battery Park, where we took off to admire the marvels of Manhattan for about an hour before the aircraft transported us to Julien's summer estate in Southampton. Throughout the tour, we were mesmerized by spectacular views of the Manhattan and Brooklyn Bridges, the South Street Seaport, and the Wall Street area. Then we flew by the Empire State Building and hovered near Central Park to soak in that stunningly verdant sight, before making a grand sweep of Yankee Stadium and the George

Washington Bridge.

Throughout the tour, I kept admiring this man next to me who appeared to have the world at his fingertips. Indeed, even the meaning of his name seemed to reinforce that idea of him: of or relating to the famous Roman emperor, Julius Caesar. Even the official calendar belonged to him, I joked quietly to myself.

Putting aside how much the tour's grandness seemed to conform to Julien's larger-than-life persona, the most moving moment was when our helicopter approached Ellis Island, and stopped to behold the Statue of Liberty from the skies. The breathtaking aerial view of that powerful symbol totally transfixed me. As I looked at the green patina covering Lady Liberty's copper skin, her torch raised so high and proud, it felt as if she were calling out to me – even congratulating me – as if to say, "You made it here too, Anissa. Welcome."

Chapter 27: Julien

Sunday, 6/22/14 at 21:45.

I've been seeing my shrink for about four and a half months, and today felt like a small breakthrough of sorts, which is all the more fitting, considering how our time together ended. Lily began our session where the last one had ended, trying to convince me to break off my relationship with Anissa.

"You yourself know that it's likely to fail," she nonchalantly pointed out at one point.

"Why do you say that?" I asked, a bit troubled but intrigued by the confidence behind her statement.

"Because you still can't free Icarus, even though you've already nursed him back to health," she explained. "You still fear, deep down, that you'll lose Anissa as soon as you open up to her about your past. So you keep Icarus caged for his constant companionship – to ensure that he'll still be there when she leaves you."

My eyebrow rose a bit. "Maybe."

"Well, there's clearly no persuading you to end your relationship with Anissa before you both get hurt, but perhaps you'll finally let me help you with the issue that will probably end things with her."

"You know our deal when it comes to discussing those details," I replied, confident that this would avoid the topic, as usual.

"And I finally kept my side of the bargain," she said with a smile that made her seem both impressed and surprised by her own decision to do so.

"Really?" I couldn't believe that she had finally called my bluff and actually visited a slaughterhouse.

She picked up her cell phone off of the desk nearby. "Yes. Here, take a look," she added, as she showed me some photos on her phone of how she had toured the gruesome meat business. I couldn't bring myself to look closely at the photos but I saw enough of them to confirm that she had indeed met my challenge.

"Wow," was all I could say, as I tried to stall long enough to figure out my next move and how I would talk about my past.

"Yes. It wasn't pretty there. And I don't think I would have done that for any other client," she confessed, as she put her phone back on the desk. "But it was worth it, if my trip produces some kind of progress with you on this issue." She picked up her pen and paper and then looked at me expectantly. "So, now it's your turn… "

"OK… Well, before I tell you anything about my childhood and how it relates to what you saw, I need to know how you *felt* when you were there, to see how much you'll be able to relate to what I share with you."

Lily seemed reluctant to answer, since it effectively turned her into the client and me into the therapist, but I think she was too curious to know where our discussion was going to resist. "Well, the sight of the blood and the animals being slaughtered was disgusting – especially the way they're just manipulated like objects before being killed…And the smell was so revolting that I nearly puked."

She wasn't being personal enough with her answer, so I persisted. "And how did seeing that make you *feel?*"

"I guess I…I felt very small…And weak."

"Why?"

"Because I was surrounded by suffering and was powerless to stop it."

"OK, good. So you have some idea of how I felt thirty years ago, as a nine-year-old, in my father's butchery."

Lily eagerly positioned her pen on her yellow pad, as she waited for more details relating to a disclosure that I had been avoiding almost since our first session. "What happened to you at his butchery?"

"He made me…" I shut my eyes and looked away. I had to get through it somehow. Lily and I had a deal and she had performed her end of the bargain. And I would need to face it again with Anissa in a few months anyway. "He made me…" I couldn't get the rest out.

"He made you what?"

"He made me participate in the actual slaughter."

"Was it a machine slaughter in Mexico, where you grew up?"

"No. He had a small shop. It was manual. You hold down the animal and you slit at the neck with a blade." I could feel my hands shaking and some sweat building across my forehead.

"And you felt small and weak there?"

"Yes. Totally impotent as my own father forced my hand towards evil."

"And how did you know, at the age of nine, that it was evil?"

"No child should be made to draw blood like that." I buried my head in my hands and paused for a moment, trying to find the strength to explain the rest. "To feel the coarse movement of a blade cutting through flesh, killing a conscious being as the floor is showered with blood to the horrific last sounds of a life snuffed out for no good reason." My face was still down, covered by my hands. I could hear the gentle tapping and scratching sound of Lily's pen taking notes on her pad.

She finally spoke. "Why do you think your father forced you to participate in that?"

"Because he thought it would make me into a man… He beat me a few times in the years before that, but he wasn't always so cruel. He had changed, for the worse."

"What do you mean? How did he change for the worse?"

I shook my head in refusal. "Sorry, Lily. That's beyond our deal. I promised to tell you more about my childhood and what happened in it to make me become a vegetarian. And I just did that, despite all of my reservations and visceral discomfort with sharing any part of that experience with anyone. You're the first to hear even that much."

"Well, I'm glad that I got you to open up at least a little."

"Yes, but I didn't promise to answer any related questions you may have about my father."

She glowered at me. "Julien, what kind of game do you think we're playing here? You of all people should know that therapy is of extremely limited value without trust. And the depth of a therapist's insight is significantly blocked when the client provides so little information. You're the one with the nightmares. How do you expect to solve them with me, or anyone else, if you keep all of the potential causes to yourself?"

"Maybe the nightmares will go away on their own. I've definitely been having them less often with Anissa in my life."

"That's a cop-out – especially because you'll lose her in the end, if you won't trust anyone with the details of your childhood."

"I'll take my chances," I replied curtly. "Anissa and I are growing closer by the day. And it's ultimately she who needs the truth, not you. Maybe she'll be satisfied with what I told you. And if she insists on knowing more, then maybe by that time our level of comfort and intimacy will empower me to reveal more. But you and I don't have that closeness."

Lily's scowl suggested bruised pride – like that of a spurned woman. "So maybe this is it for us," she replied, with a hint of bitterness in her voice, daring me to terminate her services.

"I think so. I'm happy now," I responded nonchalantly, without flinching. "And I'll be spending weekends in the Hamptons for the rest of the summer, so it wouldn't be possible to see you on Sundays anyway."

She rolled her eyes. "There are solutions to those kinds of logistical issues."

"True. We could try to do therapy via Skype video. Or I could fly you in. The mansion is big enough for plenty of privacy, even when Anissa is staying there with me. But that's not really the point."

She put away her pad of paper and pen, and started to gather her things, as if to indicate that our session was over, even though our time wasn't up. "So what *is* the point?"

"The point is that the benefits of seeing you no longer outweigh the costs."

She stopped collecting her stuff and looked up. "What do you mean?"

"I mean that I'm feeling much better about my life than when I first contacted you, so I'm not sure how much more you can really help at this point – especially since I just revealed as much as I'm prepared to share with you about my past. Thus, at this point, continuing therapy with you involves mostly downside risk."

Lily furrowed her brow. "What downside risk do you mean?"

"The risk of revealing too much. Details that are so sensitive I can't risk telling anyone else. Except maybe Anissa, if we get that far."

"So you don't trust me to keep our therapy confidential."

"We've been over that, Lily. Even the most discreet human is still human. So the safest approach is just not to tell any human. And there's another risk that's almost as important."

"What's that?"

"As you should know by now, you've been the biggest temptation in my life for a while now – the person who would be most likely to make me cheat on Anissa, and therefore the person I should probably most avoid," I noted, standing up to indicate that I considered our session over.

Lily's expression lightened a little and she stood up, leading me to the door of her office. "I guess I should be flattered now, right?" Her proud posture projected a dignified confidence, but when she looked straight into my eyes, I sensed her vulnerability, as she held the door open for me – maybe for the last time. A part of me would definitely miss her.

"Yes, you should be. Which is why this is probably our final farewell. But if something urgent comes up during the summer, or after that, I'll call you."

She looked away, shaking her head. "Funny how I'm now the one who feels used in this transactional relationship."

"Indeed. But maybe that's a sign that we both evolved a bit throughout our therapy sessions?"

"Maybe." She looked back at me with a flirty, self-deprecating smile. "I guess I'm a bit late with that kind of inappropriate sentimentality."

"You did have your window of opportunity," I replied wryly.

"And you had yours," she added with a wink.

I smiled. "Indeed. But it's probably better for both of us that we never acted on that temptation."

Chapter 28: Anissa

∾ Thursday, July 10, 2014 ∾

To My Dearest,

I'm sorry I haven't written to you in so long, but I've been so absorbed in the joys of life that it never even occurred to me that I should pause them for the sake of recording such treasures. You're still as important to me as ever, but when a simple and far-reaching happiness colors every other thought, savoring such rare exuberance seems like the best way to honor it.

Indeed, this has been the first time in my life that I've actually taken a real vacation. I spent the last week with Julien, and this must be what it's like to be on a honeymoon. Our time together began on the fourth of July, when we watched the fireworks from his penthouse balcony, which offered a marvelous sixty-third-floor view of the patriotic city spectacle. The next morning, we took a helicopter flight to the Hamptons, where we've been ever since.

It's felt wonderful just to disconnect completely from all of life's pressures and the problems of the world. I've felt so renewed by this oasis of time in which I've been aware of nothing outside of our little universe full of starry nights, ice cream by the pool, and couple's bliss.

I felt guilty not working for the MCA for the last week, but Michael was very understanding about it and gave me the time off. I'll try to make it up to him by putting in some extra hours when he needs the time for his dissertation or just to see Maria outside of the MCA. They seem to be quite happy together, which warms my heart even more and seems to validate my decision to be with Julien in the end. The fact that Maria is now not only safe, but apparently falling in love, contributes even more to my general contentment. When I described to Julien how wonderful the last week has felt, he thought that being away from the stress of the city, and indulging a delightfully slower pace – surrounded by green, pastoral beauty, near the gentle waves of the beach – might have contributed to my state, which he compared to what Italians call "*Essere in stato di grazia.*" I looked up the term online and it literally means to be in a state of grace – to feel a deep connection with the divine and/or nature that produces inspiration or love that heals and protects. That sounds about right.

As a kind of mental or psychological exercise, I tried to amplify my newfound happiness by avoiding all negative thoughts about my past, the people no longer with me, and the world at large. I tried just to be. I lived simply to savor the moment, with my love, Julien.

Our increasing closeness became apparent in so many small ways — from completing each other's thoughts, to finding humor or beauty in the same moments, to expanding each other's cultural horizons in ways that symbolically bridged our different worlds. I introduced Julien to one of the greatest Arab-American poets, Khalil Gibran, and Julien truly cherished his writing. While reading his masterpiece *The Prophet*, Julien highlighted this section from Gibran's poem on love that we read aloud together:

> *Love gives naught but itself and takes naught but from itself.*

> *Love possesses not nor would it be possessed; For love is sufficient unto love. When you love you should not say, "God is in my heart," but rather, I am in the heart of God."*

> *And think not you can direct the course of love, if it finds you worthy, directs your course.*

> *Love has no other desire but to fulfil itself.*

> *But if you love and must needs have desires, let these be your desires:*

> *To melt and be like a running brook that sings its melody to the night.*

> *To know the pain of too much tenderness.*

> *To be wounded by your own understanding of love;*

> *And to bleed willingly and joyfully.*

> *To wake at dawn with a winged heart and give thanks for another day of loving;*

> *To rest at the noon hour and meditate love's ecstasy;*

> *To return home at eventide with gratitude;*

> *And then to sleep with a prayer for the beloved in your heart and a song of praise upon your lips.*

At the same time, Julien introduced me to Octavio Paz, one of

Mexico's greatest poets of the twentieth century and winner of the 1990 Nobel Prize for Literature. I especially enjoyed the delightfully imaginative story *My Life with the Wave*, a surrealist prose poem (from his 1951 collection *Eagle or Sun?*) about a man who falls in love with a wave and tries to have a relationship with it. Julien and I read this part out loud together:

> *Love was a game, a perpetual creation. All was beach, sand, a bed of sheets that were always fresh. If I embraced her, she swelled with pride, incredibly tall, like the liquid stalk of a poplar; and soon that thinness flowered into a fountain of white feathers, into a plume of smiles that fell over my head and back and covered me with whiteness. Or she stretched out in front of me, infinite as the horizon, until I too became horizon and silence. Full and sinuous, it enveloped me like music or some giant lips. Her present was a going and coming of caresses, of murmurs, of kisses. Entered in her waters, I was drenched to the socks and in a wink of an eye I found myself up above, at the height of vertigo, mysteriously suspended, to fall like a stone and feel myself gently deposited on the dryness, like a feather. Nothing is comparable to sleeping in those waters, to wake pounded by a thousand happy light lashes, by a thousand assaults that withdrew laughing.*

With every day that passes, Julien and I have grown closer and more comfortable with each other, and I'm sure that he will open up to me about his childhood, and the source of his nightmares, within the timeframe that he promised. In the meantime, I've come to learn some rather endearing little details about him, including a quirk that I would call "hedonistic hyper focus": whenever possible, he tries to indulge in just one pleasure at a time, so as to maximize the enjoyment of whichever senses are involved. For example, if he's about to eat some delicious vegetarian meal, he prefers that any music playing be barely audible, so that he can concentrate as much as possible on the pleasure in his mouth. If we're watching a movie, and there's any interruption – me trying to speak to him, the food delivery arriving, someone sneezing – he'll insist on rewinding the film to a few minutes before the disruption, so that he can "get back into the moment" and feel as moved or swept away by the experience as he would have been had there been no interference. Similarly, when we're having sex, he prefers to keep all auditory distractions to a minimum, so that he can hear my gasping and moaning, and the noise that two bodies make when they intimately meet. To my surprised delight, the sound of me climaxing seems to bring him the greatest joy of all. Yes, thanks to Julien, I finally have been able to enjoy sex that much.

Chapter 29: Julien

Saturday, 7/19/14 at 13:18.

I probably haven't felt the need to write much in my journal for the same reason that I don't feel the need for therapy anymore: I'm too busy being happy. I can't even remember the last time everything felt so good. My fund seems to have recovered from the incident with Craig, and things couldn't be better with Anissa. I had a magical time with her from the Fourth of July through the end of the week that followed in the Hamptons, and since then we've been seeing each other four to five times a week in the city. In fact, if she didn't have to be in the city for her duties helping the MCA, we'd probably just be living in the Hamptons all summer. But she needs to be in the city, so I followed her, because it would be no fun staying in the Hamptons all alone. I can't even remember the last time I spent so many days of New York's unbearably sultry summer in the city.

This morning was actually the first time in a while that I've seen Anissa look sad. Together in bed, we read the headlines and world news on my tablet, and soon came across an article about how today was the official deadline that ISIS had given the Christians of Mosul to vacate. There was also a YouTube video of ISIS taking sledgehammers to the tomb of Jonah, removing the cross from St. Ephrem's Cathedral (the seat of the Syriac Orthodox archdiocese in Mosul), and putting up the black ISIS flag there and in other places throughout the city. The Islamist thugs also reportedly destroyed a statue of the Virgin Mary. The article mentioned that as Christians have been leaving Mosul, ISIS has been painting on their homes the Arabic letter that means "Nasrani" (from Nazrene, a word often used to refer to Christians). Next to the letter, in black, are the words: "Property of the Islamic State of Iraq."

According to various reports, the ISIS militants have also told Muslims who rent property from Christians that they no longer need to pay rent. The article grimly predicted the end of Christianity in Mosul, a city where Christians have lived for thousands of years, and the sound of church bells once mingled freely with the Muslim calls to prayer. We then spent a good hour talking about the overall situation for Mideast Christians, and some of the initiatives that the MCA was working on. Anissa explained that the Christian militias that Michael had created, with my financial support, were not numerous enough to protect every

Iraqi and Syrian city with a Christian population and, unfortunately, Mosul was one of the areas that was left unprotected.

Despite all of the time that Anissa and I have been spending together, there have still been a few days when I was in the Hamptons alone, and then – on top of not having Anissa near me, I surprisingly missed having Icarus around. I was almost tempted to bring his cage here to the Hamptons, but I thought that would be too stressful on the little guy, so I just left him there, where my housekeeper is already very experienced in caring for him, and has the vet's details, in case anything happens to him.

Lily was right about Icarus. I've been keeping him caged long past his full recovery because I fear that I'll need his soothing presence in my bedroom in the coming months – if I completely reveal my past to Anissa and she leaves me. But for now, I'm just trying to enjoy the present with her, under the blissful illusion that everything will work out.

There are a few scenarios in which my fantasy could actually come true. The most unlikely one is where Anissa relieves me of my promissory obligation after getting so close to me that she realizes how painful and uncomfortable the whole thing is for me, and she graciously lets me off the hook. But because her traumas are – objectively speaking – worse than mine (at least as far as I'm concerned), she would understandably think that it's too unfair for me never to reveal my personal horrors to her.

The more likely scenario is that I can fulfill my promise without actually getting into the details that will scare her off. With Lily, I had successfully adopted the same strategy as Anissa had used with me and everyone else (except her therapist): revealing a distorted and misleading version of the truth. But because Anissa was herself so adept at that technique, I suspect that she'll readily recognize any attempt by me to employ it.

The two of us did have one conversation that I thought might lead to the stuff I'd rather hide, but fortunately we managed to stay clear of it.

"I think I'm finally getting used to your vegetarianism," she began teasingly, just as my chef in the Hamptons brought us the first course of our dinner, a bowl of miso and soba noodle soup with roasted tofu and shiitake mushrooms.

"It's one of my odder idiosyncrasies," I admitted, bringing the bowl closer to whiff its delicious aroma.

Anissa took a spoonful of the soup and savored it for a moment. "Mmmm… This is really good!" she exclaimed.

"See that? You don't have to suffer for sparing the suffering of animals."

"Well, I understand why meat would repulse you, after you saw your dad's work as a butcher, but do you think fish are just as conscious as poultry and cattle?"

"I don't know for sure, but I'd rather err on the side of the humane. And my stomach literally can't handle it – I vomit every time I try to eat anything that used to move and perceive."

"Sounds almost like the nausea I felt each time I tried to learn how to drive," she replied.

I put my spoon down and furrowed my brow. "I remember you saying how you hate driving, but the nausea part is new to me."

"Yes, well, my phobia first started when Mohammed drove me from Homs to the international airport in Damascus… During that two-hour drive filled with so much tension and danger, and with the horrific memories of my family's murder fresh in my mind, I had to throw up on the way. And then when I began to lie to myself and everyone else about a car accident killing my parents, it got even worse."

I brought my hand to her cheek and gently caressed it. "I'm sorry, Baby," I said. "How about we overcome that phobia of yours together?"

She released a nervous smile. "What do you mean?"

"We can take one of my cars to a parking lot in the Hamptons, and you'll drive with my help. I'll have my hand on the wheel with you."

She crossed her arms and hunched her shoulders a bit. "I don't know," she replied hesitantly.

"Come on – it'll be fun. In the worst case scenario, you'll crash an expensive electric car and we'll have a laugh about it."

"No, in the worst case scenario, I'll vomit at an intersection and then a truck will ram into your car and kill us both."

I chuckled and shook my head. "Now that would be a glorious way to go – wiping your barf off of me as a truck flattens us both!"

"Seriously, if you can figure out how to stop my driving-related nausea, you'll deserve a Purple Heart, and I'll finally merit the full story of what makes you so nauseous about meat," she reminded me with a playful wink.

Chapter 30: Anissa

∽ Wednesday, August 20, 2014 ∽

To My Dearest,

I'm so sorry that it's been over a month since I've written to you. Somehow the time has just flown by more easily and happily than it has during any period since the Syrian Civil War began. That conflict – and the ever-worsening persecution of Christians – grinds on, but for the most part I've managed to give myself a break from the sadness by getting lost in an endless summer of love. So much has happened, with countless details comprising every moment, that I can't possibly summarize it all for you, but I'll try to touch on the highlights.

For the last six weeks or so, I've been going to the Hamptons to be with Julien every Thursday night through Monday night, after working out an arrangement with Michael that enabled me to handle my duties for the MCA remotely two days a week.

Towards the end of July, I again entrusted Julien to prevent me from falling to my death from high up – this time from the single-engine Cessna plane that he piloted, rather than his penthouse balcony. It was exhilarating and a bit nerve-racking at times, but I feel almost ready for skydiving at this point.

To add to the adventurous activities of this summer, he's tried for the last few weeks to help me overcome my fear of driving by acting as my training wheels while we drove his Tesla together. Progress has been slow, and I haven't made it out of the parking lot, but at least I got to the point where I'm no longer throwing up within ten minutes of getting in the driver's seat and buckling my seat belt.

The last weekend of July, on Saturday night, Julien brought me to a high-profile, benefit dinner supporting a variety of Latino causes that co-organized the black-tie gala. Julien sat on the host committee for the event and even gave a stirring speech about the great progress that Hispanics have made in every part of U.S. society – in finance, politics, media, fashion, technology, the arts, and other domains. Later in the night, he also introduced the key note speaker. To my amusement, Julien was literally one of the top prizes at the charity auction (the winner was awarded a salsa dance with him on stage). He had offered that prize (and his support as a host and sponsor of the event) long before we had ever even met, but Julien made sure to bring me along and inform everyone that we were a couple. It was fun to go out together so dressed up – him in his dashing, dark tuxedo, and me in the elegant, Elie Tahari evening gown that he had bought for me just for the occasion. That night also represented another milestone in our relationship, because it was our first highly public date – we could actually see pictures of ourselves the next day in the Latino media that covered the event.

Two days after that magical evening, my calendar reminded me to call Mohammed Rajeh and his family to wish them a happy Eid al-Fitr. After they had shown such kindness in my time of greatest need, and had literally saved my life, they will always feel like family to me. It was the third time that I had spoken with them at the end of Ramadan, and calling them for the Muslim holiday has become a kind of annual tradition for me. This time, our call felt a bit happier –mainly because the siege of Homs had finally ended, so life was a little easier for Mohammed and his family. He was, of course, also happy to learn that Maria and I were doing well and safely in the United States, but saddened by the news that our uncle and younger brother had been killed. Another sorrowful moment during our call came when he told me about the current state of my hometown. "Inās, it's better that you're there – not just because you're safer," he explained. "But because you wouldn't even recognize this place, after how much it's been battered by the war. Much of it looks like some post-apocalyptic wasteland. But we will rebuild. What choice do we have?"

During the last few days of July, I helped the MCA move into its new office on West 109th Street. With Julien's last donation, Michael decided to lease a dedicated space, with four full-time employees, who could help with fund-raising, accounting, project management, public relations, and other organizational issues. The new office will also make it possible to schedule smaller MCA meetings without checking on the availability of the university's student center, although for large gatherings, we will still need the university's resources.

Once the move was complete, the focus of my work at the MCA shifted from Syria to the situation in Northern Iraq, after ISIS had invaded the area in early August. ISIS fighters had massacred hundreds of Yazidi men and sexually enslaved their women; about seventy children died while fleeing, and about fifty thousand civilians were forced to seek refuge on Mount Sinjar after the Kurdish fighters protecting them fled the ISIS threat. The refugees were trapped on the mountain without food, water or medical care, facing starvation and dehydration.

When the crisis emerged, Michael insisted that the MCA focus all of its advocacy efforts on the dire situation there, even though the Yazidi religion is not a sect of Christianity. "They are a religious minority facing the same exact threat from Islamist militants that we Christians face, and we must stand with them," he explained. I completely agreed with him and was glad that we were doing whatever we could to help. I was angry and disappointed at the world's delayed reaction to the crisis, but finally, in the second week of August, the U.S. responded with airstrikes on ISIS units and convoys in the Sinjar area, and eventually began an operation to rescue the refugees, who were sustained by humanitarian airdrops of food and water by U.K. and U.S. forces.

Meanwhile, there was also the gut-wrenching news that ISIS terrorists had begun their promised killing of Christians in Mosul, and had started with younger victims. According to a few grisly reports, some children's heads were placed on the top of poles in a city park.

Yesterday, the entire world was finally exposed, for the first time, to the horrific barbarity of ISIS, when the Islamist animals beheaded U.S. journalist James Foley. After a North American reporter fell victim to Islamist brutality, the savage crime has been broadcast nonstop for all to see (as if this were the first time that Islamists had beheaded an innocent person). The disproportionate coverage was almost offensive on some level – like this man was somehow more valuable and worthy of global attention because he's from the U.S. and a member of the media. But perhaps there is some silver lining in this atrocity (and the special treatment that it has received from the press): this issue finally seems to be getting the attention that it deserves. On a personal level, seeing this awful incident – especially the image of him kneeling so helplessly on his knees in that orange jumpsuit – brought back terrible memories that quickly led to tears, as I recalled how mercilessly and senselessly my own family was slaughtered. When Julien tried to comfort me, he kept asking why I was reacting in such a strong way to this incident.

"What is it, *Querida?*" he asked, employing the Spanish term of endearment (which means, "beloved" or "darling") that he had started using with me. "Tell me, Baby," he said, stroking my hair and neck.

I shook my head, wiping away my tears as I tried to resist getting any deeper into the source of my distress, but I eventually relented and shared with him some new details about the massacre of my family. I told him that the James Foley news brought back horrific memories because my parents, older brother, and housekeeper were all beheaded by Islamist gunmen, and I had seen the macabre aftermath on a YouTube video made by the monsters.

Julien's mouth was agape and he just remained speechless and horrified, as he tried to hold and comfort me.

Indeed, as blissful as much of my summer was, any temporary escape from world events that I managed to enjoy would quickly come to an end whenever world headlines focused on the Middle East or I resumed my work for the MCA. In addition, my awareness of Mideast atrocities sometimes brought back my nightmares, and at times seemed to affect Julien's dreams as well. Unsurprisingly, we both had horrible dreams last night – probably because of the James Foley beheading.

But, in general – and to my pleasant surprise – the frequency of my nightmares has definitely diminished over this summer, and Julien has reported a similar improvement, which I have witnessed myself when sharing his bed. Apparently, we're good for each other's dreams!

Perhaps the most interesting news from the recent past happened last night, and that was what originally prompted me to write to you today, My Dearest, although I then got sidetracked with catching you up on the highlights of the last month. Anyway, yesterday, Julien and I went on our first double date with my sister and Michael. I was a little bit nervous about the whole thing, because I wasn't sure how Michael and Julien would get along or how we would all relate as a group. But my fears were misplaced – I forgot that Michael no longer viewed Julien as a potential rival and had come to respect and appreciate everything that Julien had done for the cause. After we all sat down for some sumptuous Mideast dishes at a vegetarian restaurant that Julien had selected, I jokingly laid down the ground rules for our dinner conversation. "OK, it's three Arab Christians against one Mexican Catholic, so let's do our best not to talk about the Middle East for the next two hours."

"Hey, and what if *I* want to talk about the Middle East for the next two hours?" Julien joked.

Somehow, in the end, we did manage to avoid discussing the Middle East for much of our dinner together, mainly by focusing on Maria's experiences in her new city and what she and Michael had done together. At one point, when Maria started talking passionately about her love of music and her dream of getting into the Julliard School,

Julien mentioned that he was actually friends with the head of admissions there and had made several sizable donations to the school in the past few years. He then very graciously offered to make an introduction, which predictably sent Maria into the clouds. Seeing my sister release such a radiant and unrestrained smile was definitely the best moment of our dinner and probably my whole week. I loved Julien even more after that.

Chapter 31: Julien

Thursday, 8/21/14 at 23:58.

I finally opened up to Anissa about my past, sitting down next to her on my bed. After the news of James Foley had led her to tell me last Tuesday about her parents being beheaded, I realized that I had made her wait long enough and that she was entitled to the full truth about my own past, for all of its horrors. It was time for me to stop hiding and just accept the risk that she might forever leave me.

I began to cry as I tried to get through the story that begins with my father forcing my hand to grip a blade in his butcher shop, in front of a conscious life about to be taken by me in an act that would forever prevent me from eating or even being around meat. Anissa held my hand and tried to sooth me, even as she encouraged me to proceed. "It's OK, *Querido*. I will love you no matter what you tell me. Please trust me. I've exposed myself to you in countless ways. Please confide in me about this. You've made me wait long enough. And if you tell me, it will only bring us closer," she concluded reassuringly, stroking my hair.

I finally managed to get all of the words out, and told her everything – every last frightful detail I could compel my memory to recall. As I feared and expected, she reacted with utter horror and disgust. "No wonder you deferred this moment for months, trying so hard to keep something so hideous from me!" she yelled. "You monster! Please don't ever contact me again – you've just broken my heart into a thousand pieces."

She tried to get up off my bed, but I tugged her by her hair and prevented her from leaving. As she struggled and screamed to let her go, I pulled out the blade that was hidden beneath the covers, held by my right hand, and with a single stroke, I slit her throat. Her last words were, "But I thought you loved me." Then I suddenly regretted what I had done and tried desperately to plug up her wound, but it was too late – there was no way to reverse that act of horrible madness born out of a soul damaged decades earlier, and the blood just kept flowing from her neck. I pulled her closer to me, pressing on her slashed neck as hard as I could, but her vital fluid sprayed out of the carotid artery where I had cut her, and soon it was all over my nose and mouth and I started coughing and choking on her blood.

And then I screamed in terror, throwing the blankets aside, as I realized that I had just had the most awful nightmare of my life. Anissa, who had awakened from a nightmare of her own a few hours earlier, gently caressed my sweaty chest, trying to calm me. "It's OK, *Querido*, I'm right here for you. As you were here for me. We'll get through our demons together."

I knew at that point that I had to speak to Lily again.

The next morning (yesterday), I called my therapist, desperate to see her as soon as possible. Lily said that she was all booked up for the day. I offered her one thousand dollars for a one-hour session, if she could find the time. She agreed to stay at the office late and schedule me in after her last appointment.

When I walked into Lily's office that evening at 7:30 p.m., there was no hint of flirty ambiguity in our relations, as had so often been the case, back when I had been seeing her on a regular basis. This was all business. She rightly sensed from the urgency of my phone call and tone that I genuinely needed her professional help – now more than ever.

We sat down in her office and I did my best to recap an entire summer for Lily, as she listened attentively, occasionally jotting down notes on her yellow pad. Her facial expressions were mostly neutral the whole time, except for a slight eyebrow raise when I told her how I was more in love with Anissa than I had ever been with any other woman. When I finally thought Lily had enough background information to be helpful, I dove right into the issue that had prompted me to call her that morning.

"I had the most horrific nightmare last night, confirming my deepest fears about Anissa… If I tell her everything, it will be over between us. But then I'll have revealed to another person what I can't disclose to anyone – including you. So I need to end it without divulging what she's waited months to hear. But how do I do that now? Refusing her the same trust that she's extended to me so many times will devastate her. And sharing those details will just add horror to the same bottom line of a broken heart for both of us. She is far too scarred already, and the last thing she needs are the scars of my own horrific past. There are no good options. So what should I do?"

Lily pursed her lips and shook her head for a moment before finally reacting. "I hate to say that I told you so. But what else can I say right now? I did try to warn you."

"I know. But a part of me always suspected that you maybe had your own interest in seeing me stay away from Anissa."

My therapist uncrossed her legs, so that her right leg was on top. "If a woman sees her neighbor's house ablaze and is happy to report the incident because she fancies the firemen on duty, does that make the fire any less dangerous?"

I rolled my eyes at her analogy, and stroked my chin a little. "Well, what do I do with this blaze now? And which fire department can extinguish it?"

She put her pen down on the pad, as if to emphasize that it was her turn to talk and my turn to listen. "I don't understand why you can't at least tell her what you told me about that day in your father's butcher shop. You've already trusted me with it, why not also trust her?" she asked, almost as if to challenge me. "Especially when you say that you're closer to her than to anyone else you've ever met."

"Because I didn't tell you the whole truth, or even the most important part of the truth – only as much of it as I could get myself to share. And my gut is convinced that Anissa would see right through that evasive approach, because she knows me so well, and because of her own experience in hiding trauma."

Lily squinted a little, like a poker player who just realized that she's been cheated by the dealer. Shaking her head in frustration, she finally reacted. "What are you so afraid of Julien? Just let it go. You were nine years old."

"If this ever got out, it would entirely change my public image. As battered as my reputation has been in the past, there would be no recovering from this."

Lily's face hardened. "Then man up to it, and accept that you're going to destroy this woman's heart. I'm sorry, Julien. There is no way to avoid both evils in this set of bad choices that you've imposed on yourself. You just have to do your best to decide which is the lesser of those evils and then manage the fallout as best you can."

"That's what I paid you a thousand dollars to tell me?"

"Apparently. Therapy is often about hearing and facing the truths you'd rather avoid."

When I left Lily's office there was no flirtatious eye contact or lingering at the door. I was frustrated and just wanted to be alone, to try to sort things out. I told Anissa that I wouldn't be able to see her that night, but that she should plan to come over the next night for our usual long weekend in the Hamptons.

I thought long and hard about what to do, often pacing around poor Icarus, who must have thought I'd lost my mind, walking laps around his cage. After a few hours of wandering ruminations, I finally crystalized the issue in the form of a single question. I asked myself, "What will you regret more: telling Anissa and then losing her after she is horrified by your past, or not telling her and wondering for the rest of your life if you might have kept her, had you told her?" That dilemma then led to a related question: "If she's really as special as you say, shouldn't you treat her that way and leave the rest to fate? If she's like no other woman to you, then you should trust her like no other woman."

In the end, I decided to tell her the next day, before our trip to the Hamptons.

And that just happened. I just told her, and my worst fears materialized. She just stormed out of here in tears – shocked, speechless, and horrified.

Chapter 32: Anissa

∽ Thursday, August 21, 2014 ∽

To My Dearest,

I've been shaking and crying for the last few hours – lost, confused, and upset. I think writing to you is the only thing I can do to try to calm myself. Maybe by recounting the details of what just happened, they'll become less potent and horrible than they seem to me right now.

At around 6:30 p.m., I finished my work for the day and exited the MCA office. Julien's driver was pulled over by the curb, waiting for me. I entered the sedan with my bag packed for a long weekend in the Hamptons, in case everything went well with the long-awaited chat in which I expected Julien to open to me completely. Technically, according to the promise he had made to me in mid-June, he still had a few weeks to reveal his hidden past to me, but I felt more unfairly exposed than ever, after what I had told him about my family, two nights ago. So I decided that it was time to give him an ultimatum, because I could no longer live with the imbalance. To my surprise, when I arrived at his place, I would quickly learn that a final demand wasn't even necessary, because he had already decided on his own that it was time for him to open up to me about his childhood trauma.

The summer air was heavy with humidity, so he suggested that we sit on the sofa in the living room by his sixty-fifth-floor bedroom, where we could still admire the splendid view with the comfort of air-conditioning around us. On the nearby coffee table, there were two tall glasses, sweating with condensation, each with a straw. He brought them over to us and handed me the cold beverage. "Here. These are freshly squeezed, organic strawberry and banana smoothies," he noted, taking a sip of his.

"Thank you." I took a sip of the sweet beverage. "It's delicious."

He looked away, and then back at me. "Anissa, before I tell you anything, do you remember what I said when I first told you about my decision to hire Craig Walkenford, even though he was a homeless man suffering from PTSD?"

I looked into the corner of my eyes, trying to recall the most interesting moments of that conversation. "You mean, when you said that there's no such thing as trust without risk?"

"Yes. That's exactly what I mean."

"OK. And why do you mention that now?" I asked, before taking another sip.

"Well, because I'm about to trust you more than I've ever trusted anyone else," he replied, resting his glass on the nearby coffee table. "And we saw how things worked out with Craig in the end, right?"

"I know, but his PTSD made him emotionally unstable – mine just gives me nightmares, like yours. But I'm totally in control when I'm awake, and you should know by now that I would never betray your trust."

"Yes, I do know that. But I also know no one is perfect. Remember what happened when I trusted you not to go into my Facebook inbox?"

I looked down in shame and nodded my head a little. "That was different, I just – "

"It's OK, *Querida*. We don't need to rehash that incident now. I'm just reminding us both that – even though you are the most angelic woman I've ever met – you're still human," he added with a gentle smile, as he lightly put his hand on mine. "So I'm still taking a risk by sharing this with you."

"I understand that," I conceded.

"Good. So before I take that risk, I need your most solemn oath that – whatever happens between us – you will never repeat what I'm about to uncover for the first time ever... " His stare seemed to penetrate my eyes, probing deep into my interior. With so much solemnity surrounding his revelation, whatever it was, I almost didn't want him to tell me anymore. "Because once I tell you this, there's no going back."

I took a hard swallow and braced myself to receive something that I could never share with anyone. "I swear to you, *Querido*, on the memory of my blessed parents, and on the future of my people, that I will never tell a soul."

He nodded slightly, as if to acknowledge my vow, and took his hand back. He let out a deep breath, and his hands began to fidget a little, as if he was trying to decide where and how to begin. I put my glass down on the coffee table, wanting to concentrate as much as possible on whatever he was about to say. After a few moments of silence, he finally spoke. "Where do you think I was born?" he asked.

"Mexico?" I asked.

"And where do you think my father is from?"

"Also Mexico, like your mother?"

"No. Both of those notions are incorrect, even though everyone assumes them to be the truth – from every personal friend of mine to the wider media."

"So where were you born?"

"In Kabul, Afghanistan, like my father."

I felt stunned and confused for a moment, as if someone had just informed me that the Earth is actually a moon orbiting the planet Mars, and not the third planet from the sun. He seemed to expect this reaction in me, and waited a moment so that I could adjust to these startling new facts.

Still trying to cling to my earlier beliefs, I grasped onto whatever counter-evidence I had. "So why is your last name Morales?"

"My mother, Leticia Morales, reverted to her maiden name after she left my father and took me back to Mexico with her."

"Why did she leave him?"

"It'll be obvious to you by the time I finish telling you everything."

I exhaled, a little nervous. "OK. So, what was her married surname? I mean, what was your father's last name?"

"It was Omar. His full name was Abdul Sayyaf Omar."

The room began to feel unsteady. Omar was also the last name of the doctor who had betrayed my father to the Sunni Islamists who murdered my family. I tried to control my shock, so that I could receive whatever other stunning facts had yet to be revealed. I cleared my throat to ask my next question, afraid of the answer, but pressing forward anyway. "So I assume that your first name wasn't always Julien, right?"

"That's right," he replied looking down for a moment. "In Kabul, growing up, my name was Jihad Omar."

I couldn't believe my ears. I looked around my surroundings for a moment. Was I in the right apartment? Was this a dream? I was totally dumbfounded. Trying to make sense out of what Julien, or Jihad, had just told me, I asked the next question that puzzled me: "And your mother was OK with the name Jihad? Was she Muslim too?"

"No, she was Catholic. But when my parents had me, my dad took that word to mean a kind of personal struggle for self-improvement, and, after he explained that to my mom, she was OK with it."

"How did a Mexican, Catholic woman end up in Kabul?" I asked, more confused than ever.

He released a nervous chuckle. "It's a fair question. She was actually Mexican-American – born and raised in Mexico, but she came to the United States on an academic scholarship, and eventually became a doctor. After she graduated from UCLA Medical School, she went to Afghanistan in 1972 as part of a special humanitarian mission to provide medical training to doctors and other medical staff in Kabul's main hospital. The program was open to any M.D. with at least two years of residency, which my mother had completed. She had skipped a year of high school and graduated college in three years, so she was just twenty-six years old at the time, and was eager to combine her love of medicine and helping people with her passion for travel and discovering other cultures."

The whole thing seemed surreal to me. I folded my arms and looked away, trying to gather my thoughts. "So how did Leticia Morales end up marrying Abdul Sayyaf Omar?" I finally asked, practically cringing as I said that name.

"He worked as a mid-level security guard at that same hospital where her humanitarian mission was based. He spoke English well, and was a charming, handsome man who was her age. She saw him quite often because he was assigned to guard her group of foreign doctors on the humanitarian aid mission. I guess it would have made more sense for her to become romantically involved with another Western doctor working with her, but there were a total of five doctors in the group and only two of them were men, one of whom was married. The other male doctor, from the U.K., quickly started dating, and ended up marrying, one of the other female doctors from the U.S. Apparently, my father was also relentless in pursuing his future wife, bringing her flowers to the hospital, helping her at every possible opportunity with translation or anything else she needed. In terms of his physique and charismatic presence, he was a really strong man who seemed to be a natural leader, and my mother assumed – like the many locals who admired him – that he was destined for things far greater than his security job at the hospital. After a few months of his persistent wooing, she finally agreed to go on a date with him, and three years later, on December 12th of 1975, I was born."

I still didn't know how all of this related to his trauma in a butcher shop, but I almost didn't want to know any more. I excused myself to go to the bathroom. I looked in the large mirror, as I held on to the edges of the stylishly designed and immaculately clean sink, feeling a bit nauseous. In the end, I didn't need to throw up, and just used the private moment to try to calm down and compose myself.

I went back to the couch and sat down. "Are you OK?" he asked. "I realize that this is a lot to digest."

My eyebrows rose and I nodded my head in agreement with his understatement. "Yes… It certainly is… So how did your father become a butcher?"

"According to my mother, soon after I was born, my father started talking about going to study in the university. She began to sense that his ambitions were frustrated by his hospital job and that he felt inferior because of her impressive education. He spoke with some friends who told him that he could earn a lot more money, and have more control over his hours and thereby study in the university, if he became a halal butcher with them. So he decided to leave his hospital job to partner up with them. He learned all of the Muslim rules and rituals of animal slaughter and shared the work duties with his friends. The first two years after I was born, he used his time off to help my mother take care of me and the house, but after I turned two, he enrolled part-time in the university, to study political science alongside his work as a butcher. My parents together made enough to pay for a full-time housekeeper who also looked after me, so that my mother could continue working in the hospital."

Julien stopped for a moment to take a sip of his smoothie. He had spoken a lot without giving his throat much of a rest. I let him pause for a moment, but I had to hear the rest, so I goaded him on with a question. "So your dad began studying in 1977, at the age of twenty-eight. But wasn't Afghanistan in a war with the Soviets around that time?"

He put his drink back down. "Yes, exactly. Afghanistan was going through a lot of internal turmoil, and in 1979 the Soviet Union invaded. And that's when my father started to change."

"What do you mean?"

"About three years after I was born, my mother noticed that her husband was becoming increasingly religious. She had converted to Islam only out of convenience – because of her marriage and her correct assumption that her life would be much easier in Afghanistan as a Muslim, for however long she planned to stay there. But my father knew that, deep down, she wasn't a true believer and he had accepted this, as long as she let him raise me as a good Muslim. I think my mother accepted that compromise because my father still wanted me to get the best possible education, and my mother personally made sure that I was exposed to science from an early age."

I couldn't believe that Julien/Jihad had just admitted that he was born and raised as a Sunni Muslim in Afghanistan. I was almost in a daze, but trying to stay focused so that I could get through whatever else awaited me. "Why did your father become more religious?"

"My mother thought it was the influence of his two partners in the butcher shop, who had begun attending a Salafist mosque. But, by my fourth birthday, my father had also become involved with a radical Islamist organization at his university, so – after she eventually learned of his involvement in that group – she concluded that this might have been a big contributing factor as well."

"And what did your mother say about this?"

"He apparently did a good job of hiding his evolving views about political Islam, until it was too late."

I felt chills run down my spine, as I tried to suppress thoughts about where this story was going. To that end, I focused on the chronology. "So by then, it was 1979."

"Yes. The Soviet invasion of Afghanistan began a few weeks after I turned four, and the country quickly became engulfed in a brutal and bitter war. I'm sure that also fueled the radicalization of my father... "

"And your mother didn't want to leave Afghanistan at that point?"

"Yes, by the early eighties, she started to prepare me for the idea that we might leave the country at some point – especially after my father had beaten me a few times for being a bad Muslim. I was around seven or eight years old at the time."

"So why didn't she leave?"

"She almost did, a few times. But she felt a moral, humanitarian duty to stay and help, with so many war-related injuries flooding the hospital where she worked and so few qualified doctors there – especially after some of her colleagues had returned to the U.S. And, of course, my father refused to leave, and – despite the occasional problems they had, like any couple – they were still married and there was still some love there. But had my mom known just how radicalized my dad had become, I'm sure that she would have just put all of those considerations aside, and at the first opportunity, she would have left work early to pick me up when my father was at his work or university, and fled the country without even telling him. But she had no idea that he was a rising member of Hezbi Islami."

I felt myself getting nauseous again. I could sense that the horrific part of his story was nearing. "What's Hezbi Islami?" I asked.

Julien, or Jihad, closed his eyes and put his hands on his face, shaking his head a little. He exhaled. "It was an Afghani Islamist organization whose ideology came mainly from the Muslim Brotherhood. Their goal was to replace the various tribal factions of Afghanistan with one unified, Islamic state."

He opened his eyes and looked at me, his eyes watering, and on the verge of tears. "What's wrong?" I asked.

Julien took a deep breath. "Anissa, I've been struggling for weeks about how to disclose this to you. I almost decided to tell you what I told my therapist, when I had to reveal *something* to her about the traumatic event, for therapy to continue."

"What did you tell her?"

"That one day, my father brought me to his butcher shop and made me do his job for him. I let her continue assuming that this was all happening in Mexico and that it wasn't any worse than a son being forced to see a lot of blood at the age of nine."

For a moment, I went from simmering at having been deceived (along with the rest of the world) about Julien's past to empathizing with his need to distort his trauma when sharing it with others – something I had been doing for most of the last few years. But now I had to know the full truth, just as he had learned mine. "So it wasn't in Mexico. And your father didn't force you to slaughter an animal?"

He shook his head and wiped away a tear. "You have no idea how hard this is for me."

I had to reassure him, or there was no way that he'd be able to continue. I put my hand on his and tried to summon all of the empathetic support I could find despite my inner revulsion at everything I had been hearing. "I know, Julien. I've been there too. Remember?"

He wiped away some more tears and nodded his head. "That's why I'm doing this. For us," he added.

"I know," I replied gently. "It really means a lot to me." Despite those words, I occasionally felt myself pulling back from a man I suddenly didn't know at all. Every now and then, I looked around my surroundings, trying to remember how I ended up in the magnificent Manhattan penthouse of a complete stranger.

After regaining his composure a little, he continued. "Before I tell you what happened in the butcher shop, there's a bit more background you need to know."

I raised my eyebrow in dread, wondering what other disturbing facts were missing from my impression of this man and his childhood. As Julien noted my reaction, he himself became more uncomfortable, and got up to pace around the living room, to avoid facing me as he spoke and maybe to release some of his nervousness.

He finally resumed his narration. "By the early eighties, the Afghans really hated the Soviets for all of the atrocities they had committed during the course of their invasion," he said, pacing about in front of me, as I leaned back against the sofa, trying to calm myself by imagining that this was some kind of college lecture on the history of Afghanistan. "The only possible exception to this rule was a Soviet Army deserter, to the extent that Afghanis understood that such a person was effectively rejecting the Soviet state and its military policies. Anyway, in Kabul, there was a Soviet man named Mikhail who had deserted the Soviet Army after seeing the crimes that his military had committed against Afghans. According to what my mother later told me, Mikhail had been a kind of 'crypto-Christian' – his family devoutly practiced and embraced Christianity in Russia, even though Communism made it difficult for any religion to be practiced. His deep Christian beliefs caused him not only to desert the Soviet Army, but also to do good works in Kabul, as he tried to make up for Soviet abuses during the war. He had become known in the community for his efforts to help Afghans wounded by the conflict, and he spent a lot of time volunteering in the hospital where my mother worked."

Julien stopped pacing and just stood for a moment, with his back facing me, as he continued talking. "But his activities weren't always limited to helping the wounded. On a few occasions, Mikhail apparently forgot what country he was in and started talking about his Christian faith to those he was helping. That in itself was already very risky, but when word got out that he was also seen a few times in the company of a local Afghan woman, his days were numbered. I think my father also viewed him as a potential rival, just because my mother had mentioned that she and Mikhail had spoken a few times at the hospital, when my father first asked if she had ever heard of him. She made it clear that their conversation was strictly about his volunteer work and the care of specific patients, but somehow my dad got the idea that he might be interested in my mom."

Julien still wasn't facing me. He leaned against a nearby set of drawers, on top of which sat a kinetic sculpture made of rotating geometric shapes. His finger pushed part of the sculpture, sending it into motion, as he contemplated its movements. As I waited for him to continue his story, I couldn't tell if he was gathering his thoughts, recovering from being emotionally spent, or just waiting for me to react in some way so that he could see how I was handling everything.

"So what happened with Mikhail?" I finally asked.

He reluctantly continued, but he couldn't seem to face me when talking, although I could see that he was wiping away some tears. "One afternoon in March or April of 1984, after I got home from school, my father came by earlier than usual, when my mother was still at the hospital and the housekeeper was watching over me. He took my hand and led me to his butcher shop. When we got there, the main entrance area had about twenty bearded men standing around a man who was seated in a chair with his hands tied together behind his back. They were all from my father's organization, Hezbi Islami. The man in the chair was Mikhail. They had kidnapped him from his residence the night before."

The room began to sway, as if the building had been erected on an oil rig. My head hurt and I decided to lie down on the sofa. I was dying to leave, but I was too deep into the story and had to hear whatever else Julien was going to share – if only out of respect for the enormous emotional effort he had invested in opening up as much as he had. But I was too psychologically spent to encourage him much, even though he was clearly waiting for some reaction from me. All I could bring myself to say was, "Go on."

His voice sounded fainter and even more unsteady. "My father read out some judicial-type sentence about Mikhail committing blasphemy against Allah, and trying to rape Muslim women, and then took a foot-long butcher blade and put it in my hand, leading me to the back of the chair, so that I was looking down over Mikhail's neck. He then ordered me to slit his throat, in front of all the men watching, so that they could all see that I was a brave and good Muslim."

I couldn't believe I was hearing this. It was as if my consciousness of the present had suddenly transformed into a nightmare. Or a bad dream had abruptly morphed into reality. It was torture to listen but this was the man that I had fallen in love with, even if I no longer was sure that I knew him. I owed it to both of us to hear him out, as awful as

166

listening any more felt. "Go on," I said, as if I were some kind of masochistic co-conspirator in our collective torment.

"I tried to resist by looking confused, but all around me, I just saw these bearded men, looking at me – waiting expectantly for me to comply. I turned to my dad, and he sternly repeated his command. Then he impatiently came from behind me, held my wrist forcefully, and showed me how and where to move the blade, guiding my hand without actually cutting Mikhail. He forcefully repeated his command, and with tears streaming down my face as I trembled in horror, I slit Mikhail's throat with the knife in my hand. Blood splattered everywhere as he screamed in agony, but he was still alive. I dropped the knife – I could hardly stand, my body was shaking so badly. My father picked up the knife, and, with a few powerful strokes, severed the man's head off."

I was definitely going to vomit soon. I could feel it. Julien and I were practically in two different worlds at that moment. He was bent over the dresser, staring at the kinetic sculpture, lost in the past but trying somehow to connect it to the present, while I was lying on his sofa, very much in the present and feeling nauseous as his voice mumbled on. To me, he sounded as if he had turned off all of his emotions and was just on autopilot.

"Back then I don't think beheadings were so in vogue among Islamists, even if there was an ample basis for it in the Koran. But I think my father's work as a butcher desensitized him, and made him comfortable putting a knife to living flesh. Beheading a man probably wasn't all that different to him than slaughtering a cow or a chicken. And that was how he had learned to kill… He wanted to teach me how to be like him… "

I gradually sat up, preparing myself to leave. Julien was still facing away from me, wiping away some more tears. I was waiting for the right moment to get up and head towards the elevator, but he was still talking, so I stayed put.

"Instead of becoming like him, I was just traumatized… That night, I told my mother what had happened, and the next day she fled the country with me. She was so horrified that she wanted to move back in with her mother, so we flew to Mexico, and we lived there from when I was nine until I turned twelve. That's how I became a native Spanish speaker… She renounced Islam and made me do the same, changed my name to Julien and our surname to Morales, and enrolled me in a Catholic school. The summer after I turned twelve, my mother was able to get a hospital job in San Diego, California, so we moved to the United States, where I've lived ever since. The rest of my secondary school education was in private Catholic schools. And, as if I hadn't already gone through enough trauma and change, six years later, just before I was supposed to start as a freshman at Yale, my mother died of cancer."

He finally turned around, the streaks of wiped tears still visible on his face and parts of his dress shirt. "There you have it, *Querida*. My whole story."

Chapter 33: Anissa

∾ Friday, August 22, 2014 ∾

To My Dearest,

I grew weary from writing to you last night; there was so much to tell, and summarizing it left me emotionally and physically exhausted – which is how I felt at the end of Julien's story.

By the time he had finished sharing his past, I was nauseous and faint, and paradoxically claustrophobic, despite the spacious penthouse in which I discordantly found myself. In the elevator, on the way down to the lobby, I ended up vomiting.

The doorman, who must have noticed me throwing up in the security camera, came walking towards the elevator, just as I was getting out. I think he just wanted to see if I was OK, but I hurried past him, rushing to get some fresh air outside while looking for the nearest taxi.

As I rode back to my dorm in a cab, a warm summer breeze blowing against my face through the open window, I realized that I had forgotten my stuff for the Hamptons at Julien's place. The extent of my shock became even clearer when – at that moment – I didn't care if I never saw that travel bag again.

There was a jarringly surreal disconnect between the Julien Morales I had known in that luxurious apartment, and the horrific past that he had finally shared with me about an Afghani boy named Jihad Omar. How could they possibly be the same person? And how could the things that Jihad was raised to believe – the things that he had done and seen during the first nine years of his life – not have influenced the adult man, Julien, that he had become and to whom I had grown so close?

And as I write all of this to you now, on some very basic level, it seems terribly embarrassing. I feel like a superficial idiot – easily deceived by his opulent wealth, academic credentials, charismatic power, and public fame. My parents had never given me any specific dating advice, but had often repeated a general warning; look at a man's childhood and parents to understand him. And I have only now – after giving my heart and body to this man – discovered the most horrific childhood one can imagine. What a fool I am.

I haven't been able to think about anything else and had to call in sick to the MCA. I wouldn't have been able to concentrate anyway and I didn't want to risk Michael or Maria asking why I seemed so down and disoriented. With so many shocking details dominating my mind, searching for a way to coexist with my earlier impressions and ideas of Julien, it seemed too easy for something secret to slip out. As angry as I felt at having been so deceived about who Julien was, I could never betray him like that, and had to avert a situation that might increase the chances of any compromising disclosure – whether because of an accidental slip or some conversational inquiry that unexpectedly forced it out. In fact, I hesitated even to tell you, My Dearest, but my sanity requires that I share it with *someone*, and you are my closest confidante. And if I can trust you with my most private facts because I keep them all in a hidden, password-protected file, then I assume that this secret about Julien is also safe with you.

But the divulgence of Julien's hidden and grotesque past to anyone else could massively overshadow all of his previous scandals – especially with beheadings in the news now – and would irrevocably ruin him. Just mentioning the fact that he was actually born and raised as a Muslim in Afghanistan would expose him to accusations of living some kind of double life, making everyone wonder what else he might be hiding.

When not busy gossiping about his scandals or spotlighting his wealth, the media have embraced Julien as a major Latino success story, and now I understood why he has so studiously helped to cultivate that image. He was genuinely proud of his Mexican heritage, but he was also understandably eager to encourage the assumption that there was nothing else in his ethnic background. I could discuss none of what he told me with anyone – not Michael or Maria or Uncle Tony or even my own therapist. It was all far too sensitive.

Indeed, when I consider just how much power Julien gave me last night to destroy his entire empire, I am humbled by the amount of trust that he has finally placed in me. But I still shudder at the thought of speaking to Jihad Omar. My brain feels bruised from so much cognitive dissonance. I can think of no psychological term or condition that more aptly describes my present state of mind: the mental stress or discomfort experienced when someone is confronted by new information that conflicts with existing beliefs, ideas, or values. Given the very human preference for internal consistency, I've been trying to reduce the Julien/Jihad dissonance by avoiding anything that highlights the cacophonous contradictions gawking at me.

Chapter 34: Anissa

∞ Saturday, August 23, 2014 ∾

To My Dearest,

It's now been over twenty-four hours since I learned the truth about Julien's past and neither of us has tried to contact the other. I assume that Julien knows, thanks to his expertise in human psychology, that I'm trying to work through his extremely disorienting revelations, and that it's probably best just to give me some time and space so that I can try to process it all. Or maybe he hasn't contacted me out of shame – he feels guilty for having let me get so close to him while concealing such enormously consequential facts about his early life that have more relevance to me than just about any other woman on the planet, given my own experience, of which he's all too aware.

I haven't contacted him both because I'm still very confused and shocked, and because talking to him just wouldn't feel the same right now – almost as if I were talking to someone I had just met, but even worse, because someone you just met doesn't cause you to feel unsure of your own impressions and beliefs about the world and the people in it. I somehow need to forget his past or reconcile it with his present in a way that makes sense to me, and I haven't found a way to do that.

In reality, people never correspond precisely to our impressions of them. So perhaps the strength of any relationship can be measured in terms of the gap that can be tolerated between who a person is in one's mind versus in reality. After all, the more someone conforms to one's expectations, the easier it is to accept that person. When Julien discovered that I wasn't in fact a virgin, that was also a discordant discrepancy between what he thought of me and what he learned to be the case. And yet he handled that surprise like a perfect gentleman. Of course, the surprises relating to his past are infinitely more jarring and hard to accept, so they put our relationship to the test that much more.

Oh, that's Michael calling my cell. I'll write more later.

* * *

I just got off the phone with Michael. He asked if I was feeling better after calling in sick yesterday. He also called to let me know that yesterday Maria and his MCA staff had helped him to organize a large protest tomorrow at Union Square, with several other organizations.

"I realized yesterday that we have to strike while the iron is hot," he explained. "The whole world is talking about the James Foley beheading, so now is the perfect time to make everyone realize that such horrors have been happening to Christians for centuries."

Trying to sound as if nothing unusual was on my mind, I said simply: "You're absolutely right."

"So can I count on you to be there?" he asked, as I feared he would. Given everything that was still weighing on my mind, I didn't know if I'd be ready to be around him and others, especially for a protest about beheadings. "Actually, why don't you bring Julien?" he added, with no idea what sort of absurd irony accompanied his otherwise polite suggestion. "We're all friends now, and he might as well feel included in the MCA's activities as a full member, rather than just a spectator passing our rallies on campus."

"That's kind of you, but I saw him the day after our dinner date with you and Maria, and I just don't think Julien wants to think about beheadings at the moment," I replied with the understatement of the century. "He's been under a lot of stress at work," I added, trying to offer some pedestrian reason for why he wouldn't be interested in the protest.

"OK, no worries. But you'll be there, right?"

"Yes," I finally agreed reluctantly. Given everything that had transpired in the last forty-eight hours, I wanted to avoid a demonstration about beheading at least as much as Julien presumably did. But I was in a quasi-leadership role at the MCA, and my sister and Michael both expected me to join them there, so I didn't really have the luxury of skipping it.

"Great, thanks so much, Inās – I knew I could count on you. Oh, and can you please spread the word on social media and email? I'm going to email you the details as soon as we hang up."

"Yes, of course. I'll do that right away."

"Awesome – so Maria and I will see you there tomorrow, along with the rest of the MCA."

A few minutes later, Michael emailed me the exact time, location, and other details for the demonstration, and I shared the information on Twitter, Facebook, and in a mass email to my full list of contacts, including the press.

Now I'm going to go for a run in the park, and try to clear my head a little. If I can calm my mind by focusing on my breathing, my steps, and my surroundings, maybe I'll get some clarity about things.

* * *

Jogging through the park was helpful, as my mind wandered through many thoughts, principles, ideas, and memories. I realized that I've also been struggling with my own prejudice, formed by the last few years of so much tragedy at the hands of Islamists. Yes, I am affected by my own biases at times – that's only human (especially after my experience) – but I also know that there have been many good Muslims along the way. The first who comes to mind is of course Mohammed Rajeh, who protected my life when I had nowhere else to go and who kept his promise to my father to take me to the airport, despite the risks to his safety in doing so; without his honorable kindness, I would probably be dead or miserable in Syria, rather than where I am today in New York. Then there is Awwad, who drove two hours to pick up Maria and Jamila from the Islamist-controlled town of Aziz, after they managed to escape their captivity. And there are the Sunni Muslim members of the Mideast Christian Association, who show their support and solidarity with persecuted minorities because it's the right thing to do, and because they oppose religious extremism.

Oh, and silly me for omitting Jihad Omar from the list of good Muslims who have made a hugely positive difference in my life. He donated twenty-one million dollars to the MCA, which helped countless Mideast Christians, including my family in Raqqa, when it was relocating to Kessab, and with the release of my kidnapped sister. And that wasn't even Jihad Omar who sent the money – it was Julien Morales, a man who considers himself Catholic and was raised in that religion since he was nine years old, when his Catholic mother brought him to Mexico.

As I think about all this, I now vividly recall one of the last things I heard my father say, when the Islamist monsters who killed him tried to get him to become Muslim and start treating only their fellow jihadi fighters: "When a bleeding man comes to the hospital, I ask which wounds to suture – not what God he prays to, or whose war he fights. And when a pregnant woman arrives, I ask whether a natural birth or a C-section is preferable, not who her prophet is."

If he were alive today, what would he say about Julien and whether I should accept his past? And what about the principles of my own faith? Doesn't Jesus teach acceptance and forgiveness?

I'm going to think about all of these things, as I go out to buy some groceries.

* * *

I just finished stocking my fridge and came back to my laptop, only to see that Julien sent me an email. Here's what it said:

Anissa, *Querida Mia*,

I know you must be in a lot of pain right now, trying to piece together the puzzle that is my past and present. I know that pain all too well, because I have to live with it every day, alone. You are the first person with whom I've ever shared it (besides my mother, may God rest her soul).

I chose you for that most intimate and dangerous of disclosures because I have more conviction about you than anything else in my life. In a very real sense, I might not be here writing this email to you but for your presence with me that night on the Brooklyn Bridge. So everything after that is "gravy" – a bonus that I can use to double down on my conviction about you. I'm all in, as they say in poker. I entrusted you with the most sensitive facts about my childhood, and – so that our relationship can be as sacred and honest as possible – I am sending you every single journal entry I wrote since the day we met. So now I am quite literally an open book to you. Like the details of my past, these journal entries are highly confidential and for your eyes only. They are contained in the password-protected PDF that is attached to this email. The password to open the PDF is the name of the restaurant where I took you on our very first dinner date.

I won't contact you again, *Querida*, because I know that you need time to absorb everything that you've come to learn about me. I also won't pressure you, because I'm obviously biased about what you should do and you are your own person, who must decide for herself the best way forward. So I'll just leave you with this parting thought:

Until last January, we were two shattered souls silently bearing their dark burdens in a cruel and lonely world. Life broke us both, but it also brought us together. Do we dare question that rarest of fortunes?

Love,

Julien

Chapter 35: Anissa

∽ Monday, August 25, 2014 ∾

To My Dearest,

So much has happened in the last few days, but I'll try to summarize the highlights in chronological order. And I should really start by telling you my thoughts on the email that Julien sent me two days ago, with his journal entries attached.

During one of our very first dates, Julien once mused about how "cheap" communication is today, compared to the days of his youth, when people wrote letters by hand, stuffed them into envelopes, wrote out the address of the recipient, paid for postage, and had to go to a mailbox, and sometimes even the post office, to send them. Today by contrast, it's all free, easy, and instantaneous, so the exchanged messages are almost taken for granted – from basic spelling to the depth and precision of the thoughts expressed. According to Julien, the quality of any given message sent today is, on average, markedly inferior to the missives sent in the days when they required so much more time, money, and effort to send. So perhaps an intense relationship is today measured more in quantity than in quality. Whereas lovers of long ago composed lengthy and beautifully crafted letters that maybe numbered in the dozens or hundreds over the course of a serious relationship, today's close couples might exchange tens of thousands of poorly drafted, sloppy, telegraphic messages during the totality of their time together. The sheer volume of communications, with its ebb and flow, becomes a kind of testament to the fluctuating intimacy between two people over time. I thought about how Julien and I have that same record, and if we were to graph the number of words sent back and forth (on every messaging platform or technology) since the day we met, an outsider could probably tell from that visual representation, when we were growing closer, quarrelling, in love, or broken up. And with this latest email from Julien, the graph would skyrocket because of how many words were included in the attachment he sent over. More importantly, that attachment suddenly showed me how – even in the era of "cheap messages" – a single communication can be so qualitatively enhanced that it stands far above the mass of regular exchanges, in terms of its impact and meaning.

Needless to say, the symbolism of his gesture was powerfully touching. In fact, I was so moved and impressed that the task of composing an adequate email reply became too daunting and I kept deferring it. I eventually tried to write my response but must have rewritten and then scrapped that email at least a dozen times. In the end, about twenty-four hours had passed since he had sent me his email, and I still hadn't answered him in any way. Part of the time was lost just reading through his journal entries, which were generally fascinating – particularly the parts where he detailed his interactions with and/or impressions of me at various stages of our relationship. There was something incredibly intimate about entering his mind and viewing how it perceived and related to me.

At around 3 p.m. yesterday, I realized that I had to leave my laptop and rush to the protest that Michael had organized, or I would arrive late. As I rode the subway down to Union Square, I decided that, upon returning from the demonstration, I would just call Julien because otherwise I might spend another few weeks obsessing over how to craft an email response that honored and reciprocated the exceptionally special message that he had sent me.

The gathering at Union Square was bigger than any of the previous ones, vindicating Michael's assumption that more people would show up and care about the issue now that the brutal barbarism of ISIS had targeted a U.S. journalist. There were speakers from the Christian, Jewish, and Yazidi communities, urgently warning the public to stop the genocide being committed by Islamist forces in Syria and Iraq. Michael was one of the three Christian leaders who spoke at the rally, and the signs held up by many of the MCA members there all echoed his core message that the ISIS threat could no longer be ignored. Maria and I stood together, each of us with a placard in one hand, watching Michael forcefully urge the U.S. to take military action.

"Wake up, USA! Islamists have been beheading us for centuries. And now they are beheading you," he boomed into the megaphone. "We have been the canary in the coal mine – serving as your early warning system, as we suffered unspeakable atrocities at the hands of violent Islamists. You preferred to look away, after growing weary of war. But today the world is too small and interconnected to run away from it. You can cover your eyes when ISIS turns Syria and Iraq into the slaughterhouses of religious minorities, but eventually they will come for you. Because you represent everything they oppose: religious freedom, human rights, freedom of speech, women's rights, and countless other values that you take for granted but are the very basis of your civilization. Like Nazism in the 1930s, the cancer of Islamist extremism will not go away on its own. On the contrary, it will fill every power vacuum it can find and take root there, growing stronger by the day."

The people gathered in Union Square listened intently and I spied Maria looking with intense admiration at her new love. She noticed me looking at her and smiled. I jokingly whispered to her, "I'm a pretty good matchmaker, aren't I?" She chuckled and nodded gratefully.

We turned our attention back to Michael's speech. "So you can destroy the threat now, when it is still relatively small, or you can fight it later, at a far greater cost. Two years ago, ISIS had under two thousand combatants. Today, in August of 2014, they reportedly have at least ten thousand fighters. They now control about 35,000 square miles of territory, bringing about six million people under their rule. By seizing banks, oil supplies, antiquities, and the property of those it subjugates, ISIS today has about two billion dollars, making it the best financed terrorist organization in the world. And experts estimate that every day ISIS makes up to another three million dollars from oil revenues. It's built an extensive and sophisticated web of connected Twitter accounts that can amplify every single message up to fifty thousand times. This is ISIS today. It quickly grew to this size because no outside force stopped it. How will the ISIS threat look a year or two from now?"

I looked around the crowd and it seemed to have grown to a few hundred people. I wondered why ISIS had chosen to antagonize the world's last superpower, rather than stay below the radar to facilitate their vicious growth. On the other hand, such a brazen move was perhaps an effective way to recruit those who might be impressed by the organization's willingness to defy and threaten the United States.

I turned my attention back to Michael, as he continued. "Does the U.S. prefer to confront ISIS when they control half of the Middle East, including much of the world's oil supply? Today it is raising a generation of children to convert or kill non-Muslims – do you really want them to get this jihadi education, so that they can later target your interests throughout the Middle East and carry out terrorist attacks in your cities? The U.S. has conducted all of about ninety airstrikes in the last two weeks since it finally decided to take action. But that is not fighting to win. Compare that to the air campaign of the Gulf War in 1991, after Saddam Hussein's invasion of Kuwait. In about one month, coalition forces flew over 100,000 sorties, and dropped nearly that many tons of bombs, producing a fast and decisive victory. But the U.S. apparently thinks that there is plenty of time to manage the ISIS threat."

Maria and I both shook our heads in disappointment, as we agreed with Michael's assessment, and held up our signs, which both read "US: Stop the ISIS Genocides." We saw that we were both reacting in the same way and smiled at each other. It was nice to share this moment with her, and I thought about how, if our parents and other siblings were still alive and in New York, they'd all be at this protest with us, equally impassioned about having their voices heard and just as impressed at Michael's leadership.

I focused again on what Michael was saying. "And weak U.S. leadership invites other bad actors into the game, like Iran. Yes, Iran, a Shiite Islamic state, has just happily offered to help the U.S. fight the Sunni Islamic State in exchange for lifting sanctions on the Iranian nuclear program. But the Islamic Republic of Iran also persecutes Christians and other religious minorities. Iran has an abysmal human rights record and is the world chief state sponsor of terrorist organizations, including Hezbollah, which – until September 11 – was responsible for more American deaths than any other terrorist group. So having Iran take care of the ISIS threat would be the height of strategic folly. That's like giving nukes to a far larger and more dangerous Shiite enemy because you're afraid of a smaller, rising Sunni enemy. There are no shortcuts here for the U.S. You can fight ISIS today, or you can keep waiting as the Islamic State grows ever more potent, and acquires more territory, fighters, and resources – and maybe eventually chemical or even nuclear weapons. But one way or another, a confrontation is inevitable."

A few minutes later, Michael introduced the next speaker and handed him the megaphone before stepping off the podium. He walked through the crowd until he reached us, at which point Maria gave him a big hug while still holding her sign. "That was brilliant," she remarked, beaming.

"Thanks, Babe. When are you going up there to speak?" he asked her teasingly.

"Can I use my violin instead of English?" she replied playfully.

"Hey, that's actually a great idea!" I exclaimed. "Why don't we organize some kind of benefit concert for the MCA where Maria performs for everyone?"

Maria's face lit up. "I would love that!"

Michael smiled enthusiastically. "Let's do it! Inās, you're in charge of the planning committee for that one."

My sister and I high-fived each other victoriously. Moments later, I noticed, out of the corner of my eye, a gathering of bearded men, some of whom looked vaguely familiar. Then I recognized them as the men who had threatened me at the last Union Square protest, when Michael knocked out their biggest member, a thug who had towered over him.

Next thing I knew, Michael was knocked down by that same guy, who came out of nowhere to push Michael back over one of his comrades who had surreptitiously crouched behind Michael so that he would trip and fall onto his back when pushed by the huge guy. After that, everything happened very fast. There were four guys punching and kicking Michael, who was on the ground struggling to parry the flurry of blows raining down on him.

"Hey, stop!" I yelled, whacking one of the guys with the wooden stick to which my sign was attached.

"Help, everyone!" Maria yelled to the people around her before jumping into the fray and hitting another guy with the wooden part of her placard.

The two guys that we hit turned their attention to us, but that still left Michael to struggle with two men, including the huge guy who was pummeling him on the ground. We were all in a brawl at that point, so it was hard to tell exactly what happened, but at one point I saw someone strike the huge guy in the head with a tablet computer, which stunned him just long enough for Michael to get on his feet and throw some powerful kicks and punches at the two men who had been beating him up. Then the loud sirens of a police car blared, and there were soon a bunch of cops standing around us with their guns drawn, telling us to freeze and raise our hands.

We were being handcuffed, but I was so shocked by everything that I wasn't even focused on the injustice of us, the victims, being arrested along with the aggressors who had attacked us for no reason. Everyone involved was bruised up a bit, but Michael got the worst of it. Yet, even the lingering pain from the scrapes and punches I had received were overshadowed by the thing that stunned me the most: it turned out that the man who had helped Michael was none other than Julien! I couldn't believe it. And he was being arrested with us.

Maria and I were taken into custody in one car, and the others involved in the melee were brought to the police station in other vehicles. About two hours later, we were all charged with public disorder and misdemeanor assault. By far, the most surreal part of the whole incident was when Julien, Michael, Maria, and I were all in a waiting room together with about five other people being held for unrelated, minor offenses (the police had the good sense to keep the guys who had attacked us in a separate room).

There was something laughably bizarre about the whole scene, with each of us, including Julien, standing there, in handcuffs, bruised up and sullied to varying degrees. Julien actually captured the absurdity of the moment with a perfect line of humor: "So whose brilliant idea was it for us to go on a double date like this? I really prefer restaurants."

The four of us shared a much-needed laugh.

"How did you hear about this protest?" I suddenly asked Julien, still confused and surprised by everything.

"Don't you know what you're tweeting?" he teased me. "I showed up a little late, but just in time to practice my tablet-as-a-weapon skills."

Michael gave him an impressed look. "Maybe the manufacturer should mention head-smashing as a product feature."

Julien nodded in amusement. "True, I guess you get one solid head smash per tablet."

I couldn't help making fun of Julien's nerdy qualities. "Who brings a tablet computer to a protest anyway?"

"Only I do, obviously. But I was doing some work on an investor presentation during the drive down to Union Square from an uptown meeting. Good thing I backed up my work to the cloud just before turning my tablet into a thug-swatter."

Michael's expression turned more serious and genuine. "It means a lot that you came to show support. And I owe you one for getting that giant off me. Actually, I owe you for a lot more than that," he added with a humble smile.

"Don't mention it," Julien replied graciously. "I figured it was time to roll up my sleeves a little with this cause I've been supporting from afar."

I was so touched that I moved towards Julien to give him a huge hug, only to be rudely reminded (by the handcuffs binding my hands together behind my back) that doing so wasn't an option at that moment. But he understood from the way I looked at him, full of love and admiration, that he was meant to be hugged by me at that moment.

"I just hate that this is probably going to end up in the tabloids," I added regretfully.

Julien tried to allay my concerns with some light irony. "Well, this city would be a lot less fun if we couldn't all read about my adventures in the paper every other day, right?"

Michael again seemed more serious. "Unfortunately, publicity about this incident could also make you a target now."

"What do you mean?" Julien asked.

"Well, if Islamists now see that a high-profile billionaire is attending rallies against them, they might assume that you should be stopped before you use your power to oppose them in more significant ways."

Julien's lips tightened for a moment of concern and then he shrugged his shoulders. "Oh well, I guess it's too late now. As Martin Luther King Jr. once said, 'If a man hasn't discovered something that he will die for, he isn't fit to live.' And at this point, Antioch seems like a pretty good candidate to me. After all, we're all here for the love of Antioch, and, in one way or another, we all connected as deeply as we did because of Antioch."

Chapter 36: Anissa

∽ Tuesday, August 26, 2014 ∾

To My Dearest,

Last Sunday, after Julien had instructed his personal attorney to find suitable criminal defense lawyers for each of us, we were all released from the police station by around 10 p.m. By the time Michael, Maria, and I stepped out into the fresh air of freedom, Julien had already left. I assumed (correctly) that he was very behind on his preparations for the big investor meeting, including the presentation that he had been refining on his tablet while getting to the protest. Yesterday, I texted Julien a quick thank you for everything and asked when I could see him again, and he said that his pressures would be done by 6 p.m. tonight, so we planned to see each other at his place at 7:30 p.m.

When the elevator doors closed behind me on the sixty-fifth floor of Julien's penthouse, I stepped right into his arms, and we just hugged for a few minutes. "It's so great to see you again," I finally said, as we released each other.

"Better here than in the processing room of the police station, right?" he replied wryly.

I chuckled. "I still can't believe that whole scenario. The entire thing is beyond surreal."

"Kind of like my hidden past, right?"

I shook my head. "No, nothing quite comes close to that."

Julien picked up a folded up newspaper and dropped it on the counter nearby. "Well, this is pretty surreal to me," he remarked, shaking his head. "I assume you've seen it already?"

I looked at the paper and saw a mug shot of each of us, side by side, next to the headline "Columbia Prof in Slammer with Student Gal Pal."

"No, I didn't see this one. I saw some of the other papers, but they didn't have our photos."

"Their photography style is a bit blander than the pics of us from that Latino benefit dinner."

I chuckled at his dry humor. "But how did they come up with the term 'gal pal?'"

"Read it, and you'll see."

I shook my head in angry frustration at the press, and began perusing the article.

"Columbia University Professor and hedge fund billionaire, Julien Morales, was arrested yesterday afternoon in a brawl that broke out at a Union Square protest calling for stronger U.S. military action against the Islamic State of Iraq and Syria (ISIS) and highlighting the genocidal campaign by ISIS against Christians, Yazidis, and other religious minorities. According to eyewitnesses, the thirty-nine-year-old, Mexican-American finance tycoon used his computer tablet as a weapon to attack a man who was among a group of counter-protestors beating up Michael Kassab, a twenty-eight-year-old Columbia University doctoral student and the founding head of the Mideast Christian Association. Mr. Kassab helped to organize the rally and spoke at the event prior to being assaulted. Anissa Toma, an eighteen-year-old Columbia undergraduate was also arrested for her involvement in the melee. Ms. Toma was enrolled in Professor Morales' Psychology and Markets class last spring, and, according to some of her classmates, was close with and possibly a lover of Mr. Morales during that time. The owner of JM Analytics & Trading (JMAT), a prestigious Midtown hedge fund, Mr. Morales is known more for his playboy lifestyle than his political activism, although he has long been a major benefactor of Latin American causes. He was photographed together with Ms. Toma at a Latino charity gala last month. Earlier in the summer, a Manhattan courier who was attacked by a JMAT security employee sued Mr. Morales for negligently hiring a homeless man suffering from PTSD to work in security."

I couldn't believe the article I had just read. No wonder the media can't cover the Middle East fairly: they can't even report on a protest fracas properly – forever labeling Julien as a "playboy," even though he hasn't thrown one of his parties in months, and then repeating the incident with the traumatized war veteran in a way that just makes Julien look bad, without mentioning that he was trying to do a good thing, that he paid huge sums to compensate the injured party, or that he continued to care for the veteran even after he was fired from JMAT. The article also failed to mention that the counter-protestors attacked us for no reason at all and that Julien was coming to the justified defense of Michael, who was on the ground being brutalized by a mob. I tried to contain my rage as I shook my head. "This is awful," I finally vented. "But how did they even know that I'm a Columbia student?"

"Well, the demonstration itself was well covered by the media, and I'm sure their reporters contacted other protestors who were there, and asked lots of questions about those who were arrested."

I then recalled that there were several Columbia students who are active in the MCA and showed up for the demonstration. "I guess one of them must have been asked about me, and said that I was a fellow student, without realizing that the reporter would then try to dig up everything else about me, including the fact that, a few weeks ago, we were photographed as a couple in the Latino media, and that I was your student."

Julien sighed. "Anything to sell more newspapers." He extended his hand, and I took it. "Come on," he said, leading me back to the same sofa where we had sat when he revealed his awful past to me. "Let's talk about more important things – like how happy I am to see you again. Here."

We sat down on the sofa next to each other. "Well, I probably shouldn't have left the way I did… I was just so shocked, as you can imagine."

"Yes, I can. In fact, I think you reacted quite calmly relative to how other Syrian-Christian women dating their Mexican-American professors who turned out to have an Islamist past would have reacted," he added absurdly.

I chuckled. "Listen, Julien, I was upset but I completely understand that you were just a boy acting under duress. And you've clearly rejected that past and want nothing to do with it. In fact, you've done everything you possibly can to repudiate it – concealing it from the rest of the world and supporting the defense of Mideast Christians, a cause that's antithetical to the Islamist worldview. You struggled with your past so profoundly that, in the end, paradoxically enough, you actually fulfilled your father's original intent when he named you 'Jihad.'"

Julien looked impressed. "I never thought of it like that, but that's a great way to spin my original name now, if anyone else knew it. But, as you can imagine, it must always remain our little secret."

"Of course." I moved closer to Julien and took his hand in mine. "Actually, as painful as it was for both of us to have all of your dark secrets come out, I think it really brought us so much closer, in ways that I'm still discovering."

"Really?"

"Yes. For example, I think I can now actually explain your recurring nightmare in which your blanket turns into razor blades and cuts you open."

"Oh, this is interesting. Even my therapist couldn't figure this one out. Although she also didn't get even a tiny fraction of the information I gave you about my childhood, so I can't really blame her. Anyway, let me hear your analysis."

"The blanket represents your father, because the very thing that is supposed to protect you ends up harming you."

He looked away for a moment, as if to contemplate the truth of my interpretation. "I think you're right!" he suddenly exclaimed, almost in disbelief. "That's a brilliant insight."

"See that? Maybe I should have gotten better than a B in your class," I quipped playfully.

He took hold of my arm and pulled me towards him. "Now who's a teacher's pet?" he asked, as he brought my lips to his while stroking my nape. We kissed, and our tongues danced with each other, as I felt myself lost in warmth and desire again.

After making out for a wonderfully long time, Julien finally gave our lips and tongues a break and offered to bring us something to drink. "I should have offered when you first came in, but that article took over our attention." He rose from the sofa to bring us some juice.

Julien returned with two cold glasses of organic carrot juice and rested them on the coffee table nearby. After he sat back down next to me, his eyes fixed intensely on mine. "Anissa, I sent you my journal entries, because I wanted you to know just how irreversibly I have committed to you. You brought me to a place of trust and love that I never knew existed."

"I feel the same about you," I said meekly, with a smile.

"Good, because I'm not sure what life would even mean to me at this point, if you were no longer in it. So, as far as I'm concerned, there's nowhere left for us to go but forward."

"Forward?"

"Yes. As a couple," he said, taking my hand.

I smiled at his mysteriously circuitous approach to whatever he was about to propose. "And how would we do that?"

"Well, it's really time for Icarus to fly again."

Now I was even more uncertain about where he was going, but played along. "Your vet said he's fully recovered?"

"Yes – a while ago, actually. But I've been worried about how empty my bedroom will feel after he's set free. So… Will you take his place and move in with me?"

I smiled at his cleverly crafted surprise. "I understand that you want me in your life, but do you really expect me to live in that little cage of his?"

We shared a much needed laugh. "Hey, you'll have a fabulous view of Manhattan, and you'll get fed very well!"

"The very best vegetarian seeds I could ever want," I bantered back.

"So, is that a yes?" he asked sheepishly.

I took my hands away. "Only if you'll accept this from me now," I said, removing the necklace that my mother had given me.

He smiled and opened up his palm to receive it.

I dropped the necklace in his hand, and he closed his fingers on it, before moving towards me for another kiss.

Chapter 37: Anissa

∽ Wednesday, September 3, 2014 ∽

To My Dearest,

It's been a very happy and milestone-filled time since I last wrote to you. Yesterday was my first day of classes as a college sophomore, and the day before, I finished moving my things to Julien's penthouse. He actually had a very special ceremony planned to honor the occasion.

Julien came home from work at around 7 p.m., and we went down to the nearby Gramercy Park together, carrying the cage with Icarus in it. We stopped in an area that was relatively empty and had a few trees nearby.

"I'm going to give you the honors," he said. "Open the cage door and let Icarus step onto your palm, and then take your hand out and set him free."

I felt my chest warm with excitement and joy at the symbolic beauty of the moment, as I crouched down a little to open the cage door and slowly insert my outstretched hand so that Icarus could climb on top of it. It was also my first time feeling a sparrow on my palm, and his scratchy little feet actually tickled my hand a bit, as did his soft feathers, which lightly grazed the lower part of my arm. He made some jerky and excited movements in my hand, which was still in the cage. Julien gestured with his head a little, as if to encourage me. "Go on. It's time. Just slowly bring your hand out of the cage, and he'll decide when to go."

I did as he said, and gradually stood up, with my open palm in front of me, and Icarus tentatively probing the air around him with little movements of his head. He stretched his wings out a little and nearly turned around in a complete circle, as if to take leave of Julien and me before flying away. Then he turned to face the direction of my fingertips, flapped his wings and awkwardly lifted off of my hand. He flew about fifteen feet and then landed by the foot of the tree near us.

Julien looked at Icarus and then at me. "One wounded soul in my bedroom moves out, and another moves in."

"Not so injured, now that I'm with you," I added with a smile. He took me into his arms and we kissed.

That was last Monday. Then Tuesday, after my first day of fall

187

semester classes, journalist Steven Sotloff was beheaded. When Julien came home and it was all over the news, I joked to him that it was as if ISIS was directly testing our relationship, to see how much we could bear together.

Julien chuckled. "I'm glad we can at least have a sense of humor about it now. In fact, in the spirit of doing exactly the opposite of what the terrorists want, we're going out tonight for a very special black-tie event, so I'd like you to get dressed up. We're leaving in about two hours," he added cryptically.

"What event?" I asked, intrigued.

He smiled mischievously. "It's a surprise, but you'll want to look your best."

A few hours later, his driver dropped us off at the Brooklyn Bridge. As we stepped out of Julien's sedan and into the pleasant night, with a late summer breeze in the air, walking onto the bridge filled my mind with memories from the last time we were in that place, and I marveled at how much had happened since then. It felt as if we had been through a decade of time – drama, pain, intimacy, love, heartbreak, renewal, and countless other emotions surrounding the story of my crazy journey with the man holding my hand.

When we got to the middle of the bridge, where, during our last visit, Julian had first opened up to me a little about the dark despair that haunted him, he stopped and faced me, this time with an exponentially happier and more confident look. He pointed towards the Brooklyn side of the bridge towards which we had been walking. "On that side of the bridge is JFK airport – the route back to Syria." He then pointed to the side of the bridge from which we had come. "And on that side of the bridge is Manhattan, where the rest of your life is waiting for you. With me."

Then he took my hand and got down on one knee, and looked me straight in the eye. "Will you marry me, Anissa?"

I was overcome with emotion and began to cry tears of happiness. I could barely speak, I was so moved. "Of course I will, Julien," I finally said, as elated joy filled my chest, and tears fell down my cheeks. I wanted to say more but I was too emotional.

He got up off his knee and took my head in his hands and brought my lips to his. I could hear the sound of a passing ship and some ambient traffic noise, but as we held each other ever more tightly and our tongues passionately intertwined, the rest of the world faded out into a moment of perfect bliss. But I eventually noticed that there was a photographer there who had been discreetly taking photos of the entire thing. When Julien saw that I was wondering who this man was snapping our pictures, he said, "Oh, don't mind him – that's Tom, one of our wedding photographers. He's one of the best in the business," he said, as he looked at him approvingly. Tom nodded in humble gratitude and continued capturing the two of us in his lens. Julien looked back at me and playfully asked, "Why do you think we had to get all dressed up for this bridge visit?"

Later, when we were back in his car, heading to the same extraordinary, vegetarian restaurant where he had taken me on our first date (The Lotus Flower), I was finally able to say what the flood of emotions had prevented me from expressing on the bridge, after Julien had proposed.

"You know, Julien, I'm just in awe every time I think back on how conflicted I was about whether to make you my first – long before I knew if you'd be the one. But now I know that you are the one. And instead of making me break the promise to my parents to keep my purity, you actually helped me to fulfill it. Not only did I indeed save myself for my husband but, thanks to you, I heeded my father's urgent appeal to help our community from the USA more than he or I could have ever imagined I would. It's as if you redeemed my decision to give myself to you when I did, and all of the decisions before that – including the selfish decision to escape and survive, rather than die with my parents and older brother.

As the geometric shapes of New York's architecture passed us by in the car windows, he pulled me over into his lap and looked down, deep into my eyes. "I can think of no greater honor than to be Anissa's redemption."

Chapter 38: For You, My Dearest

∞ Wednesday, June 1, 2039 ∞

To My Dearest,

Now you know how I met your father. Many years have since passed, and he's finally comfortable enough with his dark past that he allowed me to share it with you in our combined diary/journal. But this is only for you, My Dearest. You are the only person on Earth – besides your father and me – who has read our most private writings (minus some intimate details that will always remain just between him and me, and which I removed when preparing this for you).

Now that you're a twenty-two-year-old woman and understand the nature of trust and confidence, we have both decided to give you our combined diary/journal as a present for your graduation from college. We cherish you more than you will ever know, and grow prouder of you every day, and we felt that it was time for you to have these family secrets. You always wanted more details about how your father and I fell in love, and how we helped the State of Antioch to grow from a fanciful dream to an inspiring reality, and now you know.

If you take away only one thing from our story, let it be this: In a dark world, love is all that illuminates the path forward.

THE END

About the Author

Zack Love graduated from Harvard College, where he studied mostly literature, psychology, philosophy, and film. After college, he moved to New York City and took a corporate consulting job that had absolutely nothing to do with his studies. The attacks of September 11, 2001 inspired him to write a novelette titled *The Doorman*, and heightened his interest in the Middle East. A decade later, that interest extended to the Syrian Civil War, which provided the backdrop for his latest work. In late 2013, Zack began releasing his unpublished works of fiction and became a full-time author. He has published comedy, psychological and philosophical fiction, and romance. Zack enjoys confining himself to one genre about as much as he likes trying to sum up his existence in one paragraph.

Author links:
–Facebook: https://www.facebook.com/ZackLoveAuthor
–Twitter: https://twitter.com/ZackLoveAuthor
–Website/Newsletter: http://zacklove.com/about-me/newsletter/

And if you need a good laugh after such a heavy read, check out Zack Love's extremely objective review of his own book on Goodreads (where you can also connect with him):
http://tinyurl.com/epicGRreview

Works by Zack Love

The Syrian Virgin
(a novel – contemporary fiction, romance)

Anissa is traumatized by the most brutal conflict of the 21st Century: the Syrian Civil War. In 2012, Islamists in Homs terrorize a Syrian-Christian community and destroy everything that a young woman holds dear. Narrowly escaping death, Anissa restarts her devastated life as a college student in NY. She is bewildered and lost – a virgin in every sense.

But despite her inexperience with men and life in the United States, Anissa is quickly drawn to two powerful individuals: Michael Kassab, the Syrian-American leader working to found the first Mideast Christian state, and Julien Morales, her Columbia University professor who runs a $20 billion hedge fund.

Complicating matters, Michael is still attached to his ex-girlfriend and Julien is the most sought after bachelor in Manhattan (and has hidden demons even his therapist can't extract). Anissa's heart and her communal ties pull her in different directions, as she seeks hope and renewal in a dark world.

Anissa's Redemption
(a novel – the sequel to The Syrian Virgin)

Anissa Toma fled war-torn Syria after narrowly escaping the massacre of her Christian family by Islamists. Fortunate enough to rebuild her shattered life in New York City, the young refugee gained admission to an elite college, where she excelled. Her beauty, brains, and purity soon captured the interest of two powerful men: Michael, an activist working to establish Antioch, the first Mideast Christian state, and Julien, her professor and one of the city's wealthiest bachelors.

As Anissa's saga continues, the refugee-turned-rising-star must navigate between Michael and Julien, while trying to help her surviving relatives and other vulnerable Christians in Syria. As she gets closer to both men in a complex and evolving love triangle, can she unlock Julien's traumatic childhood to open up his heart? Or will Julien find greater solace from his nightmares and other demons in the sessions with his intriguing therapist? What will Michael do for Antioch and for Anissa, and what will Julien's role be? How far will each person go to help Anissa's remaining family and other persecuted Christians at risk in Syria? Find out in this stunning sequel to *The Syrian Virgin*.

Sex in the Title
(a novel – romantic comedy)

New York City, May 2000. The Internet bubble has burst and Evan, a computer programmer, is fired with an email from his boss. The next day, his girlfriend dumps him, also via email. Afraid to check any more emails, Evan desperately seeks a rebound romance but the catastrophes that ensue go from bad to hilariously worse.

Fortunately, Evan meets Sammy – someone whose legendary disasters with females eclipse even his own. To reverse their fortunes, they recruit their friends – Trevor, Yi, and Carlos – to form a group of five guys who take on Manhattan in pursuit of dates, sex, and adventure.

When Evan, a closet writer, falls desperately in love with a Hollywood starlet, he schemes to meet her by writing a novel that will sweep her off her feet. Sammy knows nothing about publishing but is confident of one thing: Evan's book should have the word "sex" in the title.

With musings about life, relationships, and human psychology, this quintessential New York story about the search for happiness follows five men on their comical paths to trouble, self-discovery, and love.

Stories and Scripts: an Anthology
(a collection of stories in various genres)

Thought-provoking, dreamy, sad, and hilarious, this collection of works takes the reader on a diverse and unforgettable literary journey through a variety of topics, themes, and emotions.

The anthology totals about 73,000 words and contains a novelette, four short stories, a theater play, and a screenplay. These seven spellbinding stories spanning several styles and genres include a dramatic romance, a satire of the mega-rich, a somber and soulful reflection on the problem of evil, humorous dating adventures, and stories driven by philosophical musings.

CPSIA information can be obtained
at www.ICGtesting.com
Printed in the USA
LVHW02s1714300118
564591LV00003B/570/P